THE REPLACEMENT

AN IAN BRAGG THRILLER: BOOK 3

CRAIG MARTELLE

D1521668

CRAIG MARTELLE

Website & Newsletter:
https://craigmartelle.com

Facebook:
https://www.facebook.com/AuthorCraigMartelle/

Ian Bragg 1—The Operator
Ian Bragg 2—A Clean Kill
Ian Bragg 3—Replacement
Ian Bragg 4—A Fatal Bragg

Version 1.0

Cover by Stuart Bache
Editing by Lynne Stiegler
Formatting by Drew A. Avera

Published by Craig Martelle, Inc
PO Box 10235, Fairbanks, AK 99710
United States of America

❀ Created with Vellum

To those who support any author by buying and reading their books, I salute you. I couldn't keep telling these stories if it weren't for you and for the support team surrounding me. No one works alone in this business.

The Ian Bragg Thrillers team Includes

BETA / EDITOR BOOK

Beta Readers and Proofreaders - with my deepest gratitude!
Micky Cocker
James Caplan
Kelly O'Donnell
John Ashmore
Chris Abernathy

CHAPTER ONE

"Indeed, this life is a test. It is a test of many things—of our convictions and priorities, our faith and our faithfulness, our patience and our resilience, and in the end, our ultimate desire."
–Sheri L. Dew

The unknown hovered like a dark cloud, ready to unleash its madness upon Ian Bragg's weary head.

Another delay. The flight sat on the tarmac at McCarran International, the Las Vegas airport, waiting. Hope for a quick trip to Chicago faded with the second delay.

"Today might not be our day." I wasn't sure whether to lament or not.

Jenny sipped her orange juice, served in a real glass. We didn't take our first-class seats for granted but appreciated how they made air travel less onerous. "You look like a bead of water dancing around a frying pan."

"A skillet. Water dancing, like how you check to make sure it's hot enough for pancakes. I like pancakes. Why

1

don't we ever have pancakes?" I wondered. "For dinner, maybe."

"How about we get some of that good deep-dish pizza you keep harping on from your last trip to the Windy City?"

"That was good." I stared at the seat ahead. I thought I could smell it. "Man. Now I'm hungry."

The flight attendant roamed through, taking refuse along with new orders.

The setting sun blazed through the window. Jenny lowered the cover and leaned on the oversized armrest. I leaned my forehead against hers. "Relax. It'll be okay."

"Hey! I was going to tell *you* that." Jenny play-pushed me. "It'll be okay."

"Chaz is gone. I'm having a hard time getting my head wrapped around that. We just saw him, and he was fine." I changed to a whisper. "I'm worried that his death wasn't natural."

Charlie French, called Chaz, was the other half of the team that formed the Peace Archive, my employer. Where would the company go now? There wasn't exactly a public succession plan. It was a group of hitmen implementing contracts across the US. No one knew the full story except Vinny, Chaz's partner.

"Let's see what's up before we jump to any conclusions."

I agreed. There was no other choice. We were on the company payroll and had been summoned. They had given me a great deal of latitude and an unlimited expense account. They wouldn't cancel me. I didn't know why I kept coming back to that.

"We're safe, Ian. I feel that in my bones."

"I wish I shared your confidence." I let myself get lost in the sparkle of her green eyes.

Jenny pulled back abruptly as the flight attendant

handed us two more drinks. "They're filling out the paperwork now, and we'll get in the air shortly," she told us.

"Who wants to fly in a broken plane? Better to be late than a statistic." There was no reason to be angry with her. If broken planes happened too often with an airline, we'd go with someone else, one with a better record.

The attendant nodded and moved down the aisle.

"Where are we staying?" Jenny asked.

I shook my head. "We'll call when we get there. I have no idea what part of town we'll be meeting in, and it's a big town."

After the plane finally took off, I was thankful that the flight was uneventful.

Chicago O'Hare is not for the timid. It takes striding with bold purpose, singularly focused on an objective buried in a riot of overhead signs.

Jenny and I kept pace with the crowd, turning when they turned on our way to the exit. We traveled light, without checked baggage, pulling one roller duffel while I carried a backpack over my shoulder.

I wasn't sure how long we'd be in Chicago. As was our usual plan, if we needed anything, we'd buy it. I had my laptop, which contained no information. Everything was secreted elsewhere in a myriad of cubbyholes throughout the dark web, where they could only be found if one knew the IP addresses as well as had the patience to dig through layers with varying access.

I had a phone with a direct and untraceable line to what had been Chaz's phone. The number now belonged to Vinny, unless it had belonged to him all along and Chaz had only been the delivery mule, but I couldn't believe that. Chaz had been his own man—with a wife and kids, I had learned after his death. A man with secrets he kept locked away from everyone except his partner.

Vince Trinelli.

Jenny and I had met him, but we knew less about him than Chaz. "We need to learn more about Vinny," I blurted while Jenny and I waited in the rental car line. I tapped my foot rapidly while she watched me.

"Why don't you call Vinny? I can get the car." She held out her hand. I put my wallet into it, carrying two things: my driver's license and the gold card.

I kissed her and stared into her eyes for a moment before removing myself from the line. I strolled away from the tensabarriers that guided the crowd toward the long counter where all the agencies were represented.

On the other side of the escalator, I found a peaceful spot with enough white noise from the machinery to cover our conversation. When I turned the phone on, it was impossible not to notice the time—eleven-thirty at night. I dialed the one number from memory. It was easy to remember. I had to because I had eaten the note on which it had been written.

"Are you here?" Vinny answered.

"Getting the car now. What's our agenda, and where do you recommend we stay?"

"Deerpath. There's a nice Inn. We can meet at my golf club in the morning, say ten?"

"Ten sounds good. It'll give us some time to get up there. I have no idea where Deerpath is, but this time of night, traffic should cooperate."

"It's Chicago. Traffic never cooperates. Still, if it takes you longer than an hour to get to the hotel, you're lost.

Don't eat breakfast. My treat. The Club does me up right. What do you guys like?"

"Omelet, pancakes, bacon, sausage, hash browns, orange juice, and coffee. Everything a hardworking husband-and-wife team needs."

"You want the nearby golf club. It's not the one named like the hotel. It's the nicer place. See you there." Vinny ended the call.

Cryptic. I turned the phone off. I still had my general-purpose smartphone to call Jenny and use for maps and GPS. I had no intention of getting lost in Chicago. In this case, technology was my anonymous friend, a burner phone with a pre-paid data plan. Same as Jenny's. We'd destroy them in a month or two and get new ones. We had a routine.

Jenny was first in line for the next available customer service agent. I walked around the roped area and sidled up next to her, casually wrapping my arm around her waist, conscious not to grab her backside as I had grown accustomed to doing in the privacy of our home.

She gave me the side-eye, knowing exactly what I was thinking. I winked. We were traveling, and that always led to good things after putting the chain on the hotel room's door. We had a soft spot for hotels since that was where I found her. Or maybe she'd found me.

Jenny handed my wallet back when an agent opened and we were summoned with a casual wave. I offered my Lawless driver's license and the gold card.

Ten minutes later, we were walking to the parking garage to claim our Jeep Grand Cherokee. On the way, I pulled up the hotel's number and called. I asked for a suite if they had one. Only the Palace Suite was available. We would see if the name lived up to reality. I reserved it for the three days it was open. I didn't ask the price because I didn't care. The gold card took care of those things.

Big things had to become little things to allow us to focus on what mattered. The wisdom of the gold card. It wasn't just a perquisite—a perk—it was a necessity.

"The hotel doesn't have room service this late at night." We threw our stuff in the back seat, then roamed around the SUV, looking for damage to note on the form before leaving the garage. All was good.

"Then we better get something on the way."

"I guess we are relegated to the fine-dining option of burgers." I wiggled my eyebrows at my wife.

"Kind of a letdown after the build-up to deep dish pizza." Jenny pulled up the browser on her phone. "You drive. I'll look."

I opened the GPS on my burner and typed in the hotel's address. It couldn't give me a route because it couldn't find a signal. "Is it north or south, or maybe east or west?" I didn't think we had enough time for my music. Rush waited in my pocket, but it was late, and we needed to go.

Jenny chuckled, holding up one finger while typing with another. "North."

I carefully backed out, even though the backup camera made things easy. A glance left or right, then stare at the screen. It was the modern way. I had grown up in a different era that called for a neck twist and a hard lean to look behind the vehicle.

We exited and followed the signs for any road heading north until the GPS came to life. It directed us to the interstate.

"Damn," Jenny mumbled. She tapped rhythmically on her phone. "Damn. Everything is closed or will be by midnight." The GPS said we'd arrive at twelve-fifteen.

"I guess we look for a choke-and-puke at an off-ramp."

Jenny worked her phone and came up with an answer. "I got nothing. We better use the Mark One eyeball."

"Nice use of Marine terminology. I am happy to see that my exhaustive efforts to train you have not been in vain."

"Train me, Mr. Bragg? Whatever do you mean?"

"Training in the finer phraseology unavailable to your average Joe…sephina." I had to contort my words to the feminine because my wife wasn't a Marine buddy, although she fought as well as any of them from the Sandbox back in the day. The war in the desert. Everyone from my era had had the chance to explore how sand could get into everything a person owned. That included every orifice.

I didn't pine for the good old days. I reached for Jenny's hand to hold while I drove with the other. She gave up on her search and put her phone away. Everything I needed was inside our ride. "We'll be fine, Miss Jenny. Grab a snack and get to the hotel, where I can show my undying appreciation for you."

"By serving fast-food burgers?"

"And fries. Nothing's too good for my baby."

Jenny chuckled and shook her head. "What have I gotten myself into?"

I used the turn signal for the next off-ramp. A White Castle was at the top. "Is that a burger joint?"

"Only the absolute best! They make these tiny square burgers with onions and mustard. To die for, Miss Jenny. To simply die for."

I glanced over to see Jenny making a face. "They're disgusting, aren't they?" she asked.

"I like them," I replied, keeping it as simple as I could.

"They are!" Jenny declared before we made it to the drive-through.

After the obligatory welcome, I placed our order. "One each of each of your sliders and one large fries, please."

"That's thirteen different sliders. You want thirteen, singles as well as doubles?" the disembodied robotic voice asked.

"Yes, please."

"Thirteen sliders and thirteen large fries. Anything to drink?"

"Thirteen sandwiches and only one large fries. There are only two of us. How about one iced tea, please, the largest size you have."

"That'll be twenty-five dollars and three cents at the second window."

"She's judging," Jenny said. "And so am I."

I was under a certain amount of pressure to deliver, so I hedged my bet. "Better than nothing, my lovely bride."

We paid with two twenties and received a stack of cash and change in return. It took a couple minutes to get everything done. The staff seemed to be working in slow motion, but it was midnight. The attendant opened the window and handed our drink through.

I pushed all the change she had just given me at her. "A tip for your crew. We appreciate you guys working the late shift. Everyone does it at some point in their lives. Get it out of the way and keep moving up."

"Sure," the young woman said and closed the window.

I smiled at Jenny. "I never worked fast food or in a restaurant," she admitted.

"Miss Prissy Pants," I whispered. The window behind my head opened. I turned to face the stone-faced woman handing down two bags of food. "Smells great. Thank you."

She nodded tightly and closed the window.

"What do you recommend that will disgust me the least?"

"I can't believe you put that kind of pressure on me, but let me take a wild shot in the dark. Go with the fries first. We'll see what we've got once we get to the hotel."

"We're not going to eat all of this."

"This is what decadence looks like." I tried to sound profound. Jenny left both bags closed and started looking for a radio station. "We have more than we can eat, willing to pick and choose while most likely tossing the rest, unless they have a refrigerator in the room, of course, then nothing will go to waste."

Jenny found a pop station that made my lip twitch, but she enjoyed it while we made quick progress toward Lake Forest, Illinois.

My mind was on the meeting with Vinny. I didn't know what to think about it. Too many questions that Vinny would easily answer, yet I speculated and disappeared down the rabbit hole of possibilities, wasting thought time.

Which made the drive to the hotel go by in a flash. I was surprised when the GPS said we had arrived at our destination, even though I had been driving.

CHAPTER TWO

"People have a hard time letting go of their suffering. Out of a fear of the unknown, they prefer suffering that is familiar."
–Thich Nhat Hanh

It was a short drive to the golf club, but we were eminently refreshed.

"I liked the Palace Suite. Truly palatial."

"It was nice," Jenny offered, trying to maintain a straight face, but she couldn't. It was the nicest room in the hotel and worthy of its name. "If room service sees your detritus in the refrigerator, they'll probably throw it out."

"You liked it."

"I did. We didn't need anything other than the regular sliders. They went down as their names suggested." Jenny put her hand on my shoulder while we drove the minute and a half to the golf club.

I announced our arrival. "We're early." I thought about it. "Maybe we mill about outside and wait for Vinny. I don't know what name he would go by here, so I don't want to ask for him. At ten, I'll give him a call if we haven't seen him."

We parked the rental and strolled to the front door. Our Grand Cherokee was the minimum standard for domestic vehicles in the lot. The others were Porsches, BMWs, Mercedes, and even one Ferrari.

"Looks like they prefer low-profile here. I can see how Vince would fit in," Jenny quipped.

Individuals strolling toward the clubhouse glanced at the smiling couple standing outside but didn't acknowledge them. More people left. Ten came and went. I called Vinny, but there was no answer.

"Makes me wonder if we're in the right place." I started walking back to the Jeep, but a car pulled in, a 5-series BMW, all black, with dark windows. I glimpsed Vinny through the windshield before he continued down the lot to park. I returned to the entrance to wait with Jenny.

He hopped out, beeping the locks with a casual over-the-shoulder gesture, and waved to us. I nodded.

"Sorry I'm late. In Chicago, one never knows about the traffic."

We shook hands. He shook Jenny's hand, too. "Don't you live in Lake Forest?"

"I do, but there was an accident. It should take me five minutes to get here. This morning, it took fifteen, and the police were all over the place, so I thought it best not to talk on the phone while driving."

I nodded as he ushered us inside the private club. He waved to a member, made small talk, shook hands, and we headed upstairs into a more casual dining area where the diners were not dressed in coats like those on the first floor. It dawned on me that Vinny had made no effort to introduce us to his acquaintance.

Low profile.

The attendant guided us to a table without saying a word. Vinny slipped a twenty into his hand before he gave us our privacy.

I held Jenny's chair and pushed it in as she sat. When I took my seat, Vince leaned forward, as did Jenny and I. This was what I had been waiting for and speculating about since I'd received news of Chaz's death.

"I want you to finish the little bastard who offed Chaz." Vinny added cream to his coffee and leaned back to sip it. He looked like he was waiting for me to speak. I turned to Jenny and back to Vinny.

"A little more background, please,"

Vinny sighed. He glanced to his side to make sure the server wasn't close. "Of all the garbage and waste in the world, a mugging gone wrong. Charlie was on his way back from your event. At the airport, he got rolled in the parking lot on the way to his car. They hit him while he was carrying his bag, only one hand free. He broke a jaw and a wrist, but they knifed him. A lucky strike for the little scumbags."

"You want me to find the one or all of them?"

"Just the one with the knife, but we know who and where he is. Before you suggest the police, they gave me the information and a little time to resolve the situation before they put another juvie into the system."

"He's a juvenile?" I didn't like what I was hearing.

"Built like a man. His age belies his size, and I don't care. The punk cost me my one friend. It's worth one million dollars to you."

I waved Vinny off. I didn't want to talk about money, not right now. Jenny put her hand on my leg and squeezed. We looked at each other. She gave no hint about what she thought. It was up to me.

"That simple? We know who this kid is, and you want

me to do him? Why didn't you take care of it?" I wasn't judging, but Vinny had been an operator.

"Too personal. I'd get careless. I've been out of the game for too long to be able to overcome a careless mistake. That's what got Charlie killed. He spoke as highly of you as anyone. Look at you! You're at the top of your game. You can make this quick, then we can get down to the rest of the agenda, which is you taking Charlie's place."

"*Us* taking Charlie's place," I corrected.

"Of course." Vinny smiled at Jenny. A cart rolled up with a large number of plates. Everything I had told Vinny on the phone the day before. Not great quantities, but everything had its own plate.

The server cleaned off our table, and with a masterful display of spatial awareness, made everything fit. He topped off our coffees and rolled the cart away.

"Please." Vinny gestured toward the food. He had a cup of yogurt with a side of fruit. "I remember the days when I could eat like you."

"You keep yourself in shape, eat healthy, but you're out of the game?" I wondered. It was hard not to judge. Then again, after I retired, I figured that I would stay in shape, too. It was best to live a good life in retirement. "I'm sorry. That sounded demeaning. Not my intent."

"I like playing golf. I like taking trips to warm places in the winter. If you haven't noticed, it's December in Chicago. It'd be nice to be in the Caribbean, but I want to see this through, and selfishly, I don't want to be an operator again. I know that you don't want to either, but one last one while you're still sharp."

"Someone would tell you that I'm still recovering from getting bitten by a rattlesnake and then not getting medical attention soon enough." I pointed sideways before digging into my omelet while it was still hot.

Vinny took a bite before checking the area again. "Tell me about it." He positioned a chrome water jug so he could see behind him while his eyes darted to the sides and beyond us. The server made no effort to approach.

"The Gomez case after Elena *mysteriously* disappeared during training. Tucson. Had to hit the estate from the foothills side, but with a drone. The exfil took me through the mountains, where it turns out snakes like to sun themselves. I almost got clear, but it clipped my leg. It took me another four or six hours to get into a place where Miss Jenny could help."

She snorted, licked her lips slowly, and took another bite of bacon.

"Okay. I was unconscious. She found me and fireman-carried me out and got me to the hospital. She saved my life, and I won't do a job without her."

"Bravo," Vinny said. "I don't expect you will. But there's a problem with this case. As you'll see, the target is black and lives in a drug neighborhood. You might stand out as a couple. Alone, you might be able to pass yourself off as a buyer. But you can't drive into the neighborhood, no matter what you drive."

"Throwing a lot of obstacles in my path. Tell me what you have in mind since you've been thinking about this, and I don't like playing Twenty Questions." I took another bite and waited while scowling. I pushed the food away. I didn't like being played.

"Fair enough." Vinny leaned in again. "You have to be close because he dresses like a few others in the neighborhood. You know how we feel about collateral damage."

"We don't make the hit if there's a risk," I said, my voice barely above a whisper.

"This will be a tough hit, although straightforward.

14

This guy thinks he's bulletproof. I've had him under surveillance from the point I knew his name. I will send you all that information."

"You just need me to cancel him, but I still don't see why you can't do it yourself since you've already done the hard work."

"I'm at that stage of my life where I just don't want to. Good thing is, I run an organization that can take care of things. If you want to bid it out, I'd be good with that, but I'm asking you as a personal favor. I think it will have to be done up close and personal, and I want it done now because we can't let these things languish. I have an acquaintance or three inside the force, but that's today. It could change tomorrow, and regardless, they'll need to act soon. This makes it nice and clean for them. Gang violence claims another victim. It's in the headlines every day."

I took a strip of bacon and chewed on it while fumbling beneath the table for Jenny's hand. "For Chaz." I looked at Jenny.

Finally, she nodded minutely, but it was enough to let me know she would support whatever decision I made. As she always did. I didn't want to ever betray her trust or confidence. Neither of us was happy about it.

"What do you think?" I asked Jenny. It put her on the spot, but it was a decision that wasn't mine alone to make. Not anymore.

"For Chaz," she whispered. She had met him and liked him, at least the part of him he'd been willing to share with us.

I turned back to Vinny. "Send me the information."

"I already have." Vince didn't look smug, more sad than anything. "I don't like to take no for an answer, but I would have in your case. I also would have paid whatever you asked. I respect you more that it isn't about the money. I didn't expect it would be. I'll still make a generous donation to your retirement account."

I exhaled through my mouth louder than I wanted to as I started to contemplate my next steps. I could see the setup taking shape. I was getting lost in thought, so I jerked myself back to the present.

My coffee cup was empty, but I wanted more. I held it up and turned to look for the server, but he had seen and was on his way with a fresh carafe.

"Do you have any flavored creamers hiding somewhere?" I asked.

The server hid his surprise well. "Of course." He moved off without asking which flavor. I wondered if he was going to call in an emergency order to a grocery store, but no, he returned quickly with two quart-sized containers. He leaned close and spoke in a soft voice. "This is the staff's personal stash. I can't leave it here but will pour what you need."

I held out my cup. "Two-point-one ounces, please."

He met my gaze and smiled. "Surely our distinguished guest knows that optimal is one-point-nine ounces for a cup of this size."

"Of course. One-point-nine it is."

The server poured smoothly. Neither of us had any idea how much one-point-nine ounces looked like. After the creamer, he topped off my cup with a rich-smelling dark roast. He winked before walking away.

"That's where you should have slipped him a little something for his effort," Vince suggested.

"You're much different from Chaz," I remarked.

Vinny inclined his head as if bowing at the recognition.

"I've lived my life by helping those who help themselves as well as those who don't know they need my help. It's how I justify doing what I do. This guy's a scumbag. He killed one of our own. Will he do it again?"

"Inevitably, if he hasn't already. Clock is ticking if we want to handle this ourselves. I believe this guy will be terminally at odds with law and order."

"And you're willing to place a million-dollar bet that the world is better off without him."

Vinny nodded. He placed his gold card on the table, drawing the server to us. I slipped the man a twenty when he took the card.

The meeting was over. I still had a thousand questions about the next steps for the Peace Archive, but Vince had determined that those could wait.

I needed to work out, burn off some of the calories I had just ingested, but I wasn't quite finished. I pulled the pancakes to me and cut them into huge bites that I ingloriously shoved into my mouth.

"I can't take him anywhere," Jenny said, lightening the somber moment enough that Vince smiled.

"You two make a great team."

CHAPTER THREE

_____

"A good plan violently executed now is better than a perfect plan executed next week." –George S. Patton

In the parking lot, we went our separate ways. I waited until after Vince had gone to climb in.

Jenny didn't know what to say either. "I guess we better go back to the room and see what's in the file." We drove the three blocks to the hotel in silence.

The air was crisp and cool, driven by gusts from Lake Michigan. We hurried into the old Tudor-style hotel and up the steps to our grand suite. We found the cleaning crew ready to go in.

"No need," I interrupted, waving my keycard at them. "We have a work call coming up, so we'll be in the room. We're good for today." We stepped inside and locked the door behind us. I removed my laptop from the safe and set it up on the coffee table in front of the gas fireplace. We turned it on for ambiance and to take the chill from the room.

I worked my way through the intricate maze of the dark web into the portal access of the Peace Archive. For security's sake, the location floated through dark space. One had to take a series of twists and turns, watching for the cues that indicated where the portal had gone. Then three password-protected screens to get to the information. In this case, the file on Chaz.

DeTyus Johnson. Seventeen years old. Six feet two inches tall and two hundred twenty pounds. A candid picture didn't give the impression he carried any fat. The video of the attack was bone-chilling.

Chaz held his own but was overwhelmed by being caught and forced to fight with only one arm. His bag had trapped his other hand.

He injured two of the three and they postured, but that let the big kid take care of business. Just like the punk he was, putting the cannon fodder out front so he could swoop in for the kill when the enemy was at his weakest. The murderer laughed as he cut the bag from Chaz's arm and rifled his pockets, taking what little there was: a wallet with a gold card, an ID with his fake name.

The kid walked away from the attack with his two injured buddies. He had the gall to turn back toward Chaz's body while tapping his chest and flashing the one-finger salute at the body.

Jenny hung her head while I froze the image on the screen. "I think his opportunity for rehabilitation has come to an end," she stated.

"I couldn't agree more. I see why Vinny said this thing had to be done and why it was worth a million dollars to him. This made me angry, but I can't be angry if I want to do the job right."

"You know how it has to be. Justice served cold. A debt to a new friend gets paid."

"How to deal with a world gone mad by those who remain sane." I closed the video and opened the rest of the file. An address. A map. Other statements and observations. Newspaper articles about the neighborhood. The police preferred not to go in there without taking an armored truck and a small army, but I had to go in alone.

Which meant going in under cover of darkness. The details crystalized.

A plan quickly came into my mind, as clear as they usually were when I had all the information on the target.

"We need comm, an IR camera, gloves, and a mini-drone."

Jenny waited for the rest of it.

"Comm so you can relay what you see from the mini-drone and an IR camera so I can see if he's home and in the bed that is supposedly his. If someone is sleeping there, I need to be positive that it's him."

"I'll be running the drone to be your eyes as you move into the neighborhood?"

"Keep me away from humanity. Even with a hood over my head, I'll stand out and immediately be targeted as prey."

Jenny leaned back into the couch and stared at the ceiling. "How are you going to do it?"

"I'll take a gun off a drug dealer. Shouldn't be hard to find one of those in that neighborhood."

Jenny shook her head rather than comment on the issues of society that made my statement reasonable.

"They need a politician like Jimmy to clean this place up, give them hope for a different life." I pulled up area maps of the neighborhood in question. It was like driving back to the airport, which had been a convenient hunting ground. I searched the news for other crime reports from

O'Hare's long-term parking lot. Going back a few months, the reports were telling. "Look at this."

I pointed at the reports showing weekend assaults late at night in long-term parking. "I wonder why the police don't camp out there on the weekends."

"It's mid-week, so sitting and waiting for DeTyus to show up on the weekend if it's him doing it, isn't going to meet Vinny's timeline."

Too often, I lost track of the day of the week. Days didn't matter with our lifestyle. Vegas was always happening, so we made reservations, which obviated the days.

"We'll go in tonight." I studied the map of the area, highlighting where the house was and where we could park outside the hot zone of the target neighborhood. The plan came together in my mind, but we were missing surveillance.

An accomplice. We had thousands of dollars in cash. I'd offer a grand as an incentive and see if I could get someone to sell out. I doubted it, but it was worth a try.

"Off to the store. We have stuff to buy." I didn't have a good feeling. It would be the least reconnaissance I'd ever done on a job. The potential of losing the target to the law? I was okay with that. "I'll pull the plug on this right quick and in a hurry if anything is off. Getting caught in there is no way to honor Chaz's memory."

"Is this about honoring his memory?" Jenny pressed. "It seems like this is more like a dog marking its territory. Don't mess with us."

"It may sound odd coming from me, but people need to pay more attention to complying with the law. The scumbags on the ferry back in Washington. The trio in Alexandria outside your brother's house. Cleaning up the world one punk at a time. This guy crossed the line. He wrote his own death warrant." The images of what he had done to Chaz were burned into my mind, with the final picture of him giving the body the finger as the icing on the cake.

I couldn't get angry, but I could and would make him pay.

We parked in a nondescript lot with other vehicles that didn't look like homeless people lived in them. We watched traffic of all shapes and sizes from high-end to little better than rumbling wrecks turn off the main road toward the target area.

The clock read two-thirty before Jenny turned the ignition off, leaving the radio on. I rolled down my window.

She activated the drone app on her phone with the screen brightness turned almost all the way down. I turned the unit on and held it out the window. She sent it skyward, straight up to avoid hitting any power lines, and we watched the view of the street leading into the neighborhood. She angled the camera, keeping the drone in our line of sight.

It was the best one we could find with the highest resolution camera that would deliver a feed directly to the phone. We watched until it signaled low battery, then Jenny dropped it into the middle of the parking lot. I skulked out and retrieved it. We replaced the battery and put the first on a twelve-volt charger. A maximum hover of fifteen minutes wasn't enough.

I felt the trepidation I hated. I wasn't comfortable with the lack of information. We hadn't seen a roving band, but that didn't mean there wasn't one around the next corner.

That limited view might walk me into a place I didn't want to be and couldn't get out of. I had a pocket knife on me that I had bought at the checkout counter.

I counted on my improv skills to give me the weapon I needed to complete the job.

What we hadn't seen was the ubiquitous dealer standing on the corner, ushering in vehicles to exchange cash for drugs. There had been no one on the street that we could see.

At two in the morning, I kissed my wife, handed her my wallet, and climbed out of the Jeep. We didn't say any words. Our eyes did all the talking.

I had four blocks to cover and wanted to be out by four. We had three alternate pickup points besides this one, depending on how the hit panned out.

Just in case.

I walked slowly into the shadows and stayed there, moving slowly before darting into an alley after watching to see if my movements caught anyone's attention. I took the alley to a crossroad. At least there wasn't any snow to leave a trail. It was cold, and I only wore a non-descript long sleeve shirt beneath my hooded sweatshirt. I kept my hood up, but not to cover my whole face. I'd count on the darkness to hide my face as much as possible, but I couldn't abandon my peripheral vision.

Without having eyes in the sky, I had to trust my instincts and the information my senses provided.

I vowed that I would never put anyone under this kind of pressure for a contract. For Chaz! It was reckless, and that turned my stomach sour.

But it was a job I had taken. The time for recriminations had passed. *Focus!* I ordered myself.

The roof above lacked an outline of someone watching. I hadn't expected there would be. I could not see through the dark windows. I walked to the end of the building and stopped before stepping into the faint light of a Chicago night where half the streetlamps weren't working.

I sniffed the air, but the chill and light breeze masked most of a pungency I couldn't identify. My eyes were as accustomed to the dark as they were going to get.

"Checking in," I said into the small walkie talkie, hiding it and me. A guy like me with short hair and talking into a portable radio would raise the alarm, screaming "cop" to the locals. The best defense was to not be seen.

"Acknowledged," Jenny replied. I had been taught in the Marines that short transmissions were best to keep the enemy from homing in on your position. It made sense to me. It also was important that I didn't keep the comm device pressed against my face. That would have made me look like the police in a place they were afraid to enter. I bowed my head and walked onto the sidewalk and into the neighborhood.

My eyes darted left and right, looking for movement.

Looking for someone who would raise the alarm. A car was coming from behind me and I started to stagger, playing my drunk routine. A late-model Chevy drove past. I glanced over my shoulder to find the street empty. I picked up my pace.

Three blocks to go. People were out on their porches and in their yards. A house on the opposite side of the street had a barrel in the front yard with a fire licking from it. I turned away from it and slowed my pace. Those near the barrel wouldn't be able to see into the darkness I embraced. A fire would keep them warm, but it ruined their night vision.

Two forms detached themselves from the house on the corner of the road down which I had just turned. I stared at the ground and tried to walk faster, but that wasn't working. They were coming after me. I headed for a darker point between the streetlights as far from nearby houses as I could get.

I stopped, turned, and started shaking. "Smack," I called, finding myself woefully ignorant of newer terms that might have seemed more real.

"What do we got here? Cracker's lost." Two men, hard to tell how old they were. Neither was much taller than me, but they were wider. They blocked the sidewalk before one attempted to maneuver behind me.

"I need some smack." I adjusted to make sure I didn't turn my back on either of them. If they pinned my arms, I'd be done.

"How you gonna pay?" a gruff voice asked.

"I have money, rolled a big-wig," I replied. I held out a hundred-dollar bill. With a movement much quicker than I expected, the one who didn't talk snatched it from my hand.

"What about now?" the first man asked with a laugh.

"Smack," I mumbled, bowing my head to view them both out of the corners of my eyes. They took it as surrender.

"Let's see what you're hiding." The first man reached for me. I dropped and delivered a vicious uppercut into his groin, pulling him between the second man and me when he fell. The uninjured lunged but ran into his friend.

"Cop," he growled.

I delivered a side kick to his face that snapped his head back and followed through with a right hook to put him out. I hammered the side of the groaning man's head with the heel of my boot so he joined his unconscious friend. There was no sense in trying to stash the two. Time was of the essence since the chance of not being seen was close to zero.

I patted their pockets and was pleased to find that both carried pistols—nine-millimeter Glocks without spare magazines. I recovered my hundred-dollar bill while I was at it.

Since I had to assume I had been spotted, I ran into an alley, through a backyard, and back onto the street. Between darkened houses. Anything to foil a pursuer. I found a spot of inky darkness and tucked myself into it.

I pulled out my walkie talkie and keyed the mic. "I could use some eyes because I'm running for my life here."

"Going airborne. Need pick-up?"

"No." I stuffed the walkie talkie into my pocket.

I ran down the sidewalk and turned to sprint along the parallel street to the one I wanted. I covered the next two blocks and then ducked under a heavy bush. In the summer, it would be filled with lilacs. In the winter, it was brown but still bushy, with too many branches.

No lights came to life. No one appeared on their porches to watch the crazy man running through the neighborhood. It wasn't even three-thirty, but time was compressing. The men wouldn't stay unconscious for long. When they came to, they'd light out on the warpath and alert the whole neighborhood. Then again, they might not if they were embarrassed about someone half their size taking them both down.

That kind of attention wouldn't be good. I hoped that would not happen, but as I always told others, hope is a lousy plan.

I needed to take the next crossroad. At the main street, Detritus' house was the second on the right. I had settled on my name for him, no matter how short-lived. When the contract went live, he ceased being someone deserving of a name. There would be no earning it back.

I killed bad people for a living. I believed it kept other

people safe. This guy's departure from our existence... It wouldn't bring Chaz back, but it could save the next traveler's life. It could save the next generation that wanted to escape the violent death Detritus was soon to realize.

"All clear," I reported to Jenny.

"Eye in the sky is dead. Sorry, it went out of range and disappeared."

"Roger. Moving to contact."

Before leaving the safety of the bush, I checked the Glocks. Both were the same, model G43. Single-stack, small, easily concealable. I wondered why bigger men carried them, but they did. The why didn't matter. I dropped the magazines: two rounds in one and three in the other. I stripped the two rounds out, wiped them clean, and loaded them into the second magazine. One pistol had a chambered round, the other didn't. Six rounds total.

I only needed one.

CHAPTER FOUR

"Courage is doing what you are afraid to do. There can be no courage unless you are scared." –Eddie Rickenbacker

After wiping the second pistol clean, I dumped it into the middle of the lilac bush, then wiped my new weapon down and put on my gloves. I listened intently—only the sounds of the night. Heater fans running and clunking. A car in the distance with a bad muffler. The creak of trees bending with the breeze.

I stepped out from under the bush and walked slowly with a stagger. Just some drunk no one needed to worry about. Down the side street and into the shadow beside a tree trunk. Through an unlocked gate and into a backyard, where I looked for a dog bowl or chain before continuing. I didn't need Fido sounding the alarm. I stayed close to the house, out of the line of sight of the dark windows.

I picked up an empty soup can and a nasty gym sock to carry with me.

I crouched and crawled, doing whatever it took to get through the neighbor's yard. On the target side was a low chain-link fence. I vaulted it and settled to listen and wait.

No lights. No one alerted.

After five minutes, I moved to the side of the house. It was time to use my small IR camera. It had 320 by 240-pixel resolution. Not the best, but I only wanted to use it to see where Detritus was sleeping.

Five people in the house, two downstairs and three upstairs. Downstairs seemed to be sleeping. I expected those were the parents. Upstairs, one smaller outline, sleeping. Two bigger people and a hot TV.

I continued to watch, wrapping my sweatshirt around the unit to cover the light from the screen. And I waited. I knew my target was one of the two upstairs.

I leaned close to the ground and blew out most of my breath before keying the mic and speaking. "Target has company. Standby."

"Roger," Jenny replied softly. Even in the one word, I could hear the tension in her voice. She was sitting in a parking lot, waiting for the word to come get me or for me to magically show up. I hated doing this to her. Next time…

No. There couldn't be another one like this.

Until there was since we both knew there would always be a next time. Some things couldn't be left to others, like this one. A younger Vinny would have done it himself.

While I was waiting, I wrapped the sock around and within the can with the pistol barrel stuffed into it to make an ad hoc suppressor. Doing this silently would offer my best chance to get away.

An hour passed, and it was closing on five in the morning when the two bodies came downstairs and walked toward the front of the house. I shut off the camera and eased around to where I could see the front yard but not the door. Two men stepped onto the front porch. I heard the groan from the old boards and the door slam shut. I couldn't see them since I was too far back, but I held my position.

There was no reason to expose myself now. The target was one of the two. They slapped hands, followed by the thud of chests colliding. One man walked down the steps and toward the street. The other returned inside. I waited until the visitor was out of sight before turning the IR camera back on. The target had gone into the kitchen at the back of the house.

I rushed around the side and came up on the back landing. I could see him making himself a sandwich. It looked good, heavy on the lunchmeat. Also a pile of Cheetos and mayonnaise. He returned the deli bag to the refrigerator. I tried the door, but it was locked. No time like the present.

I took aim as best I could with the front sight buried within the can. When he stopped to pick up his sandwich, I fired twice in rapid succession. A double-tap. Glass exploded inward as the first round hit him in the face. The second hit him in the chest. As he fell, I was already running.

Chicago had shot-spotters, a system that zeroed in on rounds fired and immediately dispatched a unit to check it out. If my suppressor had worked properly, they wouldn't have activated. If it hadn't, more than just the neighbors would be looking for me.

I vaulted over the chain-link and sprinted through the backyard and over the fence on the other side. I froze as a man ran toward the house. The friend. He'd at least heard the glass breaking.

It made sense that he thought it had been his friend, Detritus. Once he was past, I headed for the lilac bush as my temporary refuge to listen and watch.

How long before people started looking for the perp? I guessed not long. A silent hit would have been better, but time was not on my side. It was after five. I thought people would be getting up soon—the early work crowd if there was such a thing. Even though the neighborhood was dark, I needed to get out of there.

I jogged to the bush and disappeared into it. I thought about keeping the pistol to help me in case someone wanted to confront me, but if I was caught, the pistol would be a death sentence. I wiped it one last time and tossed it into the middle of the bush. I looked for the darkest part of the neighborhood.

Another street over.

An alley.

I ran for it, trading stealth for speed, but it was too late. Lights were coming on, and people shouted. I dove into the gravel and rolled behind a garbage can. Held my breath as my ears pounded with each heartbeat. The neighborhood rallied. It was after five, well before they usually got up, but they had roused.

They found the energy to seek retribution. At least it was December and I had a few more hours before daylight.

But with bands roving the neighborhood, it was far more dangerous than having someone summon the police. Footsteps approached, hammering a staccato against the ground. I tensed, trying to control my breathing while at the same time getting ready for a fight. They continued down the alley and into the road. I let out a breath and peeked to see that the alley was clear.

I crawled among the garbage to get farther away from the scene until I could crouch and speed up. I moved through the shadows, slowing anytime I came into a lighted area to move at an agonizing pace while in the open. Another lesson from the Marines: fast movement was easily spotted out the corner of an eye, but slow movements didn't register. A human being's fight-or-flight self-defense mechanism was wired for rapidly approaching threats.

Slow to reduce the opportunity for observation. An engine sounded a half-block away. I hit the ground and made myself as small as possible, staying behind a tree trunk, extending from it as if I were one of its roots. I buried my face in the cold dirt. The car drove down the alley toward me. As it neared, the engine revved.

I braced for impact, but it raced by. After it turned onto the road, I popped up and hurried away. I took a side street perpendicular to the way I wanted to go, finding an area that hadn't been energized by the hit on Detritus. I was covered in dirt and brush, which helped me resume my drunk persona. I jammed my hands into the pouch on my hoodie and continued down the street, staggering quickly. I covered my whole face.

Looking out of place would do more harm than losing my peripheral vision. Every move was a calculation of risk versus reward. I expected a casual observer would grunt in disgust and look away. It played a role in the strategy. I dodged into an alley and dropped down, sitting by a garbage can. I lifted the walkie talkie to my face.

"Primary in five."

"Roger," Jenny replied. I wiped the IR camera and walkie talkie down, even though I still wore my gloves. We'd make them disappear somewhere in the greater area away from this neighborhood, unlinking them from the hit.

I checked for traffic, listening and watching. A siren sounded on its way toward the neighborhood. I dropped and waited. It passed and kept going. Anyone alerted would stop looking once it was gone. I tucked my hands in and walked across the last street that formed the barrier to the neighborhood Detritus had called home.

In the shadows, I brushed myself off before pulling back my hood and appearing on the street. I walked casually like a man on his way to work. When I reached the parking lot, I strolled in like I was heading for my car. "Flash the lights and step on the brake," I said into the walkie talkie. Jenny complied instantly, making it look like I had remotely unlocked the vehicle. I walked around the Jeep to the driver's side but opened the back door, then climbed in and shut the door behind me before lying down in the back seat.

"You know the drill. Drive the speed limit and get us the hell out of here."

"Don't you ever do that to me again, Ian."

"You're not kidding. It was a touch uncomfortable in there, but it's done. I won't let Vinny leverage me like that again. I won't have it, and I won't do it to anyone else either. So what if Juvie authorities seized the punk? There was no way that kid wasn't going to live the majority of his life in prison. Sometimes, the Peace Archive isn't the right answer. But it's done."

Jenny hit play, and the somber tones of Rush's *Losing It* blasted throughout the Jeep. She used her turn signal to enter the road on her way to the interstate. She drove jerkily but at the speed limit. I reached over the center console to put my hand on her leg. She turned the music down.

"I love you, Miss Jenny. I'm tired and hungry. I expect

you're a bit of a wreck, too. How about a hot bath or a long shower?" I waited a moment before adding, "For two."

She accelerated up the on-ramp, rolling me back into the seat.

"Maybe," she replied softly, glancing over her shoulder at me, eyes sparkling and face awash with relief.

We made it back into the hotel before its restaurant opened and before the limited room service window opened. We put our do-not-disturb sign out for the second day in a row and locked the door behind us.

I used the untraceable phone I had left in the safe to dial the number I had memorized. Vinny answered on the first ring.

"It is done," I told him.

"Good. Today for dinner at the Club at seven. Wear a coat and tie." He hung up.

I looked at Jenny. "We have to dress up for dinner."

She shrugged. "I'm okay with dressing up. Looks like we're going shopping." She started removing her clothes one piece at a time, watching me watch her until she was naked. She moved close to me and put her finger on my lips. "You need a shower."

Jenny walked toward the oversized bathroom. I dropped my clothes behind me as I followed, hopping on one leg to get my pants off. By the time I reached the shower, the water was running, sending steam over the door. I headed in to find Jenny waiting for me.

I promised to apologize to the hotel for how much water we were going to use while cleaning our bodies and scrubbing our souls in the comfort of each other's arms.

Jenny held my face while her glistening body pressed against mine. "Tell me about it."

I wanted to forget about it. I ran my hands down the smooth skin of her back and over her hips. "I don't get tired of how your body feels, Miss Jenny." I leaned my forehead against hers as the water splashed against our shoulders and into the small space between us. "Two punks tried to roll me a block in. They were big but counted too much on their size. I took them out and then relieved them of their pistols. I got to the house where Detritus had a friend over. I waited for him to leave, then the young man decided it was time for a sandwich. I shot him through the back door when he was getting ready to take a bite. Getting out of there was interesting, but I managed to avoid the neighborhood's outrage."

"Why are there places like that? This is America." Jenny's forehead wrinkled as she put on her concerned face.

"I wish I knew. We grew up differently. What if we didn't feel like there was any world for us out there? I'd like to think we would fight back against a society that didn't accept us. I'd also like to think that we'd fight back in a different way."

"I'd like to think that, too. And you are fighting back in a way that makes sense. But how easy is that to say when we're in the nicest suite, unlimited money at our command?"

"Don't feel guilty, Miss Jenny. I don't have any answers for these ills of society except that the more drug dealers like the Gomez cartel or scumbags like Guano or Nader we put down, the more we help the world to be a much better place. They destroy lives on a grand scale."

"Destroyed," Jenny corrected. "What about Jimmy?"

"Maybe that's how you start fixing these things.

Politicians created it, and politicians will have to fix it. I haven't heard anything about Jimmy. I wonder how the mayor gig is treating him."

Jenny shrugged and threw her head back to let the water run over her chest. I buried my face in her neck and forgot all about Jimmy Tripplethorn and Detritus and the Peace Archive.

CHAPTER FIVE

"The secret of health for both mind and body is not to mourn for the past, nor to worry about the future, but to live the present moment wisely and earnestly." –Bukkyo Dendo Kyokai,_ *The Teaching of Buddha*

I had much less fun shopping than Jenny. She enjoyed hitting the right stores and browsing for what seemed an interminable amount of time. In reality, it had only taken ninety minutes.

"You are such a man," she told me.

"Unrepentant. I'll carry your bags, but damn! I don't understand how you can look at the same dress three times before making a decision. You spent less time sizing me up."

"I'm still wondering about that myself, Mr. Ian Bragg. You seduced me. I feel sullied."

"Who seduced who?"

"Whom. And it was you storming into my room like an uncaged lion."

"I thought it was my room. I tried to escape!" I started to question my memory.

"Your version of events."

"Why did you get ice while naked?"

"I had a bathrobe on."

"Aha! You admit that you were waiting for me like a spider in a web woven from the hotel's finest cotton. A lip bite and sparkling green eyes were bait the prey was incapable of resisting."

She dipped her head to look at me over her sunglasses. "And?"

"And I couldn't resist."

"Now that that is settled, what do we agree to with Vinny? Are we willing to move? What are we willing to do for this?"

"Those are good questions, Miss Jenny. Maybe we discuss the particulars away from Vince after he's laid things out. I don't want to do anything in front of him again. That took us to a place I didn't want to go. But the persuasion. I see how good Vince is as a salesman. I bought it hook, line, and sinker."

"Me, too, Ian. I could have said no."

"I don't think either of us could have said no." I drove into the Club's parking lot and picked a spot closer than last time. It had a light dinner crowd, or maybe this was the usual. Places like this were insulated from the routine based on a nine-to-five job that rippled through the rest of the world.

Seven in the evening on a Thursday, and we were standing tall outside our Jeep. Besides a stunning low-cut red dress that accentuated Jenny's curves, she had purchased a nice overcoat from Kohl's that cut the wind and kept her warm even though we didn't need to spend much time outside. Still, we had to maintain appearances. I had to buy everything from socks to shoes to a suit, shirt, belt, and tie.

"You look dashing," Jenny purred.

"And you, my dear. Scrumptious, even."

Vinny rolled in right at seven and parked next to us. He wore a sport coat with jeans. I turned to Jenny.

"You should see your face," she remarked and started to chuckle. "It's okay to dress up."

"Sure," Vinny said and vigorously shook my hand. He hugged Jenny before gesturing toward the door.

"I don't like half-truths, Vinny. You could have told me..."

"What's the fun in that?" Vince replied. He held the door for us. Inside the Club, we found more were dressed like us than Vince. "They let me dress down as a major benefactor. It's better for guests and new members to play it closer to the line. You dressed properly, Ian."

"New members?"

"Yes. I've already added you for consideration, and before you ask why, I'll tell you that half of the Archive's revenue has come from contracts made within this building."

I covered my mouth and whispered, "They know what you do?"

"They know I fix things that need to be fixed. No questions asked."

I looked around before speaking again. "What about the government work?"

"Chaz said you were sharper than the average bear." Vinny didn't expound as we were ushered into the main dining area, where there was plenty of space between tables. We were put into a private area off the main room, where a lone table was set for three.

"I hoped your wife would be joining us," I said casually.

Vinny waited for the server to leave before answering. "I don't have a wife. I have the business."

"But I thought…" I stopped when Vince smiled. "I thought what you wanted me to think."

"And that is how you operate at this level, Ian. I pressured you into the hit on Chaz's murderer. I really wanted to see that person erased, but I'll tell you now that I would have been good with you saying no as long as you provided an alternative. You seemed on the cusp of that with bidding the job out."

I clenched my jaw. I did not like to be played, especially not by a supposed partner. I glared at Vince until he held his hands up in surrender.

"Please forgive me. I wanted you to see the harsh realities of this side of the business. People will always try to play you for the greater good, ask for impossible deliveries, and try to make you feel like they're doing you the favor. You won't ever forget this. It's the difference between success and the feds crawling up our asses."

"No one wants that," I agreed. "About the gold cards. How are they not tracked?"

"Exclusive agreement with our bank in the Caymans. They never share that information with anyone. If the law changes, then they'll destroy the accounts after a single transfer of all remaining funds to a Swiss account. Now, the Swiss might share the information, but the individual transactions will disappear. There is nothing coming down the pipeline which threatens our anonymity, but if it does, I'd need anyone holding a gold card to go underground for a short while."

The server appeared with menus that showed meals but no prices.

I selected a twelve-ounce prime rib, and Jenny went with a petit filet. Vince ordered lasagna.

"Do you know something we don't know?"

"I'm Italian, and I love their lasagna. Their steaks are good, too. I wouldn't get the fish because this is Chicago, a long way from the ocean even though it's a quick flight from the coast. Still, get fish when you're in San Francisco, but not here."

Jenny and I looked at each other. "We generally don't get the fish. Maybe if we miss a workout, but then we'll go with lighter fare overall." I buttered a warm roll that had appeared on the table. The honey-butter made it taste more like dessert than bread. "How many people have gold cards?"

"We deactivated Chaz's before it could be used. Since it doesn't look like a normal card, I don't think they realized how to use it. Otherwise, five regions and me, but only two of the regions have the card. That makes three in circulation. We have a couple million against it and keep that topped off, so it's not an issue. Nobody abuses it by trying to buy a yacht or something."

"What about the other regions?" Jenny asked. "Why didn't they get one?"

"It wasn't the right incentive for them. Not everyone gets the same benefits because not everyone delivers at the same level. Our director in Atlanta will run the next retreat. I want you to go down there and give him a hand."

"What is my status?" I asked. I wanted to pin Vinny down.

"A good question. If Chaz was here, he would say equal partner. Since it's just me, I'll tell you that you're the XO, the executive officer, and when I retire in a year, then you'll become the CO. The partnership worked when it was Chaz and me, but I don't want to do that moving forward. This organization will work with one person at the top." He took a drink of his sparkling water. "You may have to move to Chicago because this is where the deals are made."

"Half the deals," I countered. "What about the government contracts?"

Vinny leaned over the table. "Those have been coming with greater and greater frequency over the past few years. You've spotted a number of them. We have a special place for those, one-hundred-percent online. We use an old BBS out of California and a VPN to get there. We say we're coming from Canada as the last place for the USG to be worried about."

"They know where to go?"

"It seems to be an open secret."

"Sounds like an opportunity for a setup from an overzealous agency." I shook my head. "I think we need something a little more secure to minimize the exposure to our people."

"When you figure out what that is, drop a note into the backroom of the old bulletin board where those projects take shape." Vinny smiled. "See, you're already taking charge of what needs to be controlled. We're nothing without our people. We have forty-one active operators, five directors, and me. You'll dual-hat until you can find a replacement. That shouldn't be hard. Who doesn't love Vegas?"

"I don't love Chicago. This traffic is horrible."

"You don't have to move here until I retire, but you'll need to come here fairly often between now and then to make sure you get to know the people you need to know and to learn the ropes. This job is tough. There are certain words you can't use, just in case we ever get recorded. And there are people you need to get to know so they can trust you."

I moved over to let the server deliver Jenny's meal and

expertly put everything in its place for the rest of us. She nodded before walking away, knowing there was nothing else we would ask for.

I didn't attack my prime rib, even though I was hungry.

"Build trust," I started. "These look like old-money people, which means they won't accept a blue-collar guy like me because I'm a new-money upstart with no right to walk the same hallowed halls."

"As long as you know your place and you deliver something these members need. I'm not accepted as their peer. No one they didn't grow up with can be, but they'll tolerate you as they do me. And for your information, since you are now inside these hallowed halls, you don't want to be their peer. Their money makes a difference. You make a difference, but they personally have no impact on the rest of the world. Their affairs are not the affairs of common folk like you and me or any of our operators. You don't want to be them."

I studied Vinny's expression. He maneuvered a forkful of gooey lasagna into his mouth and closed his eyes to savor the bite.

"For the first time, I feel like you are being completely honest with me. I can work with that. We'll call them colleagues, but outside these walls, they won't be seen with us." I cocked my head as I thought about it. "And that's probably best."

I returned to my thoughts as I dug into my prime cut. It wasn't the best I had ever had, but Jenny and I had eaten at as many five-star steakhouses as there were in Las Vegas. We enjoyed a high standard. I scanned the crowd of diners —insular group. Probably ate here every night.

Vinny was right; we did not want to be them. We could work with them. That was all that mattered, and Vinny had taught us a valuable lesson about working through the subterfuge and dissembling that would come to refine the contract into something that could be put into the hands of the directors. I looked at Jenny, and she smiled at me.

She hadn't missed the nuances. She didn't want to be them, either.

I took another bite of my steak and chewed slowly before speaking again. "You mentioned Atlanta."

"You should try this lasagna," Vinny offered. I started to push the plate for my dinner roll toward him, but he was waving for the server. "Could you deliver a small portion of lasagna to my friends, please?"

"Of course, Mr. Trinelli. At once."

The server hurried toward the kitchen.

"Atlanta. Meet with the regional director, a man by the name of Phillip Treglow. Talk him through what you did, maybe give him the classes you prepared. He's going to need a lot of help. Where you seemed to be a natural, he is not. You may have to attend."

"That creates a link between the two sessions. I'm not so sure."

Vinny took another bite, savoring his dinner as he chewed. The server brought us fresh portions of the lasagna, about two bites' worth each.

Jenny and I tried it while waiting for Vince. He wasn't wrong. I looked from my steak to the lasagna, wanting more lasagna, but I wasn't decadent enough to trade my meal for a new one. Neither was Jenny.

She knew what I was thinking, as she usually did. "Next time," she said softly.

"With a nice chianti."

Vince finished chewing and smiled, pleased by our reception of his recommendation. "As long as no one is on your trail, then there is no link between the two. Did you use your name?"

"No. I used a made-up business name that I found out later actually existed. I'll make up a new business name. The link will be the gold card."

"That's circumstantial at best since it'll be Phillip's card used. The numbers won't match, and the bank won't give them any data. No. I think you need to attend."

"I know this is the place where I'm supposed to push back if I feel you're wrong, but I don't. The vision for training isn't something others will share. Train the trainers. But Jenny and I will talk privately before we agree to anything. Last night's job was a total goat rope. I'm not going to put myself into that position again."

Vince nodded. "I understand. There's an old saying that comes to mind. 'If you want it bad, you get it bad.' But there are some people who can overcome the lack of information and imminency to excel. It's a rare gift. My compliments to you, Ian. To you both. I get two for the price of one."

"I still don't know what I'll be doing besides having ubiquitous meetings with people at the Club and trolling the backroom of an old bulletin board site, trying to find the government contracts where they have to keep our secret for their own self-preservation. And we know who those people are because of their digital signatures. I'll give you all that information."

I didn't like the amount of information I was going to be given, but there was no way around it. I wouldn't be able to memorize it all, at least not right away, which meant I'd have to store it. More information in the hidden rooms of the Peace Archive, a place no search engines could reach. There was a great deal to learn.

"How much revenue does the Archive get in a year, and how much does it pay out?"

"Now you sound like the people around here, but it is

a valid question. This year, we have taken in two hundred and seventy-four million dollars so far. We've paid the operators two hundred of that. We covered our overhead costs of fifteen million. We add ten percent annually to a contingency fund, that was twenty-seven-point-four million, and Chaz and I split the remaining thirty million. The contingency fund contains nearly two hundred million. That's enough money for our directors and us to disappear off the face of the planet and leave scorched earth for anything related to our operations. The operators can all disappear. They have their own funds."

"That's almost real money. What about when you retire?"

"It all moves over to your control, but upon implementation of the emergency protocol or a drawdown in operations, I'll get a cut of the contingency fund. No other monies are due to me."

"You are going to hand over an operation that makes you fifteen million a year?" I questioned.

"Despite the allure of the shiniest gold, there comes a time when a person has enough money. Everything I want is already paid for. I'll keep my gold card, of course, because it's nice never to see a credit card bill. Or any bill, for that matter. I'm not sure how I feel about seeing anything that says I owe someone money. How gauche."

Jenny and I chuckled. We, too, had fallen for the magic of a card that paid for everything without any further complications.

"We have four and a half mil in the bank."

"Did you count the extra mil I sent you this morning?"

"I stand corrected," I replied. "And I get you. We have what we need."

Vince waited for the server to clear our plates before

leaning close to examine me and then Jenny. When he spoke, it was a simple observation. "I sense a 'but.'"

I took Jenny's hand under the table and gripped it tightly. "I believe in what we do. I believe it makes a difference when the targets are properly vetted and found worthy to be on the receiving end of a contract. What we do makes the world a better place."

"And that is why I'm comfortable handing it all over to you. Go back to your hotel. I've had a bottle of champagne sent to your room for you two to celebrate privately. And tomorrow at noon, be back here to get your membership cards and meet one of our clients. Later in the afternoon, we'll meet another."

Jenny's eyes sparkled under the crystal chandelier, and for that one moment in time, everything seemed right with the world.

"What about you? Are you okay being alone?" I asked.

"Who said I'd be alone? I've got a good woman waiting at home for me. She promised to make a nice dessert if I promised her I was good with retiring in a year. I think it'll be sooner than that."

I was confused. "You said you weren't married," I blurted.

"I'm not. Maggie and I have been together for twenty-five years, but we never got married. That's old-people stuff."

I rolled my head sideways to look at Jenny. She bit her lip to keep from laughing out loud.

"So many assumptions, Ian. I have the business. Maggie and I are the best of friends, and," he leaned close and whispered conspiratorially, "we sleep together." He stood to go. "They'll put it on my tab. Stay as long as you'd like. I'll see you tomorrow around noon."

He strolled away, nodding at various people as he

passed. He stopped to talk to the hostess, shaking her hand and filling it with cash before he left.

"I feel like I'm on the receiving end of a running joke."

Jenny daintily wiped her mouth and put her napkin on the table. "The fact that Vinny can joke with you is a good sign. This business is tough, so finding the lighter side whenever you can is a good thing."

The concern on her face touched my heart. "I'm happy to have met you and that you married me, despite it being an old-person thing. I would have never figured Vinny for a hippie."

CHAPTER SIX

"The Best Way To Get Started Is To Quit Talking And Begin Doing." –Walt Disney

Morning came quickly after a quality evening spent by lovers with a bottle of champagne and chocolate-covered designer strawberries. We'd appreciated the gift from Vinny.

And we had appreciated each other.

I turned on my computer, accessed the VPN, changed settings, and then started the laborious process of getting to the backroom of the Peace Archive, where Vinny had stored the information he thought I needed to know.

There was far more than I had expected. In the beginning, they had documented a great deal and kept fairly meticulous records, but only as they related to setting up and running the business. The financials were screen captures from the main bank account, with extra captures of the secondary accounts.

I dug into the numbers. No one balanced the books

since there weren't any books. Everything went through the bank, and according to the records, Vinny and Chaz took a trip to George Town on Grand Cayman once a year to meet with the bank director to review the numbers.

It looked to be a vacation as much as anything. The scheduled meetings weren't long. I had no idea how they turned out since there were no after-action reports or minutes.

What kept drawing my eye were the vast sums of money moved into and out of the account. Vinny or Chaz personally made the payments to the operators, half up front and the other half on completion. I looked through the annual reports and counted forty-one current operators.

I went through the pictures twice to make sure I hadn't missed anything. Two hundred and fifty-four payments, which meant one hundred and twenty-seven hits this year, and the year wasn't over yet. The Archive had earned a grand total of two hundred and seventy-four million dollars. I calculated the averages. That meant an average of three hits per operator at average earnings of six million. They took home four mil a year and we kept two. I was good with them making more than me even if I included our costs incurred on the gold card.

The account access information was included in one of the files. I looked at it to memorize it, looked away to recite it, and then looked back. I would do that another dozen times before attempting to log in.

I heard the television come on. Jenny had propped herself up on pillows and was still tucked under the covers. It was Chicago, and there was a chill in the air even though the room was mostly warm. She pulled the covers down enough to show off her bare skin before shivering and pulling them up again.

From the television came "Jimmy Tripplethorn…"

Our heads snapped toward the screen, and I exclaimed, "Turn it up!"

Jenny was already mashing the remote's buttons. I stood and moved closer as if that would help me.

"I say again, the vice president has stepped down amid the Forsberg scandal. He vowed to continue fighting the allegations while refusing to let the case impact President Mastersmith. On the party's advice and consent, Seattle mayor Jimmy Tripplethorn's name has been forwarded to the Senate for their consideration as the next Vice President. This is Breaking News. Please stay tuned as we learn more about these shocking developments."

"'These shocking developments.'" I smirked at the talking heads. "I like how they tell me how to feel. I hate watching stupid people telling me the news, but I'm glad you had it on."

"When I saw you watching me, I stopped surfing so I could try to seduce you. Call it the luck of the draw."

I shut the top of the computer, removed my clothes, and crawled under the covers to get next to Jenny's naked body.

"I guess we were destined to know. Karma," I offered.

Jenny wrapped her arm around me and pulled me tighter against her than I already was. "What does this change?"

"I don't know what you mean."

"He owes you his life and the renewed relationship with his wife." Jenny kissed my head.

"I don't know. I've never had the vice president owe me before." I skooched up on the pillow and propped my head in my hand. "I would like to think it doesn't change anything."

"It will. I'll bet you he comes calling."

"Wouldn't that be something—an illicit meeting in the White House to talk about snuffing people out. Nah. I think his handlers won't allow him to ever meet with an operator like me."

"There are no other operators like you." Jenny turned to face me and sent her hand roving down my body.

"Chaz was an operator like me." I turned Jenny's face with my free hand to stare into her eyes. "Is his the end we're all destined for?"

"Vinny is doing pretty well and planning to retire. I give it three months."

"Another guesstimate. The Jennitor, Mystic and Seer."

"The all-seeing eye!" She put her finger to the side of her head. "I bet I know what's going to happen next." She seized my wrist and pushed me onto my back. I didn't fight very hard.

"Where's your coat?" Vinny asked after we got out since he was there before us.

"It's back in the room. Don't tell me…"

"I'll wait." He headed inside.

I looked at Jenny. She shrugged. "It's almost like a game with him," I complained.

"They have standards here. As members, we'll get to read the rules so we can avoid being embarrassed by getting denied service."

"There is that. At least we're close." We hurried back to the hotel. My suit jacket didn't look like a sports coat, but it was close enough. I put the tie in my pocket just in case. When we returned, Vinny wasn't outside, so we let ourselves in. We found him in the lobby, engaged in a casual conversation with another member. The two men shook hands, then Vinny joined us.

"This way," he said without preamble or greeting. We followed him down the hallway to an admin office, where we were warmly welcomed. The room looked more like a high-end lawyer's office than a room where administrivia happened with new members.

A young woman had us sit up straight in our chairs and took our pictures. She handed us clipboards with an extensive list of questions while she retreated into a back room. When she returned, our faces were emblazoned on shiny new membership cards. I finished the form quickly and handed it over. Jenny was still on the first page as she wrote neatly, taking up the offered space to give detailed answers.

I made eyes at her until she looked at me. I held my finger and thumb out and then moved them closer together in the universal gesture for "shorter."

She gave me the side-eye but abbreviated the rest of her answers.

"I assume you're the primary member," the young woman asked. I shook my head and pointed at Jenny.

The young woman smiled innocently and waited for my wife to finish filling out her form. She manually entered the information into the computer. "Jenny Bragg and Ian Bragg. You are confirmed as members. Welcome to the Club. Your sponsorship packet will be mailed to your home."

"Thank you," Jenny and I replied in unison. Home? I wondered what Jenny had put as an address. We shook hands and left to find Vince sitting in a wingback chair in the hallway, doing nothing but waiting for us.

"You look exceedingly executive," I told him.

"I've worked hard to achieve this look." He nodded once.

"What address did you put on the form?" I asked.

Jenny looked confused for a moment before her eyes shot wide. "My home in Washington."

My mouth fell open.

Vinny chuckled. "None of that matters. I've told them your address, right here in Lake Forest."

"Don't tell me you've bought us a house." I crossed my arms until I realized the posture I had assumed. I uncrossed them and tried to look casual.

"Not directly," he replied. "It's my house. When I retire, I won't need it. These old bones aren't as welcoming of a Chicago winter. It has a guesthouse you can use at your leisure until we move out, which will be before next winter sets in."

He stood and gestured for us to follow.

"First up is an appointment with a man we'll call Mr. Smythe, spelled with a Y but pronounced US-style."

The nuance didn't matter to me, but Vinny said it for a reason. I needed to pay attention since he didn't waste words. He used words with multiple meanings to keep from pinning himself down in case anyone was listening.

Imagine a conversation getting replayed in court, I told myself. *Don't say anything you don't want to relive.*

Vinny directed us to a table where we were able to put our backs to a wall. "This is the business table. You will meet all our clients here. The Club has a special dampener in this corner that foils any electronics. Check your phone."

I removed my burner. "No signal."

"It's more than that. Try to record something."

I looked for the app and found it. I had never used it before. I pressed the record button. "Mary had a little lamb. Its ass was in a jam. Along came Jenny Bragg to free the little fleabag."

"Nice." Jenny didn't say it like she meant it was nice. I was rather pleased with myself. I pressed play and heard only white noise.

"Now *that* is nice."

"Despite the fact that you gave certain personal data to the Club, this is one of the most secure facilities on the planet. Your information is in a safe that cannot be accessed except by three people who know their part of a trinary combination. If the safe were seized, any attempt to access it by other means would result in a thermite meltdown to destroy everything within."

"Who started this place?" I wondered.

"It's not who started it but who made it what it is today."

"Don't tell me. You own the Club."

"Just fifty-one percent of it. Chaz and I owned that together, but with his passing, his share rolled over to me. Once I retire, you will be my proxy here, but I'll retain my ownership because I like this club, and I just can't let it go. I'll tell them you're the new owners and that's how you'll act. Owner proxies."

"You are the owner, and you sent me off to put on a suit jacket."

"We have standards." Vinny smiled. "And we have a secure area to do business where a certain sum of money for our operations remains above board. There is nothing like a legitimate business behind which to hide where the real money is made. Prohibition was a grand adventure in Chicago where money-laundering and backroom deals flourished. Some of those lessons continue today. I present to you the Club."

"The little things we would never know. When Chaz

talked about a sales team, is this what he meant and not that the Archive actually had a separate layer of employees?"

"The sales team was Chaz and me, but it helps morale for the operators to think we are more robust."

I chuckled and shook my head. "No one knows anything out there, so I prodded Chaz to talk about the organization. It's my fault that I put him on the spot. Maybe it's better to keep details about the Archive secret. The thing about disinformation is that once it is proven false, the house of cards falls. While we're here, I think we need an alternate identity capability. Leaving forty-one people to figure it out on their own could get us exposure we don't want."

"You're not the only one who asked for that. It's something we might be able to leverage through here. The Prohibitionists are alive and well, with no trust in the government. I think we can trade a job for a hundred fake IDs or something like that. I'll introduce you to an individual who might be able to help. You can take that one and lead the effort."

An older man using a walker approached. He moved at a glacial pace. Jenny was on the outside, and when I moved to get up, she knew what I was going to do. She stood to help Mr. Smythe sit.

"Please allow me," Jenny told him and pulled out his chair to help him get into position.

"If I was only forty years younger, my dear, or a little richer, you could make me very happy."

"I'm flattered," Jenny replied. "I'd like to think that my husband keeps me plenty happy." She pointed at me.

"Does he know about us?" the old man asked before falling into his chair and inching it forward.

"Not yet, but I'll break the news to him when he's

feeling down." Jenny settled him and returned to her seat. My darling vixen winked at me.

"I like you. Let me guess. You're the replacement." His tone turned somber. Vinny and Chaz had been fixtures at the Club, and judging by the kindness in the man's rheumy old eyes, they had been well-liked.

"I'm Ian, and this is Jenny."

"A stunning beauty, my young man. Don't ever lose her." He turned to Vince. "You're looking good, young fella."

Vinny glanced at us. "Now you see why Mr. Smythe is my favorite."

"I'm sure a finer gentlemen has rarely walked these hallowed halls," I remarked.

Vinny waved for an attendant to bring us drinks. He reappeared quickly with four mimosas.

When the attendant left, Vinny spoke. "You said you had something that needed done."

"Always working, this one." He stabbed a gnarled finger at Vinny. "But such is life. The finer things don't come easy or cheap. A friend of mine talked about a problem he was having with a security racket moving into his neighborhood. The shakedown artists are out in full force, and he'd like them removed. Permanently."

"Where are we talking?"

"The Big Apple."

"Do you have better details?"

"All kinds." He slid a memory stick across the table. Vinny pushed it toward me. I palmed it and shoved it into my pocket. "Says it's worth two large to him."

"Two million," Vinny clarified. "How many targets are we talking?"

"At least two, might be four."

"But they take their orders from someone with an

57

entrepreneurial spirit. Having to root that individual out will take quite an effort. I think three-point-five is more in the ballpark for a job of this magnitude."

"Three is all he can go. After that, it's a wash as to which direction he throws his money. But with success, the neighborhood is clear for his kids and their kids." He pushed his hand toward Vinny, and the two men shook. "I'll let you let me go now. Bye, beautiful lady. I miss you already. And you, too, Ian. I wish you all the luck in filling Chaz's shoes. It was an awful thing that happened to him. I hope the police solve that crime soon."

I nodded but didn't answer. Jenny jumped up to help Mr. Smythe to his walker. He reached out to grab Jenny's butt, but she danced out of reach. He smiled at us before trundling away.

Vinny shrugged. "I know it's not okay, and before you ask, the men here are used to seeing women in positions of power. Some are a little more old-school and have more money than sense, as you can tell from his three ex-wives."

"Is there an ex-wives club?" Jenny quipped.

"There is. It's called the Better Club." Seeing our skepticism, he continued, "I'm not kidding. It's on the other side of town."

"There's something very right about that," I offered. "But back to business. Three to get one or four. There are a lot of unknowns in this contract."

"I'll hand it over to the northeast director to work it up." Vinny threw back his mimosa, which was light on the champagne, heavy on the orange juice. "Tell them your favorite drink, then you only need to snap your fingers and it will appear."

"As the owner, you made me pay for the meal, but…" I wasn't sure where I was going with my thought.

"Really?" Vinny fixed me with a one-eyed stare. "What

58

do you say we stop by the house and take a look? You can stay there or in the hotel. Makes no difference to me."

"The hotel is nice, but their restaurants close down early."

"You'll have time tonight to partake. We'll hit the house now and be back here before dinner to meet with Lance Bingham. You've seen how it's done. You can take this next one."

"I'm not sure I've seen enough to say I have any idea how it's done. They make an offer, and I counter at fifty-percent higher?"

"No." Vinny headed out, and we had to hurry after him. He nodded and waved at people as he passed. I noticed that he greeted the staff as eagerly as the members. I could respect that.

We took Vinny's car for a drive that lasted less than five minutes. His oversized colonial stood within a fenced compound at the far end of the golf course. He pulled around the center fountain and into the farthest bay of a four-car garage. The middle two stalls held classic Grand Prix-style race cars, and the closest bay held a Grand Cherokee that was the twin of the one we rented, but this one was cherry-red.

Inside, a tall and graceful woman greeted us. "You must be Ian and Jenny. Call me Viv." She dispensed with the handshakes and went straight for hugs. Vince stepped out of her way. "My, you are a beauty."

I stared at Vince. "Were you messing with us?" He had said her name was Maggie.

"Maybe." He smiled slightly and stared back at me.

"I'm going to develop a complex. Mr. Smythe seemed quite smitten." Jenny smiled. I couldn't help but laugh.

"Mr. Smythe lost his ability to woo the ladies twenty

years ago. He puts on a good act." She turned to Vinny. "Everything turn out okay, dear?"

"As usual. We're good for this one, and we'll probably get another contract this afternoon. Two in one day. Not a bad introduction for Ian."

"Do you want me to show them the house so you can retire and we can go someplace warm?"

I snorted. "I see who the real boss is."

Vinny narrowed his eyes and looked down his nose at me. "I'd be lying if I told you you were wrong." Vince showed us his first-floor study, which overlooked a wooded backyard through which we could see a green and a sand trap from the Club's course. He remained there while Vivian showed us the rest of the two-story house. It was furnished minimally and decorated with an eye toward the Renaissance. Oil paintings hung throughout—not originals like those that hung in the Louvre and the Uffizi, but copies that made me wonder.

When we finished, we returned to the kitchen for glasses of sparkling water we drank while looking out at the backyard. "There is very little we'll be taking with us. We have a vacation home on Grand Cayman that will be our permanent home as soon as we can get there. You two are a godsend."

I squeezed Jenny's hand. From operator to running a quarter-of-a-billion-dollar operation. I worried about when the rug would be pulled out from under me. "I don't know if I'll ever be ready to fill both Chaz's and Vince's shoes. I can only promise that I'll do the best I can. The best *we* can because I'm not alone in this."

"I didn't realize you were in the business," Viv said to Jenny.

"I'm a schoolteacher, but Ian has shown me his world."

"Jenny can hold her own," I added.

"I don't have anything to do with Vinny's business. Maybe I should have, but I have my own career that is wrapping up. I ghostwrite stories for some famous authors. I'm out of gas and ready to retire."

"You don't need to work," I blurted. "I'm sorry. Everyone needs to have a purpose."

"And that was mine. With Vinny's business as it is, I couldn't do anything where I was highlighted. People can be nosy. Not at the Club. They tend to mind their own business there. So ghostwriting was perfect for me. My stories are on the bestseller lists four to six times a year. I have no complaints."

Vince reappeared. "Did you show them the guesthouse?"

Viv chuckled. "Forgot that part."

He kissed her on the cheek and headed for the garage. We followed him through and out the other side. That led into a home about a quarter the size of the main house but every bit as well-tended. Two keys sat on the counter. "There you are. Come and go as you please."

Jenny slipped them both into her pocket. Vince offered his hand.

"Sooner rather than later."

I took his hand. "Feeling your mortality?"

"Is it that obvious? Since Chaz cashed in, it's been weighing on me. I want to get out while I still can. Now watch me have a heart attack on the beach a week after I retire."

"Shall we meet up with Mr. Bingham and then call it a night?" I suggested.

"Capital idea." We piled back into Vinny's car and returned to the Club.

In the entryway, we met Lance Bingham, a man in

perfect physical condition who sported just enough gray to scream "executive." He introduced himself as a lawyer.

We maneuvered our way through the main reception area to the back room where the table we had sat at earlier waited. "The owner's table," Vince had called it.

We settled with our backs to the wall, as we had before.

Lance sat and tossed his head with a devil-may-care attitude. "I have an issue that needs your gentle touch," he stated.

Vince pointed at me.

"And what would that be, Mr. Bingham?" I asked.

"Call me Lance. We're all friends here." I kept my expression neutral. Bingham was the opposite of Smythe, immediately unlikeable. "A client needs a competitor removed from the marketplace. He's being held back, and no one is getting the service they need."

"Then your client needs to work harder to earn his market share," I said evenly, not bothering to look at Vinny for validation. They had said in Vegas that they didn't take bad contracts.

"Okay. You're onto me. Vinny put me up to that."

"I suspected," I replied, even though I hadn't. I had just assumed the worst about this guy. "The real issue is a gross increase in crime, and it's all because of a dirty cop."

That sent ice into my veins. I waved at the attendant. "Sparkling water, please." I wanted to buy time.

"Do you know who the bad cop is definitively and who he or she is dealing with?"

"Those are good questions. We have suspicions, but that's it. I'm not going to lie. Seeing how there's been an exponential increase in crime with a decrease in successful arrests tells me there's something rotten. We can only surmise there's a leak and the cops can't get close to the real perps."

"What is it worth to you to fix?"

"My client. It's worth at least," he glanced over his shoulder, "a cool million."

I smiled. The sparkling water arrived, glasses for Jenny and me. Vince and Lance declined anything. "No. Give me a real number because what you've described is the second-highest-risk job I've ever heard of. Trying to clean up a dirty cop shop isn't something to be taken lightly, even if it's only a single officer, which it probably isn't. I doubt one person could keep that kind of secret. This will take a soft touch, lots of time, and a great deal of money if we want to make sure the neighborhood is properly cleaned up, which means turning the clean cops loose."

He hung his head. "I think it's the chief of police."

"Which makes it even spendier. Give me a real number," I pressed.

"Four mil."

"That's more like it. Where is this questionable department?"

"Right here. Downtown Chicago." Lance looked less than confident as he stared at his clasped hands resting on the table.

"Give me what you have, and I'll look into it."

"Transfer as usual?" He removed a thumb drive from his pocket and held it out. I took it quickly and tucked it into my pocket.

"As usual, yes," I replied, though I had no idea what the usual was.

He nodded once, eyed Jenny, stood, and walked away.

"I don't like him," Jenny said once he was gone.

"No one does," Vinny confirmed. "But he gives us more work than anyone else. He is an influence broker working deals for people across the country, and he moves a great deal of cash."

"Sounds like we're both unanimous and okay with our dislike for the man, but it doesn't affect our business relationship. In that regard, we'll have to see how we can be accommodating, and *you* will need to explain what happens next. As in, what is 'the usual?'"

CHAPTER SEVEN

"Tell me and I forget, teach me and I may remember, involve me and I learn." –Benjamin Franklin

Once back in our hotel room, I disappeared into the computer to figure out the details of how an initial request for bids worked. It started with the agreement and then more from the thumb drives. First thing was to scan the drive before allowing it to access any information on my computer. I used three different scanning processes to find out if anything was embedded.

Both were clean.

Smythe's and Bingham's requests were similar: clean up the bad influence from a neighborhood to allow businesses to flourish. The two jobs were significantly different. One could be satisfied with a surgical hit and the other with an anonymous exposé delivered to the media, showing the dirty cop and forcing those who opened up the neighborhood to the predators under the scrutiny of the public and internal affairs. Cockroaches run for their lives when the light is turned on.

Would that contract make more sense? Collect info rather than make a martyr of a dirty cop. The message had to be sent in a way that would best resonate across the whole department, maybe get leadership fired. Then those who wouldn't turn a blind eye could be put into positions of authority.

"What if we put out a hit that isn't a hit?" I asked.

Jenny had dressed up and was reading while she waited for me so we could stroll downstairs to eat at the hotel's restaurant.

"I don't understand."

I explained my thoughts.

"It's better if people don't die if Bingham wants a long-term fix," Jenny agreed.

"I think that's the right answer if we want the Archive to evolve. The hit is nothing more than a targeted media exposure with enough facts delivered anonymously to the station, newspaper, and TV news all at the same time. The police would have to act on the allegations, and the public would demand that something be done."

"There you have it. Doing right by killing people where it matters."

I sucked my teeth as I looked Jenny over. "I'm going to have to contemplate that over dinner."

"I'm hungry for lasagna," Jenny stated.

"We *are* owners now…"

Jenny shook the keys to the rental. It was seven in the evening. "Indeed. Our first meal as throbbing members, then we're off to Atlanta tomorrow. I'll put on a coat."

I went with jeans and a dress shirt with my suit jacket. "We'll dump the dress clothes at the guesthouse on our way out of town."

"I guess we're obligated to get more, too." Jenny smiled.

I didn't see the pleasure in shopping, but I enjoyed watching Jenny model new clothes. Maybe there was pleasure to be had in shopping.

"More lingerie," I blurted. "I mean, 'Yes, dear.'"

"Incorrigible. I married an incorrigible man."

"And there's nothing you want to change about me, either. What do you say we partake of that fine lasagna, Mrs. Bragg?"

Hartsfield-Jackson Atlanta International Airport was one of the largest and busiest in the world. We were happy not to have checked baggage once again. We followed the signs to proceed through the underground concourses connecting the terminals on our way to baggage claim to snag a rental vehicle.

I had not yet contacted the regional director to set up the meet. I'd have to make the deposit and wait for his call. I wanted to talk to each of the regional directors. The Marine in me wanted to talk to my seconds in command.

General Bragg. I chuckled at the thought.

"What are you laughing at?"

"Thinking of myself as the general in command of the Archive. I'm thinking I need to talk with each of the regional directors to establish my expectations and the ground rules."

"Like Dave?" Jenny referred to the one who'd tried to strong-arm me and had an operator hold Jenny hostage for leverage.

"Especially Dave. I think it's time we had a nice conversation with that fella. Maybe I can smash his face into a fruit smoothy again. And using an operator on a personal mission? Tsk, tsk."

"Can I watch?" Jenny wondered.

"I'm not sure we can go back to Seattle yet. We should probably avoid that place for a while."

"It's been over a year, Ian."

I pulled Jenny close and kissed her. "As you wish. We'll go see Dave, but maybe we'll fly into Spokane and drive from there."

Jenny shrugged one shoulder. "I'm good with that."

We caught the automated people-mover to take us to the rental car center, which was a massive affair all by itself. We upgraded our rental to a BMW 550 and headed into the garage to pick it up. Once we checked it over and settled into our seats, I looked at Jenny and she looked at me.

"This is a little different than the first car you chauffeured me in, Mr. Bragg."

"Just a little. Where are we going?"

"Atlanta," Jenny replied without missing a beat. I stared at her until she removed her phone and looked for a high-end boutique hotel nearby. "How about the Artglore? It's in midtown, and there's a pizza place nearby."

"Midtown means nothing to me. It's like saying north and south when I'm in a parking garage." I messed with the radio while Jenny hurried to find the directions. If I brought up Rush before she found the directions, we'd listen to my music the whole way. I scrolled quickly to *Marathon* and punched play. I put the car in gear, looked both ways, and slowly rolled out of the parking spot on my way toward the city.

"Fine," Jenny said as she put her burner into a recess in the center console. As soon as we were outside, I followed the signs that directed us toward the city. When the GPS came to life, it told us to keep going in that direction.

"An unerring sense of direction," I stated proudly.

"What next, Ian?" Jenny asked. "Are we going to travel around the country meeting with the directors and then move to Chicago? Split our time between there and Vegas or someplace else?"

"Good questions all. What do *you* think we should do?"

"I was wondering if you were going to ask."

"Ouch." I dialed the vehicle's performance to sport so I could listen to the engine growl while we were caught in traffic. "We have a job to do, and if we can adjust things to make sure that not every case is a hit, then we win. Fixing things without having to kill anyone."

"You know that's not how it's going to work."

"Always the voice of reason. I know. Sometimes there is only one right answer, but we'll have to look to see if there are other options before we race to the conclusion that is irreversible once implemented."

"And I'll say it again." Jenny slid her hand slowly toward the music player. "That's why you are the best person for this job. You are the best person to teach other people about this job. You are the best person to provide oversight of those doing this job."

"If I didn't know better, I'd think you were trying to stroke my ego." I inflated a little since Jenny was being sincere. But words weren't actions. I had to stay sharp every day if I wanted to continue to deserve the praise.

"I don't need to butter your muffin. I'm just being honest." I put my hand over the music player to block Jenny. She casually looked out the window as if she hadn't been trying to swap Rush for the radio. I tried to think through what a conversation with Phillip Treglow was going to look like. I also wanted to give all the directors back-door access to a secure communications area of the Peace Archive so we didn't have to keep spending money to make phone calls. We parked hit packages in that area. I wondered why Chaz and Vinny had decided on the process to make phone calls by going through the bank.

Incentive. It made it an expensive proposition to carry on a conversation, which meant that the fewer of them were made, the less the exposure. Everything had to be hard; otherwise, it increased the risk.

Chaz and Vinny were pros. I didn't want to undo that. I'd hold off on revamping communications. It would cost what it cost until there was something better that was equally low exposure. I needed to learn the ropes before I looked at changing anything except matters that related to the frontline operations. I knew how operators worked. I carried that mindset.

"Never forget where you came from," I reminded myself.

Jenny casually turned her head. "I've never been to Atlanta before."

"You are in for a treat!" I declared. I waited for a moment. "Me neither. Not anywhere besides the airport, that is."

Jenny worked her phone to find out what else was around the hotel. "The Art District. We are going to a museum, Mr. Bragg."

"Yes, dear."

That earned me a punch in the shoulder. "And you're going to like it."

"I appreciate art." I pointed at Jenny's body. That earned me another punch. "We need to get back in the gym. It's been three days. Four days?"

"No kidding. I feel myself getting weaker by the minute." Jenny flexed her bicep.

"Could you be an operator?" I wondered.

"No. I couldn't take a contract and carry out a hit. That's not me. That psychopath Jack? That was different. I can protect myself, thanks to you, but I can't do what you do, Ian. I'm sorry for sniping you earlier. We're in this together, but this is your business. You don't need me to do any of it."

"But I want you with me. Balance. Decency."

Jenny pointed at the next off-ramp. The map app strongly suggested we take it.

"With great power comes great responsibility," I added.

"What could you do if you activated all the operators at the same time?" Jenny asked.

"That's something I never aim to find out. But how about Jimmy? We haven't talked about him. Vice President. That means his father-in-law is now an even bigger power broker than he was before."

"It's like something out of a weird thriller novel, as if Vinny's wife wrote it."

I nodded. That wasn't far-fetched. Maybe she *had* written something like that. She had never given up who she wrote for, even though there was no doubt the Archive leadership could keep secrets. That was one she wasn't willing to share.

It was better for people to keep their secrets. Not everyone needed to know everything.

The GPS guided us through the turns to deliver us to the front door of the multi-story boutique hotel in the heart of the Art District. "I like it."

"Artists see the world differently than the rest of us," Jenny explained. "Ours is to appreciate their vision. I look forward to strolling through the museum."

We parked the car. It was mid-afternoon, which meant the hotel's parking garage wasn't full yet. The early departures had gone, and the newcomers had not yet arrived. Jenny took the roller bag and I carried my backpack into the lobby, where we found a king suite was available. We reserved it and moved in.

"Museum closes in thirty minutes," Jenny lamented. "But it opens at ten tomorrow morning. We can work out, eat, and then enjoy a casual stroll."

"We can't miss," I agreed. "Let me do that money transfer thing and see how long it takes for our man Phillip to call us."

I opened my computer and went through the process of getting online through the VPN and to the dark web to where the banking data was hidden. I opened a new window to the bank and deposited money from the administrative funding account into the one identified as the southeast regional director's. I made two deposits to give him the number to my untraceable phone.

After that, I pulled up the two new packages. I wanted to do more research on them, but that was no longer my job. I put a tag on the Chicago contract to list as something requiring surveillance and information to build a public media package. Evidence to share but not to make it a hit. I named it a living case and dropped it into the central region's folder. I sent the package to the northeast region to clear out the protection racket. I gave him a budget of two million to work with. I gave the central region the same budget.

It was a lot of money for being a private investigator, but it was high-risk to go after the authorities, and that was where the cost came into play. If only the dirty cops got killed, it would send a message to the others that it was time to step back into the light.

That was my plan, anyway. We had to give the operator the latitude to do as he or she saw fit. We could influence the contract's deliverables, but ultimately, the operator decided.

And that was why the training sessions were critical. It all tied together.

"Maybe we can work out and then catch dinner?" Jenny suggested.

My mind instantly jumped to the wrong conclusion. I shut the computer and jumped up with a stupid smile on my face. "Oh. You meant 'work out.'"

Jenny stood there in her shorts and t-shirt and sneakers. "That's what I said. Work out. Did you always have such a libido problem?"

"It's not a problem," I countered. "Because only with you. I'm always at a heightened state of readiness if you know what I mean."

"How could I not? You know you missed our anniversary."

"I what?"

"One year. It was six weeks ago."

"I feel like I should be more remorseful than I am." Jenny bit her lip. "Those things don't matter to me, but if they are important to you, then I'll make sure I don't miss it again."

Jenny studied me intently, hand casually stroking her chin.

I didn't know what to do with the silence. "I try to treat you like it's our anniversary every day. Just last night, we had lasagna, and we were treated like royalty."

"Because we're the owners now. They were obligated."

"We tipped well. Very well."

"Money talks," Jenny said, watching me do the striptease to get undressed. "Look at us. Best suites in the hotels, five-star dinners, and owners of the Club, with a house that is a mansion. All ours. I don't feel like we deserve it."

I stopped dancing and pulled my shorts on. "I know. I feel a bit guilty, too. We're in this position because Chaz is gone."

"They were pulling you up to their level before Chaz was killed," Jenny argued.

"Chaz was too slow to retire. Don't let that be us."

We performed the pinky swear before I finished dressing, and we went to the hotel's workout room. We were the only ones there.

Treglow called in the middle of a bench press set on a universal machine. I put the weight down and pulled the phone out of my pocket.

"Phillip," I said.

"Who is this?"

"My name is Ian. Vinny asked me to give you a call, talk about your upcoming retreat. We're in Atlanta and staying in the Art District. Can you meet us here tomorrow?"

"I'm only three blocks away. I can meet you in ten minutes if you'd like."

"We are in the middle of a workout. Meet us for dinner, then. Pick your favorite place nearby as long as we can have some privacy. We are wide open on what we'll eat."

"We?"

"My wife and I. We are a package deal."

"I hadn't heard anything about that. I didn't think it was possible."

"Then we have a lot to talk about. Where are we going to meet?"

"A pizza place with big booths about a block from the art museum. Riordino's. I'll meet you there. I'll be wearing a brown leather flight jacket."

"I'll be wearing a plain windbreaker and have a supermodel hanging off my arm."

Jenny poked me.

"See you in an hour?"

"An hour. Riordino's. See you there." I ended the call and returned to my set.

"I don't like when you call me a supermodel." Jenny assumed a defiant pose with her hands on her hips and her head upright.

"You have no idea how you look through my eyes. You need to simply accept it because you are. And now you're getting paid like one, too."

"I...I..." she stammered. I finished my set. Added more weight and pushed another full set before turning the bench over to Jenny. She stuck the pin at her chosen weight and laid back to push it up.

She hit four reps before I had to help her with the fifth.

"You're throwing more than your body weight now," I said. "My supermodel."

"Just between us, you can call me that all you want."

We rotated through for a quick ten minutes on the stair stepper. By the time we finished our race, my blood was pumping. A ten-minute sprint to the top of the Eiffel tower, twice. I nearly fell off the thing trying to stand, but with Jenny's help, we managed to walk out of the mini gym. In the hallway, our legs settled down.

A shower, and then we'd take care of business.

CHAPTER EIGHT

"It is not fair to ask of others what you are not willing to do yourself." –Eleanor Roosevelt

We spotted the regional director before he spotted us. We made it to him and stood there briefly while he scanned the area.

"Right here, Phil," I said softly. He nearly jumped out of his skin.

"How did I miss you?" he wondered, shaking his head. "You're good."

"The targets never complained," I replied. We shook hands. He hesitated before offering his hand to Jenny. She raised one eyebrow as she looked eye to eye with him. Phil was shorter than me and older.

We went inside and snagged a booth.

"Jenny and I are an equal team. It makes things a lot easier."

"I always got the impression that this was a lonely business. I've chased away some fine ladies because of it."

His exceedingly average everything suggested he was exaggerating. I took it in stride since everyone's tastes were personal. I'd proven that with Miss Jenny, where I had fallen hard for her from our first night. There was no going back.

"It's okay, but tempering how you discuss our company is something that has to happen in the right way. Can't have a breakup with someone who has insider knowledge."

"Gotta have an *up* before a breakup." He passed out the menus. "I figured." He stared at Jenny. "Are your eyes green? Gosh, you are beautiful!"

Jenny blushed.

"Don't make her kill you. I think we can call you Mr. Smooth."

"And you're an operator, too? You are amazing!"

Jenny shook her head. "Sorry, Phil. I'm not an operator. We train constantly, but that's not my shtick."

His face fell, and he looked at the table until the server stopped by. We ordered a couple of thin-crust pizzas.

When we were alone again, I spoke. "We're here to talk about training the operators in your region."

"I'm all ears. You're the guy who ran the other session. How did that go? How many people did you have? Who gave the sessions? Where did you have it?" I held up my hands to stop the tidal wave of questions. He wasn't showing that he was all ears.

"I'll send you the package I put together for it to show the various classes I prepared, but we only did half of them. It could have been all directed discussions, roundtables. Strategically, you need to find an exclusive place to hold it. This is the most critical thing you can do to make sure it goes well. After that, good people will make the right things happen. They'll talk about what's most important to them and share their experiences. We had thirteen operators with a good variety of experience."

"Thirteen! Wow. I only have five in this region."

"I haven't reviewed what kind of contracts we've gotten, but is that enough?"

"Not by a long shot. I've only been able to fill half the contracts without bumping the bids up. We're costing the company money."

Until I met the other operators at the Arizona retreat, I had assumed most came from the military. The most effective ones were those who didn't stand out in a crowd, with the exception of Elena. She stood out, but that was exactly why she was effective. Phil was average, and no one would be able to pick him out of a lineup. "Were you a corporate guy in a former life?"

"Fed." He smiled at the surprise on my face. "I know. I'm the odd man out. I was an IRS auditor." He leaned across the table. "Turns out I have a certain skill with poison and booby traps. Those science and chemistry kits I grew up with came in handy."

"How many successful contracts do you have?" Jenny asked. I wasn't sure why.

"I have seventeen," he looked around before speaking in a voice barely above a whisper, "and never a hint that they were anything other than an accident."

"That is impressive. But you only have five bidders. I'm going to have to look into that side of the business. I don't have any idea how it works. How did you come into our employment?"

The server arrived with the drinks and an appetizer of hot wings. He nodded at her and she hurried away.

"I have a gift with women, as you can see. I think how I got my start is for a different place." The table beside our booth filled with people my age. We nodded politely at them.

"Think about where you can have your event. For us, we went with a dude ranch. Exclusive, just us for a three-day meeting, with open days on both sides to make it easy traveling in and out."

"No airport?"

"Not even close. People flew in to airports at all points of the compass and then drove in. It worked." I didn't mention any of the other troubles we had with the event. I refused to believe that would happen again. "Maybe we can combine a couple events to bring people from the northeast region, too. We paid everyone a little bit to show up."

"That's good. Money talks, or so they say." Phil stared at the wall, deep in thought. His fingers twitched as if he were imagining himself on his computer. When he returned to the moment, he turned his head toward Jenny. "Did you discuss what it was like being a couple in this business?"

"We did. There was a great deal of interest in how to make that work," Jenny replied. "I think how Ian shaped the conversation was important to how I received it. That's not a viewpoint any of them had. It also made a difference that someone tried to…" She stopped mid-sentence and changed course. "We had some issues that we had to deal with, but Ian was calm and helped us both through it."

"Another topic for a different time," Phil said.

"It is." The group next to us was engaged in a lively conversation. "The number you called me on earlier, memorize that. I have an untraceable phone, and I prefer not having to do deposits back and forth."

Phil took a drink and kept glancing at Jenny.

"When you see the information I send you, I think

you'll feel a lot more comfortable about the retreat." I knocked on the table in front of him. "You act like you've never seen a woman before. You're making me uncomfortable."

"Sorry. Maybe that's why I'm good at what I do—because I'm so bad at the other stuff."

Jenny nodded. "Work on it. I'm a person just like anyone else. You have to deal with it; otherwise, you might get your ass kicked."

He sat up straight. "I thought you said you weren't an operator?"

"I'm not, but I have learned how to fight, and I've taken down an operator who was executing her own contract on me."

"Catfight!" Phil blurted. Jenny buried her face in her palm.

"Phil, you are killing me."

"I'm nervous. We missed a contract, and the operator disappeared. Now I have to do it…" He paused as if waiting for me to tell him he didn't, but I wasn't going to tell him that. It was his responsibility to see it through. I had learned that lesson the hard way. "It's on for tomorrow."

"Good luck," I replied nonchalantly. "We'll stay around to backstop you if needed, but I'm sure you've got this."

He didn't look sure. I expected more from a director. I couldn't ask him the details. The pizza joint was a little too public. Our meals arrived, and we hadn't eaten any of the wings yet.

"My mouth is watering. Let's get down to the important business of finishing off this pie."

"Can thin-crust be a pie?"

"Don't harsh my buzz, Phil. It's always a pie because that's what I call it. You can call yours whatever you want.

Every meal is a feast and every paycheck a fortune. Every day is a holiday."

"That is a surprisingly positive way to look at things." Phil dug into his meat special.

"Did the IRS suck all the joy from your soul?" I asked, going for the wings.

"Mostly, but I have always had a different sense of humor." Phil seemed pleased with his answer, even chuckling before taking another bite.

Jenny bit her tongue and fidgeted. She couldn't get out of there fast enough. I tried to watch Phil, but he was as uncomfortable as we were. A solo man in a job that fed his need to be alone. I was sure he wished to be anywhere else besides there with us for dinner, but I was the boss.

"We'll finish this up and be on our way. You get a good night's rest and then see that contract through."

He nodded. There was no need to talk.

We ate quickly, boxed up a few leftovers, paid the bill in cash, and hurried out. I shook Phil's hand outside, and he settled for a chin tip since Jenny had crossed her arms.

He walked away with his head bowed. We held hands on our way back to the hotel.

Jenny didn't need to comment on how she felt. I sensed the tension drain from her with each additional step between her and Phil.

"I will never introduce you again as a supermodel," I promised.

"You know, I don't think that was it at all. Phil is so uncomfortable around people that it would have been grim no matter what you had said, but I appreciate it. What do you say we get a bottle of champagne and a jug of orange juice? We can make our own mimosas."

We had no idea what the next day had in store, but I knew what I needed to do. I forwarded my notes from the first retreat to Phil's area in the backrooms of the Peace Archive.

I then trolled through the information Vinny had provided to learn more about the company while looking for any notes about recruiting. I was sorely disappointed. There was nothing about how they brought new operators on board.

I needed to ask Vinny. Maybe even talk with my old skipper, the one who had recruited me. The answer eluded me while I paced the room, trying to think.

"Talk to me," Jenny said, sitting cross-legged on the bed.

"I don't know anything," I complained. "Nothing about this business. There isn't a manual or a website to look up how to run something like the Archive. And Vinny is less than forthcoming. Am I supposed to learn as I go? It gives me the willies, trying to solicit for work. If I had my choice, I'd move it all online except for the people I knew and could personally vouch for."

"Which is exactly how it's set up now. Chaz and Vinny know all the people they get contracts from."

"But *I* don't know them."

Jenny looked at me as if the answer were obvious. I waited since it wasn't.

"We need to spend more time at the Club. Play some golf, help out in the kitchen. You know, do owner stuff and get to know the people."

"Oh, man! Chicago?" I grumped as I looked at the floor. "Can't we move it to Vegas?"

"Old money isn't moving."

"I was liking Vegas."

Jenny climbed off the bed so she could hug me and pat my head as if I were a child who had lost his favorite toy.

"You promised me that we would never get to settle down, and now we have an opportunity to do just that. What's wrong with that?"

"But it's in Chicago."

"Where there's an airport you can fly anywhere in the world non-stop from."

"Almost anywhere. Same could be said for Vegas," I complained in my best petulant voice. "We better go shopping so when we get home, we can look sporty."

"My Ian, wearing a suit to go to work. Brooks Brothers is going to get some of that sweet gold card money."

"What's a Brooks Brothers?"

"Your new favorite place to shop."

"My best disguise is my homeless-person look. Will I ever get to put that on again?" I held Jenny at arm's length to give her my most winning smile.

"I sure hope not." She frowned and stared back. "While we are on the subject of things we won't be doing, please tell me that we won't be seeing Phil again. He could be the most awkward person I've ever met. He makes me feel uncomfortable, and when you add that to his favorite *tool* of poison, then he's downright creepy."

"Helping awkward people out of their shells. Maybe we could get him some professional help." I chuckled. "Then again, we probably have enough work in the Archive that we could put our own psychotherapist on exclusive retainer."

Jenny lifted my chin. "They have outlet malls here."

"I feel like my life is no longer my own." I tried to be somber, but Jenny's smile and sparkling eyes drew me in. I pulled her to me and kissed her slowly. "And I like it. After a year in my world, it's now time to explore yours. You take the reins, *sensei*, and teach me, but only enough to look like I belong in the executive ranks. Not enough to where I'm an expert at fashion. I think that would turn me into a total knob."

"My Ian will never be a knob. And I don't know anything about being an executive, but I do enjoy shopping. I've never shopped with a purpose like this before. I look forward to the challenge."

"I surrender to your superior position. I guess we're going to have to get dressed."

Jenny pointed at herself. "I'm ready to go now."

I looked down at my shorts. "I guess I better get dressed." Jenny pulled clothes out of my backpack and handed them over. "Shirt's wrinkled." I smiled.

"Wear a coat," Jenny suggested before taking my laptop and putting it into the safe. I dressed, even putting on socks since I expected we might buy dress shoes even though I already had one pair stashed in the guesthouse. "You look like a little kid getting dragged to a back-to-school sale."

"It's not that," I started, but I had nothing else. "Okay. It's exactly that."

We laughed as we headed out. We had to kill time until we heard from Phil for one last meeting, then we'd buy our tickets to return to Chicago.

That was the plan.

CHAPTER NINE

"Ability is what you are capable of doing. Motivation determines what you do. Attitude determines how well you do it." –Lou Holtz

I dragged the big suitcase down the hallway to our room. Jenny had dutifully filled it with all manner of things necessary to help me fit in at the Club. Jenny had bought some clothes and shoes for herself, too.

It had been a good day with a lot of laughs. It had felt like a vacation. In the room, I tossed the suitcase on the freshly made bed and started removing items one by one to take off the tags.

Jenny pulled out a Victoria's Secret bag and headed for the bathroom. She wouldn't let me go into the store with her and hadn't let me see what she had bought. I was intrigued to the point of extreme distraction and could think of nothing else.

When my special phone rang, it made me jump. I tapped the green button and waited.

"Who is this?" an unfamiliar voice asked. I immediately pressed "End" and turned the phone off. I dug out my computer and rushed through accessing the net with my VPN. I dug into the depths of the web, looking for anything on Phil's target.

A failed attempt on the life of…

My head spun. In the news, I saw a picture of the police putting a handcuffed Phil into a squad car.

"We have to go!" I yelled. Jenny was right behind me, wearing a red negligee that would have been heart-stopping under different circumstances. "I'm so sorry. But we need to be out of Atlanta right now."

Jenny flew through getting changed while I loaded our stuff. In less than five minutes, we had packed and were wiping down the room. We casually strolled down the hallway with our luggage and out the front door, then loaded our car and headed for the airport. We didn't need the GPS since the highway's signs directed us.

I took out my phone and handed it to Jenny. "Call Vinny." I dictated the number. She handed me the phone when it started to ring.

Vince answered but didn't say anything.

"Vince, it's Ian," I said.

"I'm assuming there's a problem."

"A big problem. Double contract failure. First the operator, and then the director was caught and taken away."

"That's not good. I'm activating the emergency protocol to send everyone to ground. Why don't you and the Mrs. take that round-the-world cruise you've been talking about? Right now would be good."

"We're on it. I'll check in in a week." I ended the call and glanced at Jenny. "We won't be going to Chicago."

I took the next off-ramp and followed the road to a

grocery store. We parked and pulled out our phones, frantically looking for a long cruise.

"Here's one. Out of Fort Lauderdale, leaves in a week," Jenny noted. She showed me her phone.

"Where's it go?"

Jenny looked at me like I'd grown another head. "Does it matter? It's one hundred and eleven days, forty-eight ports."

I reached into a pocket for my wallet and handed it to her. "Book us the nicest cabin you can get. I'll call the rental company and see if we can deliver the car to Fort Lauderdale instead of the airport here."

Jenny started tapping. "Need your passport." I reached behind me for my backpack and pulled it out.

"You have the entirety of my documented life in your hands."

She smiled and returned to her phone.

"I'm at your mercy. Maybe you should tie me up."

"I'm confused," Jenny said. "Are we laying low as in running for our lives, or is it playtime?"

"I always look for the humor in high-stress situations. It's what made me a good Marine, and it's what keeps me sane. Get us a cabin, Miss Grumpy Pants, and I'll take care of the car."

I connected with the rental company and explained what I wanted. They said there would be a thousand-dollar surcharge. I told them to add it to the card already on file. A few seconds later, they confirmed that we were good.

"Done!" I declared as if I'd won a race.

"Suites are sold out, but they have a mini-suite with a balcony. Reserving now. Lots of info." She tapped and tapped and tapped while shifting from one document to another. After fifteen minutes, she entered the gold card numbers and hit one last button. "Done. A quick ninety thousand later, here we go, Mr. Bragg. And you know that I didn't change out of that little red thing."

Jenny unbuttoned enough of her shirt to show red silk underneath.

"I guess we better get as far away from here as we can." I returned to the highway and headed south while Jenny brought up the GPS.

"We can be there in nine hours if we power straight through."

"I'll settle for crossing the border into Florida. What's that look like?"

"How about four hours?" Jenny said, sounding dejected.

I blew out a breath and accelerated onto the interstate, matching the speed of the fastest cars in the fast lane. "I guess it'll be about four hours then. Once in Florida, we can take our time. Six days to drive five hours' worth? We can do that."

When we were out of Atlanta and firmly heading south, Jenny verbalized what we were both thinking. "What about Phil?"

"I expect Vinny has already cut off his access, so even if Phil were to give all his passwords, none of them would work. Will Phil bag on the Archive? I don't think so. We didn't even tell him our last name."

"The car is rented in my name," Jenny noted. "Phil doesn't know a whole lot. He'll come off as a crackpot...won't he?"

"Just a nut trying to poison someone. If he takes the attempted murder charge, he'll be out in less than ten years with good conduct. He doesn't need to tell them anything. And when he comes out, he should have plenty of money available. In fact, with seventeen successful contracts, he should have enough cash to hire the best lawyers money can buy. If he said nothing at all, they might be able to get him off in entirety."

"We have four months for them to stop looking for us." Jenny peered out the window, watching the world go by.

"*If* they're looking for us. The one bit of advice that I was given besides to always complete the contract was that if I got caught, say nothing. Silence is the criminal's friend."

"Weird," Jenny said softly. "I don't think of you as a criminal."

"I don't either, but I know how the justice system would see me. The best place for us is out of the country, at least for a little while. I'll stay in touch with Vinny, checking in weekly. And we'll keep our ear to the ground with Phil's case. They should press charges and all that good stuff, but it'll be a year or more before it goes to trial if it ever reaches that stage."

"He was trying to kill a person." Jenny stated the cold hard fact. "He can get off by denying everything?"

"You would be amazed. Deny everything. Without a confession, it's royally hard for prosecutors to get a conviction."

"See that on TV?"

"In a former life, one of my friends went to law school and became a DA, a district attorney. That's what he told me. That kind of information sticks."

"I'd crumble."

"Don't say that. You wouldn't because their interview methods are much more constrained. They try to be your friend. They are not. I know who *my* friends are. You, Chaz, and the first sergeant. Two of those people are dead."

"You mean you're not friends with my big brother?"

I snorted at the jibe. Jenny was starting to understand how to deal with stress. "If Phil buckles, what would they learn about us? I paid in cash at the pizza place.

Nondescript man and woman walked away. If they had a camera, they could try and follow us, maybe even question the hotel. But we were ghosts. If they searched the world for Eldon Lawless, what would they find?"

"That he doesn't exist."

"Only questions and no answers. If they search all the databases at the airport, they'll find a Jenny Lawless who rented a car. They can match the gold card payments, but they won't be able to dig further. I didn't put the license plate on the form. If they are able to link us, then kudos for the good detective work, but they'll lose our trail in Fort Lauderdale because we won't take a cab from the rental car return."

"But they'll have our pictures."

"From a distance and only a guess, plus facial recognition isn't allowed in court, thanks to it not working right. In any case, deny everything. We were here to check out the art scene and do some shopping, but all questions will be answered by 'no comment.' They can't hold us for more than forty-eight hours, and no matter what, we say nothing. You'll be able to survive it if it happens because you have to. If we say anything at all, then they can start unraveling the threads, leading us back to Chicago, our real identities, and those types of things. They don't get to take our fingerprints, so don't touch anything."

"What about a lawyer?"

"We have over five million dollars in the bank and the full horsepower of the Archive. Demanding a lawyer will be the first thing we do. The promise of a hundred-thousand-dollar retainer should sweeten the pot. Unless we need to pay a quarter of a million, then we'll do that."

"I'd rather do that from the outset." Jenny frowned while staring at the dash. "Let's hope it doesn't come to that."

"We are in a risky business."

"And the man you saved is now the Vice President. You have a trump card if you have to play it."

"Jimmy won't acknowledge I exist if it ever comes to that. And I won't ask him to. We got out with our skins intact. Same as in Tucson, and now we can add Chicago to the rough hits. I doubt the police will dig too deeply into any of those, but for some reason, they liked the target enough to save him and bring Phil in. That's weird, but you wanted to talk less about that and more about the road ahead. Forty-eight ports. Which one are you looking forward to most?"

Jenny leaned her head back and closed her eyes. "That's a question I am happy to explore. The boat leaves Florida on its way to the Panama Canal, through and out the other side to Mexico, then Hawaii. Lots of stops in New Zealand and a few in Australia, the Pacific Islands, and into the Indian Ocean. That's all I remember, but forty-eight ports and one hundred eleven days underway. A day and a half at sea for every day in port, and we have a mini-suite to enjoy the ride."

"Going south means it'll be warm for the first couple months and then coming back north for the spring and into the first part of summer. I like the weather plan. I have to admit that I've grown accustomed to weather that doesn't include snow or freezing rain."

"As a perpetual Washington girl, I don't miss the rain." Jenny unbuttoned her shirt all the way and flung it open. She looked at me until I glanced back.

"We are not going to get to Florida fast enough," I muttered through a big smile. We continued in the fast lane, passing everyone without being the fastest car on the road. I remained a respectful distance back from the pacesetter. The airhorn of a semi shocked me out of my reverie.

Jenny put her shirt back on. "An inadvertent peep show. That was meant for your eyes only." She dialed up the music I liked and let it play, selecting Rush's *Moving Pictures*.

"It doesn't get much better than this," I offered. "Except that little thing where we're running from the law…"

CHAPTER TEN

"There is, one knows not what sweet mystery about this sea, whose gently awful stirrings seem to speak of some hidden soul beneath..." –Herman Melville in *Moby Dick*

With the rental car turned in, I breathed a sigh of relief. I expected the BMW had a tracking device attached that would have led the authorities directly to us if they had made the connection between the couple who left the hotel and the rental car reserved with the same last name, although we parked in an area of the lot where I hadn't seen any cameras.

They were probably there, but the precautions I had taught myself in my first year as an operator continued to serve me well. One needed to maintain a certain level of paranoia to remain in our business.

Phil had seventeen hits and had gotten himself caught. Maybe he'd been out of the game too long and lost his edge.

Maybe.

Before we checked out of the hotel, I verified that Vinny had activated the nuclear option. Each operator had been given one million dollars as an advance against future work in order to lay low.

I thought we should have just given it to them, but this was still a business with overhead and costs, even though Vinny and Chaz had built up a huge stockpile of cash that was now mostly depleted. It was for a good cause.

As I had learned from Phil, having enough available operators was a problem. That would take more cash. We needed assets to grow.

It wasn't like we could go to Quantico and hang flyers, hoping to draw in Marines and FBI wannabes alike. It would continue to be by referral only, like the skipper and the first sergeant had done with me, until we could figure out something better.

Thinking about recruiting and sales fried a hole in my stomach. My two least-favorite things in life. It was like drinking vinegar and milk mixed together.

We reported to the ship at the appropriate time, taking a different taxi service from the one that had brought us to the hotel, which was nowhere near the port.

That made it hard for an investigator to track us down.

We held up our passports as we approached the counter to check in and get set up. We received labels for our luggage that were pre-filled. I carried my backpack, and we checked the big bag with our dress clothes and the small roller bag Jenny had been lugging around. We strolled toward a staging area and tried not to look nervous.

I pulled Jenny to me. "Only took us a year to get our honeymoon."

"We've been on our honeymoon since the first day we met," she replied.

I rested my forehead on hers and whispered, "I love you."

"Bragg!" came a shout from near the gangplank. My heart sank, and I wanted to run. I glanced sideways to avoid looking directly at where the call had come from—a yeoman with a clipboard.

"Come on," I said, taking Jenny by the hand. We strolled casually toward the man. Jenny squeezed my hand so tightly it cut off the circulation to my fingers. "Easy."

She let up. When we reached the man, I announced myself. "You called?"

"Are you Ian and Jenny Bragg?"

"We are," I replied.

"Please follow me," He walked toward a set of stairs and down to a small, closed tent set up next to the gangplank to board the ship at the lower level. He held the flap. I looked at him, and he was sweating. Inside, two security officials and two police waited. Jenny pulled my hand in a brief moment of panic, but I clamped down with my grip.

"Thank goodness," I said loudly. "You found our lost luggage, but I really don't want to file a complaint." I let go of Jenny's hand and walked forward to offer my hand to the security guard. He took it, as did the second one.

The police hooked their thumbs in their belts, not taking their eyes from mine.

"I'm sorry. Is anyone going to speak? You're making me supremely uncomfortable."

"Mr. Bragg. Is this your bag?" I looked at the four bags before turning to Jenny. "We only had two bags. A big one with dress clothes, a suit, shoes, a couple shirts, three nice dresses for my wife and shoes and a purse of course because you can't just buy a dress without the accessories. The smaller roller bag is ours, and that one has toiletries and some casual clothes. Nothing of any value."

"What about these two?"

"They're not ours." I tried to step closer, but one of the security guards stopped me. "I told you which ones are ours."

"Open your bag, please," the taller police officer requested. I put my backpack on the table and opened it. He went through the bag, pulling everything out and setting it on the table. He opened the computer, but it was powered off. He tried to access the phone, but it was powered off, too. "Can you turn these on?"

"Of course. Can you?" I countered. His expression turned cold. "I don't appreciate getting stressed out over something that's not an issue. Before we take one more step, I'm calling my lawyer. Phone, please."

My mind raced. I didn't have a number for a lawyer, but I could call 4-1-1 and get one.

"There's no need for that. Just power it on so we know it works. Same with the laptop."

I turned on the phone but didn't access it. Same with my computer.

"You can put your stuff in your backpack."

I glared at the officer as I repacked my bag. Jenny was starting to sweat profusely.

"I'm sorry. The fun and games are over. Do you want to let us in on your little joke? The problem when harassing people with a lot of money is that they hire the best lawyers to get their ounce of flesh."

"Mr. Bragg, please. We had to make sure you weren't associated with these bags." He stepped aside and pointed at the tags on the strange luggage. "These were handwritten and not the ones that you were given. We have a favor to ask."

"You have a horrible way of enticing me. I want to say

go bang yourselves because of the way you tried to high-stress us."

"I'm sorry, Mr. Bragg. Only you two can help us. You see, we want to send this luggage to your room. We want you to be waiting there for whoever tries to collect it. That's when we'll swoop in."

"And what are the local cops doing here? These guys have no jurisdiction at sea." I stabbed my thumb at them while talking about them as if they weren't there.

"They have jurisdiction on shore in case these were yours."

"You already knew they weren't ours. This is going to make for a long and uncomfortable cruise with this kind of welcome aboard. You know what would make it less uncomfortable? An upgrade from the junior suite to something nicer. Otherwise, I'm going to have to tell you no. You see, I understand how business works. This risk is all mine. This op could go sideways twenty different ways, and it only works in one way. You can send those two bags to the suite we used to be in while we lounge on the top deck in the best accommodations. Then these perps have no idea we were in on it because we're not. It's all you, Pierre."

I didn't know if that was his first or last name, but it was on his name tag.

He looked confused for a moment. "That makes better sense. Let me check."

I turned to my wife. "Are you okay, Miss Jenny? Maybe we'll get mimosas the second we're on board."

She worked on calming her breathing. Despite trying to prepare her for the confrontation, when it came, she hadn't been ready. And the police were wary.

"Why do you look guilty?" one of them asked.

I stepped between Jenny and the officer. "What kind of

garbage question is that? You came after two innocent people with allegations of whatever the hell and try to high-stress us. I was in the Marines, not my wife. She isn't used to dealing with overly aggressive might-makes-right people. How about you pack your bags and leave since we're not the droids you're looking for?"

The shorter officer stepped forward. "You have a nice day, sir." The two studied us one last time before leaving the tent.

"We had our hearts set on this cruise, and all of a sudden, the planets came into alignment. Here we are, getting harassed before we even board. Puts a big damper on our unbridled joy," I deadpanned as the officers walked out.

The two security guards remained and looked apologetic. An executive from the cruise line arrived and asked us to sit before realizing there weren't any chairs. I stared at him.

"Please accept our apologies, but we need to catch these people who think they can use our ship for smuggling."

"What's in those two cases?" I asked, and as expected, he simply shook his head.

"Nothing as of now, but we still need you. We expect the ones who added the luggage to yours saw you. That means they'll be expecting you to answer the door when they knock."

"What is being thrown into harm's way worth?" I pressed. Jenny finally stepped up beside me, holding my arm in a way that reminded me of a child who was afraid. I wrapped my arm around her shoulders and hugged her tightly to me. "You've scared my wife, and I'm not very happy about that."

"Ma'am, please accept my apologies. The police suggested this course of action, believing you were in on it.

It was clear to us from the start that you were not, but we had to follow their direction."

"I'm still not very happy about this situation, but I'll wait in the cabin for this scumbag and help you take him down if you make it worth our while."

"I'll be there, too," Jenny said. "I'm not going to be somewhere else." Her eyes told me she was thinking about Vegas and how an operator had visited her while another tried to work me. And now I was Dave's boss. When the time was right, I'd contemplate what that meant.

The supervisor moved closer to us while the cruise line's security guards faded into the background. "Upgrade to a special suite in an area that is inaccessible by the other passengers, with your own private steward at no additional cost. Tomorrow night, you'll dine with the captain. All of your land tours are included as well. Will that make it worth your while?"

I looked at Jenny. I didn't care about the cost of anything, but being in a private part of the ship with our own personal steward? I exercised my self-control to keep from smiling. Jenny's eyes darted to my flexing jaw muscles. She winked at me while continuing to cower beneath my arm.

"We're in. Now tell me your plan…"

———

We hung out on deck with the others as the crew maintained control of the lower decks to deliver the luggage. At the appropriate time, ten minutes before the passageways were opened, we were escorted to the crew elevator and down to our deck, where we wove our way down the passage around the mounds of luggage to the junior suite. A key card opened it for us. We blocked the door open to move the four pieces of luggage inside, cleared the area in front of the door, and closed it.

Eight minutes until they opened the gates and the passengers headed for their rooms. We were still tied to the dock. We had to run through the appropriate muster drills for lifeboat training before we could head out to sea.

One minute after the passageways opened, a knock came at our door. Jenny remained in front of the luggage, and I answered the door.

Two young women stood there, midriffs bare, with short shirts and too-tight pants, twirling their hair with a finger. "I'm sorry, but I think you might have our luggage," the blonde said in a high-school-girl voice.

"You mean, luggage with our name and cabin number? How could such a mistake have happened?"

"I can't imagine," the young woman replied, her voice chilling at my lack of response to her approach.

"You know this luggage isn't ours. What's in it?" I asked.

"Just our stuff. You know, bikinis, lingerie, and toys to make the nights more exciting."

I snorted, trying to contain a laugh. "Of course they do. Take your garbage and go." I backed into the bathroom entrance to give them room. Jenny stepped beside the bed.

"There's such a nice view from this cabin. Would you like to switch with us? We have a lower deck interior room."

"Yes, that's not a problem. We prefer an interior room, but when we booked, this was all they had left," Jenny replied. I hoped the security team listening to the conversation through the room's comm system was having a good laugh.

Jenny held out her key card. I held mine out. They took them without offering theirs. Jenny snapped her fingers and then tapped the palm of her hand.

"Yes, I'm sorry." They produced key cards and the sleeve with the room number.

"Seven tac one-twenty-three. We'll be able to find that, no problem. We'll be on our way, now."

"No one trades a suite for an interior room that quickly," the brunette countered, voice rough and deep.

I shook my head. "You can feel the sway all the way up here, and we haven't even left the dock yet. Have you ever been seasick? The interior of the ship moves less than the exterior and light-years less than these higher decks on the outside. The way a moment arm works is that there's a central point around which lateral movements are exaggerated the farther away they are." I had no idea what I was talking about but tried to make it sound convincing. I even demonstrated with my hands. "You're doing us a favor. If you don't mind, I want to get downstairs before we start the pukefest."

Both women laughed. Jenny maneuvered our big bag with her small roller on top toward the door. I waited for her to go into the corridor before I followed her out. "Good luck, ladies. I hope you brought plenty of batteries." Jenny yanked my arm as I let the door close.

We found the security guards waiting in the hallway. We handed them the new keycards and walked past. Without a knock, they opened the door and rushed in.

"Well-played, Mr. Bragg."

"I think your execution was brilliant, Mrs. Bragg. Cheerio!"

At the end of the corridor, a large and brutish man stopped us. "I'd like a word." He reached for my arm. I hit him in the throat with a finger strike at the same time Jenny delivered the toe of her shoe on the bullseye between his legs. He went down hard, gasping and choking. The security guards were going the other way.

"Hey!" I yelled. "You forgot one." One of the guards detached himself from the entourage and hurried toward us.

When he arrived, he found the big man struggling to breathe.

"You might need some help," I suggested.

"What did you do?"

"We protected ourselves, something the ship's security team seems hard-pressed to do." The big man flailed while digging for his pocket. I stomped on his forearm. He grunted and returned to his pitiful gasping.

"Who are you?"

"Just a guy trying to have a vacation. Those women are lackeys, probably well-paid. Here's your muscle, but the brains behind this operation isn't going to be obvious. We may never know who he or she is, but once you toss these three overboard, the big boss will lose their teeth. Now, if you'll excuse us, we're off to start our adventure."

Jenny and I hopped the nearest elevator to an upper deck, where we strolled toward the aft section and into an area that looked like a small building. The only access had a sharply dressed purser in front of it. Before we could show our welcome aboard packet, the real one and not what we used to access the junior stateroom, the young woman smiled and said, "Mr. Bragg and Ms. Lawless, welcome to the luxury premiere. I'll escort you to your room."

The door opened of its own volition, and we followed her inside. She clapped her hands, and a second young woman came running to relieve us of our luggage. She took a hard left and opened the first door, where we found a thousand square feet for our exclusive use. The room had its own hot tub, along with a living room and two bathrooms.

"What's not to like about this?" I said. Jenny smiled and shook her head.

"You can dine at your assigned location for dinner, or you are always welcome to dine in. Menus are on the nightstand."

"We'll eat in tonight," Jenny said. "It's been a trying day, and it's time to relax."

Our personal concierge moved our luggage into the walk-in closet and left.

Jenny sat down on the bed and started to cry. I left her to herself for a moment while I started the water to fill the hot tub. I then sat on the bed and pulled her to me. She buried her face in my chest. I let her get it all out.

"I self-destructed. If we're caught, Ian, I'm going to get us both put in jail for the rest of our lives."

"You did fine. The best defense is to say nothing, and that's exactly what you told them. Nice comeback with the dynamic duo, by the way."

"You saved us again. You were magnificent, my husband."

"I was mad, and that's not the best way to stay on course. They were all bluster and no substance; otherwise, things could have gone south in a big way. But they didn't. We have four months to relax, and when we come back, it'll be a whole new world ready for us to bend it to our will."

"Bend it to your will," Jenny mumbled. She pulled away and wiped at her eyes.

"You look beautiful," I told her.

She pushed at me. "I do not." She smiled beneath puffy eyes.

"Maybe you can help me understand. We had all afternoon for recriminations and self-condemnation, but you made it through the arrest of the smugglers and up here before having a good cry."

"We were in public. I couldn't look like this out there." She went to the mirror to look at herself.

"You are in complete control of your emotions, even when you're not. I don't understand."

"And that is how it must be, my dear. What kind of view do we have?" Jenny checked the hot tub and turned the faucets off before crooking a finger for me to follow her onto the balcony. The view looked down on the entire world.

"This is worth the price of admission," I said while hugging Jenny from behind, brushing her ear with my lips. She relaxed enough to take a seat on one of the deck chairs.

"I'm going to give Vinny a call and see where we are." Jenny gave me the thumbs-up and returned to her thoughts while looking at the port of Fort Lauderdale.

I dialed the number and waited through three rings before someone answered the call. Silence on the other end.

"Vinny, it's your favorite director."

"Ian. Nice to hear from you. I think we may have acted too quickly on the nuclear option."

"Time is not on our side. We have to act quickly to protect the company. I like the bit about the money being an advance. I suspect we'll see a rash of million-dollar bids come in when we open things back up." The shipwide broadcast announced it was time for the lifeboat drill. "What makes you think it was premature?"

"Inside scoop suggests they're treating him as a loner who is not all there."

"I'll admit that he is a bit off." Someone knocked at the door. "Gotta go, Vinny. We'll be out to sea shortly and back in four months. Maybe then we can bring the company back up to full speed."

"Probably before then, but enjoy your vacation. You've earned it, and once you get back, you'll be busy. Expect it but don't worry. There is nothing that you can't handle. Go enjoy yourself with that hot wife of yours." The line went dead.

Jenny held the balcony door for me. She closed it after I came inside.

"Vinny told me to enjoy that hot wife of mine."

"Vince said that? He doesn't strike me as a totally hip kind of guy, but I'll take it. He wasn't wrong."

"That's my sweetheart, back at the top of her game."

We opened the door to find our personal concierge. "Your lifejackets are right there." She pointed inside our room. We dutifully snagged them and put them on under her watchful eye. "Your station is right outside this door with our other premier guests."

She glanced at Jenny, whose face was still a shade puffy.

"I'm fine. That little issue earlier finally got to me, but your company has been extremely gracious. You've been great, thank you." The young woman nodded and Jenny continued, "Will you be with us the whole cruise?"

"The whole cruise. There are three of us who watch over the luxury premiere area, but we can always summon reinforcements if you get to be too much."

Jenny chuckled. "I hope we're not all that. You won't get any trouble from us, and if you need anything when we go ashore, don't hesitate to ask. We'll bring you whatever you want."

On the premiere level, only twenty people stood around a smaller lifeboat with an oversized davit to get it beyond the side of the ship and down.

We received our briefing, nodded that we understood,

and were turned loose to return to our suites. There were ten couples in the five suites on the premiere level. Six of the ten were in the twilight of their lives. The other three men were about the same age as Jenny and me, each with younger wives. Taking time away to enjoy life.

I expected they were venture capitalists or money brokers of some sort, taking their trophy wives away to show off their wealth. Maybe it was expected.

We went back into our room, drew the curtains, and stripped for a casual soak in the tub before we got underway and it became too rough to keep the tub filled.

"I like this part," Jenny offered. She seemed to have completely recovered, but I knew we'd have to talk more. She needed to be able to present her cast-iron side if the situation called for it. Then again, maybe the kind woman I had married could never delve as deeply into the dark world as me.

CHAPTER ELEVEN

"Give me six hours to chop down a tree and I will spend the first four sharpening the axe." –Abraham Lincoln

"Vinny, you big husky hunk of man-candy. How's it hanging?" I said into the phone.

"I think you've had too much vacation, Ian. Is it hot where you are? Have you suffered a heat stroke or a brain aneurysm?" Vince taunted.

"Just checking in from sunny New Zealand. I thought I saw new contracts going out for bid."

"We're back up and running. Just because we stopped didn't mean the world stopped with us. Work needed to be done, and there's nothing you need to do. Enjoy the rest of the cruise. The second you get back in the US, I'll need you to come straight to Chicago. I'm putting together a better turnover package. You can read and memorize while you're cruising. I think I might retire this summer, which means you will have it all."

"Damn, Vinny. That wasn't what I was expecting to hear."

He didn't answer. My expectations were meaningless. Only reality mattered.

"You know I'm going to be reading everything about everything as well as working up packages from here, and ship internet is slow."

"I know. Don't work too hard."

"Easy to say. Not so easy to do," I replied.

"I know," Vinny answered again. He wouldn't have given his company to me if I wasn't going to work for it. I suspected he didn't take enough time off, so he was trying to show me the necessity of it.

Build a strong company that can stand on its own.

"Thanks, Vinny. We'll see you when we get back." I looked at the screen on the phone as if it would tell me something before I powered it down. It remained unrevealing. The answers I needed weren't to be found there. They wouldn't be found anywhere as we traveled around the world.

The answers were in Chicago.

We dined at our assigned seat only a couple times a week, preferring a meal ashore if we could get one and then relaxing with a movie or other diversion while we waited for room service. We tipped well enough to be our personal concierge's favorite. We brought them candies from onshore. We grew fairly close to the crew who took care of us and no one else. We didn't have anything in common with them. We had money, but we weren't from money. Our people were blue-collar, and my work was to protect them from those who preyed on them.

We settled into a routine where we worked out in the morning before others got up, so we had the ship's gym mostly to ourselves. In rough seas, we'd use the rowing machine. Calmer and we'd use the treadmills, but always the universal machines. We didn't get to spar as much as we liked.

We barely did any full-contact workouts. I felt like I was losing my edge, but we'd get back to it as soon as we could. We worked out hard to get stronger and faster.

"We can't live in fear. We can only prepare ourselves to face what we're afraid of." The view from our balcony as we pulled out of port was spectacular. We never missed the opportunity as long as the sun shone or the city lights were bright. The Greek isle of Santorini was the best of the best. The port consisted of the caldera of an ancient volcano with the city balanced on its highest ridges.

"I don't know what I'm afraid of, Ian." Jenny's voice was soft among the low rumble of a nearby tug's engines mixed with our ship's maneuvering thrusters. I slid my deck chair next to hers and leaned close to make sure I didn't miss a word.

"Loss of freedom. Just like me." I took her hand in mine. "I don't mean the luxury premiere, but simply being able to walk down the street. I don't want to be torn away from you. That's my fear."

"Your job puts me on edge, but if it weren't for your job, we would have never met, never gotten together. If it wasn't for your job, we wouldn't be able to live this life, but I have to admit that I'm good if we don't go on world cruises or stay in the best suites in a hotel. I don't feel like we deserve that."

Her words resonated in the base of my soul. I didn't feel like we deserved it either. "But it takes the edge off the hard job. There are very few people out there who could do what we do."

Jenny interrupted, "Do what *you* do. Don't kid yourself that I can do the job because I can't."

"I know," I muttered. "As long as there are people like Jimmy who don't know how much they need to count on someone like me, I have to stay in the game. I have to."

Jenny faced me. "And I'll be by your side, supporting you in every way I can. Just don't ask me to fly a drone."

"Sounds like we need to spend time training on drone flight operations. I think we need more drones and will probably even create a squadron, something like Eagle Eye Squadron to the flight line. Start your engines."

Jenny smiled and nodded. I stroked her leg and turned it into a caress.

She stopped my hand before I went too far. "Your engine is always running."

"In a good way because we never know when the last time might be."

"That right there, Ian, is what I'm afraid of. That I have to live with that thought in the back of my mind."

"I always think like that. Plan for tomorrow, live for today. It's what I've said since the first day we met. It's not because I'm doing anything high-risk. How did you feel when you found out your parents were dying?"

"Like crap."

"And there was nothing you could do except try to make up for lost time." I hesitated as her eyes glistened. "And your sister and brother left you to handle it. You lost respect for them. I don't want any remorse that we didn't live life to its fullest, Miss Jenny. Every single day, I want to treat you like it's our anniversary because I don't know when something will take it away from us. Maybe we'll get lucky and won't notice as we age gracefully. That's what we'll call the optimal state."

"Aging gracefully," Jenny repeated. "I've always been too young to think about my life in those terms."

"Look at the difference we're making in the world. If

we never did another thing, we've already left it a better place than we found it. How many students did you put on a better trajectory? You influenced them well beyond your classes. You've done great things for others. You made it so your brother and sister could go about their lives."

"And you made it so people could live in peace. You kept hope alive when the average Joe didn't know how much their future was threatened. Maybe the risk is worth it." It was too dark to see the beautiful green of her eyes.

I leaned in for a kiss. "There will always be risk. Are we doing everything we can to mitigate it? That's what I need to beat into the operators' heads. Starting with whoever the new director of the southeast region will be."

"My sexy man is dominating those personnel issues before he goes caveman on the sales and marketing team."

"I *am* the sales and marketing team," I lamented.

Jenny knew that. She stood and pulled me toward the sliding door into our suite. I slid it shut behind us and closed the curtains. She slowly unbuttoned her shirt.

"Am I that easy to manipulate?"

Jenny didn't hesitate. "Yes."

"Are you feeling better?" I swooped in to help with the disrobing.

"I am. Simple rules. Leave no trail, and if we get detained, deny everything. The alternative is you stop doing what you're doing, and the world isn't ready for that."

"Not yet, but someday," I whispered, helping with the last layer of clothing before Jenny started on mine. Every port, we made love like it was the last day. Now we both knew why. As if every day was the last day.

Live for today…

I bought our plane tickets as we were pulling into port at Fort Lauderdale. We had acquired a second suitcase and filled it with nonsense...I mean, souvenirs and additional clothing. It had been exactly one hundred and eleven days since we departed. I was ready to get off the ship.

We had put our bags in the passageway the evening before as directed, but we didn't have to compete with the other thousand people trying to send their luggage ashore when the morning came. I carried my backpack, and Jenny went with a shoulder bag she had bought in Italy.

The movement ashore was less convoluted for the premier passengers. We checked through immigration with our passports sporting a great number of new entry and exit stamps from a laundry list of countries. We picked up our luggage and rolled through the Customs inspection. A beagle and her handler trooped past, not the least bit interested in our luggage. We both wanted to pet the dog, but there was a sign requesting we didn't.

We continued to the curb where we caught a taxi to the airport. We were five hours early for our flight. I was good with that. We'd been gone too long. I had work to do, and it involved more travel. I wondered about combining the regions into a west, a central, and an east since we only had three directors. We only had forty-one operators, too. I wondered how many would return after the hiatus.

More operators, more directors, more sales, more contracts, and more money. I could feel the weight of the world crashing down upon me.

"You look like hell," Jenny said, pulling no punches. "What do you need to get yourself back on track?"

"Meet with Vinny. Build a work plan. And dojo to energize my mojo."

"Judging by last night, there's nothing wrong with your

mojo," Jenny purred. "And I'll help with the work plan. We'll split it up, break it down, and get it done."

"I was hoping you'd be all in on the way forward. We need to get you a laptop like mine."

Jenny laughed. "After that trip, do we have any money left?"

"They should call that the give-us-all-your-money cruise. We'll need to get some cash."

"You're not going to stiff me, are you?" the driver said over his shoulder.

"Of course not. We'll take care of you," I replied. That told us not to continue our conversation, but we had couched our words carefully as we had taken to doing.

We wanted to lower our risk, not raise it by talking about killing people. We avoided those terms since we'd had the opportunity to step back from the pointed end of the business. At least for the last four months.

I had checked the papers for Detritus, but his death didn't even make a byline. Phil Treglow received little press, too. Once they determined he was a can short of a six-pack, they dropped coverage on him.

I paid for the taxi ride with the gold card and tipped the minimum. He shouldn't have eavesdropped.

We could only check in four hours early, so we snagged an area to the side and watched people come and go. I set up a rental for when we arrived in Chicago.

"Rush hour," I whined.

"I can do sales," Jenny said casually while looking out the window at the busy airport drop-off.

I glanced at the back of Jenny's head. She turned, unbuttoned one more button on her shirt, and stared at me. "Sounds like about three mil to get it right. Now tell me again exactly what you want so we can both be sure of the number."

She cocked her head slightly to encourage an answer.

"Damn." I didn't have any more words.

"It's tearing you up, Ian. You are more afraid of that side of the business than the one that is critical. I've been thinking, and I believe that I can do it. Well, more than just do it. I think I can do it well. How much of a burden would that take off your shoulders?"

"All of it. Well, the worst part. I'll still worry over getting the contracts right." I buttoned Jenny's top button. "You'd do that for me?"

"I'd do that for *us*. We're a team. I've been thinking about it for a while. You've been so fixated on it that I thought you wouldn't want to give it up, but I see now that you have to. I'll take care of the sales. You handle the other part, and together we'll make this work for everyone—us, forty-one operators, three directors, and the soon-to-be-retired Vince."

"I don't deserve you." I didn't get any more shmoopy than that, but I felt like the Grinch, and my heart had swelled three sizes bigger.

"I know you don't, Mr. Bragg, but I'll let you ride my coattails for a little while longer because you are still lots of fun, despite the dinner you're going to feed me tonight."

After a deep breath, I confirmed her fears. "White Castle drive-through, here we come."

CHAPTER TWELVE

"Life is never fair, and perhaps it is a good thing for most of us that it is not." –Oscar Wilde

When we approached Vinny's driveway, we saw a black Chevy Suburban with heavily tinted windows parked where it could observe the drive and the house. I continued past and around the bend, maintaining an even speed. I could see at least two people in the vehicle.

"This is where a fake ID would have been best to rent the vehicle. Now they've tied your name to this neighborhood."

Jenny shrugged. "It's not a crime to buy a house in a high-rent neighborhood."

"It *is* a crime to have money we didn't tell the government about," I replied.

"Deny everything and stay silent. It's on them to prove guilt, right? I don't need to tell them where any of our money comes from. That's on them to find."

"The Club is our road to legitimacy. I see why Chaz and

Vinny bought it and are running it. Not money laundering, but everything is aboveboard. And we still don't admit to anything, don't share anything. Dammit! Who is watching Vinny's house?"

I drove to the inn, where we registered into a regular room. We left the biggest luggage in the Jeep Grand Cherokee. We had liked it so much on our last trip, we rented one again. The luxury ride wasn't as comfortable, in our opinion, and they didn't have any high-end vehicles available anyway.

Thanks to the luxury premier suites on the ship, they had done our laundry, and everything we carried was clean and neatly folded. But we had more pressing matters. I called Vinny.

He answered on the first ring.

"You have company."

"I know. I think it's the feds."

"We came to the hotel instead of the guesthouse. See you at the Club in the morning?"

"I think that will be best. My retirement needs to happen soon, but I don't want to leave you a stinking mess, so we'll do what we can to get this resolved before I move on."

"Maybe you can take them coffee and fresh doughnuts first thing in the morning."

"I like how you think, Ian. I'll set it up from the Club and see how they react."

"See you at ten, then."

"See you there," Vinny confirmed.

I shut the phone down. "Tomorrow will be interesting."

I felt a dark cloud materialize over my head just when I thought we had regained control of our lives.

"I heard," Jenny said. "We'll deal with it when it comes. If they had anything substantial, they would have already arrested Vinny. This is harassment designed to influence Vinny to stop doing what they think he's doing."

"Look at you with the theories." I poked Jenny's arm. She rolled her eyes at me. "Same thing I was thinking. We'll find out what it's all about soon enough."

"On a completely different note, we should probably hit Vinny's gym in the morning and have ourselves a righteous workout, including sparring. Free weights! Oh, how I've missed you."

"Now you're singing my song. That sounds like a plan. We need to make it early so we can get cleaned up before heading to the Club. That means I need to get my styling sports coat out of the bag in the Jeep."

"In the morning. I'm more tired than I expected. Travel takes it out of me."

"Sitting around an airport for five hours isn't as easy on the body as one would think." She shut everything down and crawled into bed, where our shared warmth was all we needed to drift off to sleep.

I was happy about Jenny's change over the four months of the cruise. We had started with her mortified by the police, and we ended in Chicago with her shrugging off a potential threat. I felt better about it, too. Vacation had been good for us, plus we got to see every time zone the world had to offer.

We strolled into the Club like we owned the place.

Because Vinny told us that we did. We were early, so we browsed through the staff. They all knew who we were and greeted us cordially. We shook hands and asked names as well as thanked them for working there. Most had been there for at least a year. The longest was twenty years and had worked through three different owners.

We greeted the members as well, being polite to all while we waited.

At five minutes after ten, Vinny strolled in. He greeted us warmly with a big smile.

"You are a genius, Ian."

"I feel like I'm being set up for something," I replied. Jenny nodded vigorously.

"The doughnuts and coffee worked. They didn't want to see me at all. They were waiting for you!" He clapped me heartily on the shoulder and strolled toward the deal-making room.

"Breakfast on you," I stated. "How can you drop that nuclear depth-bomb and walk away?"

Vinny slipped me a piece of paper. I moved to the side with my back to the wall and opened the note.

The Vice President wishes to have a private meeting with Mr. Ian Bragg.

I showed it to Jenny. "How did they find us?"

"A question for Vinny, but I bet he added our names to the title on the house. I wonder why we weren't intercepted en route."

"That could have come across as more hostile than they intended? I think this is legitimate."

"I don't want to work for the government." I stuffed the note into my pocket. Vinny was across the entry area, talking with the host. He waved us over.

"Even though you're not wearing a tie, we'll make it work."

I held up one finger and with my other hand, removed the tie from my pocket. Jenny tied it for me while I firmly gripped her hips.

"Stop that," she whispered, trying not to smile. "I feel like a weight has been lifted...again."

I shook my head. "We need another vacation."

Vinny leaned his head next to ours. "It's time to get to work. You don't get any more vacations until I retire, and then you won't be able to take any. But don't let that dissuade you. Our table's ready."

They put us at the table we'd had before, in a secluded alcove off the main room. After a vigorous workout, I was ready for protein and significant amounts of water to quicken the muscle recovery. The server tried to hand us menus, but we declined. She immediately took our orders.

After she left, we were free to talk. I checked my phone to confirm that the dampening technology was active. "The owner's table is pretty nice."

"Of course. We can't have private conversations becoming public," Vinny replied.

I looked at Jenny. She began, "I'll take over the Archive's sales and work with the clients and potential clients."

"Good because he's horrible at it." Vinny tilted his head toward me.

"Thanks for that," I grumbled. "It makes the most sense. Now, let's speculate on what Jimmy wants to see me about."

"It's either good or very good for the company. There are only two choices."

"What if he wants us to shut down operations?" I wondered.

"That's not it. He could turn a blind eye easily enough. He risks himself by meeting with you. You'll need to pass the nice men in the Suburban your phone number."

"Well now. My super-secret untraceable phone will be listed at the highest levels of the government."

"Think about what you just said," Vinny suggested. He

waited until I shook my head. "It hurts them a hell of a lot more than it hurts you. Think Watergate. Having their number wasn't good for a defense claim of ignorance."

"I'm not too keen about anyone using me as a pawn."

Vinny sat relaxed, with his elbows propped on the table and his chin resting on his hand bridge. "No one will know you exist besides the people most interested in keeping your relationship secret. Ian, this will make the Peace Archive a real entity with the potential to expand our business, even if they ask us to cancel all other work. If we do only government contracts from now on, we'll have top cover if anything goes awry."

"I don't want anything to go awry," I blurted.

"None of us do, but I only see upsides to this, and that is why it'll take a plastic surgeon to remove this smile from my face." He grinned at us. "I can retire in peace, knowing that the company Chaz and I built is in good hands and will remain a functioning and effective business for years to come."

I snaked my hand under the table in search of Jenny's to feel the warmth of her fingers while I contemplated Vinny's words.

"Okay. I'll meet with him."

Vinny was taken aback. "Was there any doubt you would have to meet with him? That man holds all the cards. How you play it? That's what will keep us in business. All the while, Jenny is making sales."

"I'm not meeting Jimmy without Jenny by my side. He should expect it."

"As you wish, Padawan."

"I would have never taken you for a *Star Wars* fan. I see you as more of a Clint Eastwood fan."

"Alas, you would be right, but I have a classical

education. Bruce Willis, Arnold, Stallone, and Harrison Ford."

I turned to Jenny, who cocked an eyebrow at me. "You are a strange man, Vinny."

"Thank you. I try. Too bad you didn't get to know Chaz better."

On that solemn note, our food arrived. We dug in rather than try to force a conversation.

Vince was right. We did wish we could have gotten to know Chaz better. He was a decent sort who had started a business to assassinate bad guys. Some might not see him as a good guy. Or me, for that matter.

The question remained, what did Jimmy Tripplethorn think of me?

"So, what do we do now?" I wondered.

"You take a note out to the parking lot and hand it to the nice men in the Suburban."

"What if they want me to come with them?"

"I wouldn't do that. You need to set up a neutral location, and for the VP, it is probably going to have to be in DC."

My face fell. I turned to Jenny but found no empathy there.

"You said I'm going." She smiled. "I'm good with that."

I wrote my number on the back of the note Vinny had given me. "I'll be right back." I backed away from the table and stood. Jenny mirrored my movements.

"I said I was going."

"I thought you meant…never mind." I took her hand, and we walked out as Vinny asked for a fresh cup of coffee.

Outside, we found the government vehicle at the end of the parking lot. It waited for us. When we arrived, the passenger's window was down. A man with mirrored aviator sunglasses looked out. I gave the note to him. He opened it, read it, and handed it to the driver.

"Get in."

I leaned close enough that I could punch him if I needed to. "That's not how this is going to work. I don't care that you're the big bad feds. This isn't hardball, as much as you're trying to act like it is. This will be a congenial meeting between colleagues."

The man rolled up his window, and the vehicle pulled out. We stepped back but remained on the balls of our feet in case they tried something.

Once they were gone, we relaxed. "I don't trust them. I have become master of the obvious."

Jenny looked at me. "I don't trust them either, but I'm okay with that. We shall see what happens."

We had taken one step toward the main building when my phone rang. I looked at it for a moment before pressing the green button. Expecting it might be a handler, I made it easy for them by saying, "Hello."

"Is that you, Ian?"

"Jimmy." I tried not to let the surprise creep into my voice.

"I find myself in a unique position that would not have happened without you. I owe you for that, but I also have a compelling need for someone of your talent. We need to talk."

"Jenny and I can come to DC whenever it is convenient."

"Good. Be at Arlington Cemetery at six in the morning. The men you just met will be waiting for you. They will bring you to me. Trust them, Ian. They are my personal security detail and will not cause you any grief."

"Tomorrow. Arlington National Cemetery at oh-too-early. Got it. Until tomorrow."

I ended the call and put the phone in my pocket. "We need to be in DC by early tomorrow morning and at the top of our game. This meeting will determine the future of the Peace Archive."

"I'm sure Vinny will be happy to hear that." Jenny strolled casually with a new spring in her step.

"Why are you so happy? Another plane ride. Joy," I deadpanned.

"The Vice President of the United States has asked for your help. That makes me happy, Ian, because of what you did for him when you didn't have to. When no one else raised a hand. Because you are the most decent human being I've ever had the pleasure of knowing."

"That's not how I'd put it, but it sounds pretty cool hearing it out loud. Let's finish our breakfast and get our tickets. Then back to O'Hare."

"I think we have sales meetings this afternoon. We'll fly after those, but I need to make those sales happen for me and for us."

We went back inside to find Vinny at a different table, chatting with an elderly couple. We returned to our table to find the server hovering with fresh coffee, ready to pour. There were small cups of designer creamer for me.

Vinny rejoined us, and once the server departed, he waited with raised eyebrows and wide eyes.

"Jimmy has a proposition for us. We need to meet him in DC tomorrow morning."

"Sounds good. I'll take the two meetings this afternoon so you two can be on your way."

Jenny shook her head. "I'll do them. We'll leave after we've seen what kind of deals we're going to have and what we need to do for the next steps. Our people are out there without work. Idle hands are the devil's playground."

Vinny and I looked at each other, and he started to

laugh. "That's the spirit. I'll see you when you get back. I'm going home to start packing."

"Not so fast, big fella," I interrupted. Vince stopped halfway through standing up. "We need to understand a lot more about the process. How do you arrange the meetings with these people in the first place?"

"They leave notes for the owners in the office."

"We have an office?"

"Of course. We're the owners." Vinny stood. I gulped my coffee before Jenny and I followed him out. I stopped and returned to toss a couple of twenties on our table. *Never forget where you came from,* I chided myself.

The owners' office was on the second floor, complete with a secretary at a lavish wooden desk in an antechamber containing overstuffed armchairs to make it more comfortable for those waiting for an audience.

"Gladys, you know our new owners," Vinny said and continued through to the big wood-paneled office.

We stopped to shake her hand. "As with most big companies, I expect you are the one who's running the show."

"Ah! An enlightened soul. It will be a pleasure to work with you, Mr. and Mrs. Bragg."

"I hope we live up to your expectations. Just let us know what we need to do. The Club is the centerpiece of our world, and it looks like the members are happy. Whatever it takes to keep them that way. Maybe sushi night?"

Her eyebrows knotted. "I'm sorry, what? Have you seen the average member?"

"No sushi then, huh? I'm devastated, Gladys, but I'll recover," I joked. "I would like to have a members' night once a month on the Club as a celebration and recognition."

She glanced toward the office before leaning close. "How much are you willing to spend?"

"Fifty?" I ventured.

She stabbed her thumb upward.

"A hundred?" I tried.

"Now you're talking. We can do something nice for that. I'll get on it. Last Friday of the month, and welcome to the Club. I think you'll like it here."

"We can't miss, knowing there are good people like you running things."

She nodded and immediately started making a list for a monthly members' event.

We closed the door behind us in the big office. It looked little-used, without wear and tear on the plush deep-green carpet.

"Are you spending the Club's money already?"

"It's what we do best," I replied. "Happy members will solicit more contracts. It only takes one extra to pay for a year's worth of events."

"You have to make sure you don't mingle the money. Club money can't get supplemented by Archive money. That's why it's important for you to spend a lot of money here."

"It's not money laundering if we get a five-star meal out of it."

"The Club was our answer to bringing clients on board without the risk of open sales. They come to us because we have a solid reputation. You need to leverage that while building on it. We only have to be present, and they will come to us."

"It's as simple as that?" I stared at the floor as I thought it through. "If you build it, they will come? It seems far-fetched. All of the old-money here has to know what you do."

"None of them *know* anything. There are a lot of problems out there. They are comfortable sharing them with us, and we make them go away—for a price, of course."

"You don't worry that someone will turn you in?"

"The process of talking to the client and turning it into a contract happens well outside the borders. There is no direct link. These people transfer money offshore all the time. Tracking it is impossible. Otherwise, they'd probably all be in jail for tax evasion. They're not because their lawyers are better than the government's lawyers. And it doesn't hurt to have a few judges who are members of the Club."

Jenny leaned forward. I rested my hand on her back. "This is its own ecosphere, insulated from the outside world, and that, in and of itself, is what protects the Archive. These are completely separate worlds in which the players move. Those who would see issues where the leather walks the sidewalk can find no connection with those here. The genius of the arrangement is mind-boggling, and all it took was time and the first successful contracts. You didn't start in here at all, did you?"

"No. We started out there. Took care of business when a meth lab tried to move in next door to someone who had enough money to make them go away without calling the police." Vinny tapped a couple keys and looked at his computer. "I ordered coffee. I hope you don't mind."

"It only took one who introduced you to a friend, and then another and another."

"Something like that. Plus, I enjoy a good round of golf. Out there," he pointed out the window, where we could see the golf course within the brown of winter trees, "is where deals have been made. It would behoove you both to get up to speed."

"I have to play golf?" Jenny blurted. Her jaw dropped, and she looked frantically back and forth between Vinny and me.

"Used to play. I can get back into it. I expect we have a pro who gives lessons?"

"Of course. You shall want for nothing except a good putting stroke."

"We had best get our flight set up so we know when to leave."

"Gladys will do it for you. Give her your passports, and she'll take care of it." Vinny waved a hand dismissively.

"We have people now." Jenny held out her hand, and I dropped my passport into it. She ran her hand up my arm on her way out. I watched her go. She glanced over her shoulder, happy to see me staring.

"Golf, huh?"

"Yes. You should probably brush up on your bridge, too. There are tournaments on Sundays." Vinny leaned back in the leather captain's chair behind his desk with his hands clasped across his trim stomach.

"The sacrifices you've made for this company." Vinny didn't rise to the jibe. "I can't tell you what it means that you trust this to us."

"I had to trust it to someone, and there's no way Phillip Treglow was going to fill Chaz's shoes."

"That doesn't feed my ego. Have you heard how he is?"

"He has the best lawyer in the South. He'll be off on a technicality, but they may bring him back in if they can resolve the issue. I think he'll get out of it, but he's done when it comes to us."

Jenny returned and took her seat.

"I was thinking of combining the five areas into three. Save us from having to find a new director in the short term."

"Sounds reasonable. Yours was the biggest region. If you could handle that, then others can handle theirs, too. You see that we don't always have a lot of contracts. You slowed things down with your package-building. We had to shunt some of your contracts to the northwest and central directors."

I clenched my jaw before I said something untoward.

"Relax. You're here, aren't you?" Vinny put his hands out in the calming gesture. "Your contracts were better-handled. There's a lot to be said for good prep. Go slow to go fast, right?"

"I like the term 'intentionality.'"

"It's a good consultant word that would resonate in these halls."

"Why don't you use this office and Gladys to help with the Archive?"

"We do, even though it's important to separate the Club from the Archive. We get the contracts in here, but there is no one else who knows how we work. And none of us," he waved his hand to take in himself, Jenny, and me, "are going to tell the authorities anything. The way to keep a secret is to tell no one."

"There is no statute of limitations on what we do," I added.

Vinny touched his nose. "Don't put anything Peace Archive-related on a system in this building, just in case we get raided. It's best not to leave breadcrumbs. Gladys knows how to not leave a trail. She has an eidetic memory and doesn't need to write anything down."

"I knew there was a reason for everything you do."

A knock on the door, and Gladys entered. She handed our passports back and an itinerary for a flight leaving at five and landing at Reagan National. She reserved the hotel in Arlington for us, the same one we stayed at before. She did not bother with a rental car.

"You are an absolute gem!" I jumped up and kissed her on the cheek.

She looked at Vinny for a few heartbeats before leaving us alone.

"We're her new favorites," I chided Vince.

"Of course, you are. I haven't given Gladys as much of an opportunity to do what she's capable of. You see, I have a hard time trusting people. Chaz and Gladys had a great relationship. You are more like him than me. She appreciates that."

"We better get down to business," Jenny said, checking her watch. "Who are we meeting this afternoon, and what are we going to talk about?"

CHAPTER THIRTEEN

"The successful warrior is the average man, with laser-like focus." –Bruce Lee

Jenny sat with her back to the wall while I was off to the side, talking to the server who watched over the area. Two other tables had members. One group of four played bridge. I hadn't broken the news to Jenny yet that we had been advised to take up the game in addition to golf.

It was almost like running the Club was going to be a full-time job.

The realization dawned on me when the server asked about time off for a funeral. I didn't have an answer since I didn't know who managed the staff. I didn't want to upset anyone's schedule, but the server was on the verge of tears, so I sent him on his way for the last two hours of his shift and took up his duties delivering drinks and cleaning up the tables.

I strolled through the tables, asking about refreshing drinks. At least there were only six people in there, and everyone had what they wanted. Jenny ordered a whiskey sour. "If you can't pay, ma'am, we'll have to come to a different arrangement." I winked at her.

She perked up. "As a matter of fact. I need my own gold card."

"As a matter of fact, we'll get you one!" I declared. I would have to ask Vinny how to do that. After every meeting, I added more items to a growing list of things I didn't know.

I returned to the bar to order Jenny's drink. "Whiskey sour, my good man."

The bartender started working on the creation. "You know, that server you let go goes to a funeral every week. He has to belong to the unluckiest family in the world, or he enjoys his time off."

"Interesting. I always try to give people the benefit of the doubt. What if he goes to funerals to help other people cope with their loss?" I leaned on the bar casually, glancing around the room to see if anyone had run dry in the two minutes since I last walked through.

"Could be. He is a sensitive soul."

"What about you? How long have you been working here?"

"I've been here five years. This is a great job for me. I'm not a late-night kind of guy. Other bar gigs want you until two or three in the morning. We're out of here by ten no matter what is going on."

"I can't imagine anyone here is a late-night partier. What about New Year's?"

"We all work, but it wraps up by about twelve-fifteen."

"I tell you what. This year, although it's a ways off, we'll invite the families of the staff that has to work. We'll celebrate together."

He shook his head in time with shaking Jenny's drink. He

stopped and poured while pointing with his chin toward the group playing bridge. "That won't work, Mr. Bragg. Upstairs, downstairs. One doesn't associate with the servants. These people are old money. It's how they were raised. There's a certain decorum that is maintained here, and that is why they are comfortable spending their time and money in the Club. I'm okay with not bringing my family here to be looked down on. Despite your best intentions, it won't work. They will barely tolerate you, and only because you're the owner. For the time being, maybe status quo is best."

I contemplated the sincerity in the bartender's eyes before replying. "You may be the smartest out of all of us. Who is in charge of the personnel, scheduling, and all of that?"

"Gladys. She's upstairs. I'm surprised you haven't met her."

"I'll have to spend more time with her to learn fully what she does. She's like you, an absolute Niagara Falls of information." I didn't like showing my ignorance, but the amount I didn't know vastly outweighed what I did.

A middle-aged man strolled in wearing a three-piece suit. Executive-gray in his short haircut highlighted his temples. He stood opposite Jenny while she sat. He stared her down while she repeatedly gestured for him to take a seat. I carried her drink over and set it down. "Miss Jenny will be handling this side of things from now on. I ask that you show her the respect you would have shown Chaz or Vinny. They retire and the next generation steps up, trying to do half as good a job."

"You're Ian Bragg," the man said and offered his hand. I didn't want to take it but I did, nodding for Jenny to stand. She glared for a moment before standing and offering her hand. He looked at it without taking it.

"Are you going to be a problem? You're here because we make problems go away. Now shake my wife's hand, then sit down and talk about the problem you need taken care of. The time for posturing is over. We have mutual interests. Let's explore them together while we figure out how to resolve your issues. Everyone goes away happy."

"Vince said to expect something different with you. I'm not sure I like it."

"I'll send a drink over for you. I don't want you to be uncomfortable, but if you know someone else who can do what we do, then you are free to contact them."

"What do you do, exactly, Mr. Bragg?" The man crossed his arms. He still hadn't shaken Jenny's hand. She sat down and took a drink of her whiskey sour.

"That is a good question. I'll answer by reiterating that we help people with their problems. That's all. Now tell Miss Jenny your problems, and she'll tell you what it'll take for us to help you with it."

He sneered as he looked at Jenny, who was casually sipping her drink. "This is a man's business."

"Is that so? Maybe you should just leave. We don't need your business."

"You're going to throw away two million dollars because you are forcing me to talk with her instead of Vince?"

"Do you have a problem that needs resolved or not? If you only want to show dominance, spend your two mil buying hookers and having them cower at your feet. But this is a serious business and an august place in which we conduct it. You'll respect these halls and the people within. We showed you courtesy from the beginning. We expect to be treated in the same manner. That is the minimum standard of conduct here at the Club. I don't care how much money you have. You will not disrespect my wife, me, any other member, or any of the staff."

His mind churned with the idea of walking away, but the problem that hung over his head was serious enough to make him pause. I pulled out the chair for him.

"Take a seat, and I'll bring you a drink. What are you having?"

"Single malt. Something older than fifteen years, not any of that blended crap."

"Of course, Mr.… I'm sorry. I didn't get your name."

"I am Brandon Segway." He said it like it was supposed to mean something. I'd never heard the name before, but I'd been insulated from the Chicago power families for a number of reasons, not the least of which was that I hadn't cared before we became the Club's owners.

"Mr. Segway, your drink will be right up." I walked toward the bridge players, who had stopped playing, to see if they wanted anything. I went to the last occupied table before going to the bar.

At the bar, the bartender chuckled to himself. "Let me guess, the best single malt in the house."

"It is what it is," I replied. He poured two fingers into a highball glass, neat, and swirled it. "Is he a jerk to everyone?"

"I can't speak badly of the members, sir. I hope you understand."

"That's a good policy. I've already formed my own judgment. I will do my best to enforce a modicum of decency even if they reject it. I'll drag old money into the new century, and they won't even notice because I'm pretty subtle about it."

"Subtle," the bartender said slowly. "Yes, sir. Very, sir. I doubt I've ever seen anyone more subtle in my whole life, sir. Your subtleness…"

I held up a hand to stop him. "You win the Sarcasm of the Day award. Call me Ian. What's your name?"

"Prince Markle."

I held the forgotten drink and stared. "Are you messing with me?"

He rolled his eyes. "My parents did me no favors. I was their little prince, so that's what the birth certificate says. And then, when a Markle became royalty, I was doomed for all time. Just call me Mark. That works better than anything."

"Will do, Mark. I'll be right back."

When I arrived at the table, Jenny was speaking. "That's way more than two." She pointed upward with her thumb."

"It's easy," he shot back. "Just take him out."

"He sounds like a man of some stature. Without being able to get close, the complexity is magnified, as well as the time it will take to resolve. One week and two becomes six weeks and three."

"But that's not going to work for me. I need him out of the way by next week."

I waited behind his shoulder while Jenny controlled the conversation. "You'll have to describe why the rush because that changes the price, too. Speed comes at a much greater cost."

Jenny's articulation was better than I could have managed. It wasn't that I doubted her or thought I would do a bad job, but I had failed by not considering she would be good at it. And she was.

Brandon Segway was on his heels because her questions were sharp but not aggressive. I didn't even have to threaten to beat him up.

"A hostile takeover is coming, and we cannot let them get in before us. That means now."

"A hostile takeover, which means one corporate entity

buys another using share purchases to leverage and not through an outright sale or even that the company is for sale?"

"Something like that."

"This competitor of yours. I failed to ask what crimes he has committed?"

"He's a problem to me, and you solve problems."

"I'm sorry that I labored under the misperception that this was valid. Sounds like you'll have to outmaneuver him, maybe even outbid him. If you can't outbid him, then maybe the takeover isn't worth it."

"I'll be back in touch." He drained his glass and stood. He looked at me, then back at Jenny, and reluctantly offered her his hand. She stood before taking it and shaking firmly. She had a good grip. Weightlifting assured that.

He nodded tersely and strode out.

"I couldn't be more proud of you," I said softly. "The business will flourish because of you. The contracts will improve, and I think the sun will even shine more brightly."

"This is Chicago. I'm not sure about how brightly the sun is going to shine." She smiled.

"I think your talents were wasted in a classroom."

"Not at all. Teaching is simply selling a different product. Getting teenagers to embrace knowledge requires ninja skills, and there is some transactionality involved."

"You made that word up." I worked my way in beside her and hugged her close.

"But it sounds impressive." Jenny put her head on my chest, and I closed my eyes to take in the scent of her hair. Always different. I'd make sure we had the stuff I liked in the guesthouse's shower.

Someone cleared their throat. I opened my eyes to find Mr. Smythe standing there. "Our two pm is here."

Jenny ran her fingers through her hair while I stood up to help the elderly gentleman into his seat.

"Mrs. Bragg handles the initial conversations now, as Mr. Trinelli is preparing for his retirement.

"I would much rather work with this lovely creature. You can go." He waved a wrinkled and shaky hand at me while looking at Jenny.

"What can we do you out of, Mr. Smythe?"

"I have a friend in Los Angeles…"

I lost the rest of the conversation when I made my rounds to take the next drink orders.

At the bar, I had to lament the trials of my position. "Mark! When is my shift over?"

"Whenever you want. We have extra people in the dining rooms who can cover. It's not a busy time."

"Why didn't you tell me this earlier?"

"I've never seen an owner wait tables before. You're good at it. You should consider a second career."

"Call Gladys and have someone spot me so I can put my feet up and try to recover from the physical challenges of the day. And we have to get going. Got a plane to catch."

I turned over the orders and waited while he made them. As I took them to the tables, Mark was on the phone getting someone to backfill me.

"How do they pay?" I wondered.

Mark nodded. "I know all of them. They have tabs, and I tally up their drinks. They get a bill at the end of each month."

"That's the peak of efficiency. I like it. Let's do more of that."

Mark raised his eyebrows at me. A server entered. She couldn't have been more than eighteen.

I glanced at the table where Jenny was holding Mr. Smythe's hand, probably to keep it from shaking the table. She looked intense.

"No need to make rounds right away. They just got refreshed," Mark told the server.

"Damn." She drew the word out. "It's slow on the other side, too."

I slipped her a twenty and gave two to Mark. "Thanks for your help."

"You're welcome, Mr...."

"I'm Ian Bragg."

"The new owner. I'm sorry. I should have known." She looked down as if she were ready to be punished.

"I should have done better at introducing myself to everyone. How long have you worked at the Club?"

"Six months, but it's the best job I've ever had. I make enough that I'm putting myself through college."

"That is what this all about. Helping people to help themselves."

"Thanks, Mr. Bragg," Mark added.

I looked at the server. "If you need to know anything, right here." I pointed at Mark. "Or Gladys, as I've discovered."

"There are a few more. Betsy and Clive. You need anything, you ask them. Anything at all. They have connections that are out of this world." At my blank look, she put a hand on my arm and explained, "They put people into their seats in the main restaurant and upstairs."

I glanced over again to find Mr. Smythe struggling to stand. I hurried over to help him into his walker.

"Thanks for saving me, young fella. My girlfriend would be embarrassed if I fell over." His laugh was dry and raspy and ended in a racking cough.

"Don't you die on us, Mr. Smythe. How will your girlfriend ever live without you?"

When he was able to speak again, he said, "Now you're talking, sonny." He trundled away, taking his time to cross the room, stopping to joke with others around his age.

"Segway is a no-go, but Smythe's Los Angeles friend has potential." She showed me the thumb drive in the palm of her hand.

"We'll have to look at that in DC or just give it to Vinny to work up. I'm not too keen on carrying it around if we don't have to."

Jenny nodded. She put her lips by my ear and whispered, "Six million for a single human trafficker. I personally want to see this guy go away if what the old man said is true."

"Me, too. We'll give it to Vinny to hold as we'll probably be back tomorrow."

"Well, Mr. Bragg. It has been a most excellent day. Shall we surrender to the rigors of travel and see what tomorrow will bring?"

"I am most curious, Mrs. Bragg. Most curious indeed."

CHAPTER FOURTEEN

"Big brother is watching you." –George Orwell

"This is an absolutely ridiculous time of day," Jenny muttered while standing out front of the hotel in Alexandria, a few blocks from her brother's house and a short taxi ride from the cemetery.

"I love this time of day. Kudos to Jimmy for picking it." I smiled and bounced. Only one cup of coffee in case it took a while to make it wherever we were going.

The cab arrived, and we traveled in silence to get dropped off at the entrance to the Arlington National Cemetery. Sunrise was imminent, preparing to spread its glory over the solemnity of the rolling hills. Equipment and a small detail of workers suggested there would be a burial that day. Maybe more than one.

I couldn't take my eyes off them until Jenny nudged me. "Our ride is here."

A black Suburban drove up and stopped. The man we'd

talked to jumped out of the passenger seat and opened the back door for us. Jenny climbed in first. Once we were settled, he closed the door and returned to the front seat.

"Hi, guys!" I said as jovially as I could.

They dutifully wore their sunglasses.

I had to talk to them because it was a game. I had to see them crack. "I served in the Corps," I started. "And I understand you. Loyal to the Vice President, but that doesn't mean you can't retain your humanity. I'm sure you guys are Chatty Charlies when you're alone. We won't tell your secrets. Where are they hiding the alien bodies?"

The man in the passenger seat turned and faced me. I stared back without blinking until he turned away. I blinked rapidly and rubbed my eyes, proud of my effort. Jenny elbowed me. Through the windshield, downtown loomed before us. We passed various monuments on the way to Pennsylvania Avenue but then turned away. We followed a route that led toward Dupont Circle and then away from the downtown. We accelerated to the northwest along Massachusetts Avenue until we arrived at the Naval Observatory, home of the Vice President. The agents pulled up to the side entrance, where a canopy protected the identities of those exiting a vehicle.

Jenny's door opened, and she climbed out and scanned the area before us. I followed her into an entryway covered with vinyl and through a single door with thick bulletproof glass. Jenny pulled it open, and we walked through. I reached behind me to close the door, but the security guard was there, mirrored sunglasses and all.

We put our minor possessions on the table and walked through the metal detector. The security guard buzzed the detector as he walked through, staying close to us while we recovered our goods. He moved in front of us.

"Please follow me." He took us into the building and through the back passages into an area away from the living quarters where the Vice President maintained an office where he could meet guests. Jenny gripped my hand so tightly it cut off the circulation to my fingers. I looked wide-eyed from one place to the next.

Jimmy knew what I did for a living but had still brought me here. He didn't want to be associated with me but was inextricably tying himself to me. I didn't think that was an optimal political move, but Jimmy was savvy, and I was just an operator. We would learn soon enough.

We were waved past a receptionist and into an executive office, where Jimmy sat behind an exquisite wooden desk. The guard excused himself, shutting the door to leave us alone with Vice President Jimmy Tripplethorn. He walked around his desk to shake our hands.

"Congratulations, Mr. Vice President."

"You used to call me Jimmy."

"And you are still that man. Please don't change, Jimmy. Remember where you came from."

Jenny remained silent. She hadn't spoken the last time we had met. Jimmy cordially shook her hand, but his focus wasn't on her. He wanted to see me.

"I don't, and that's why you're here. I have security guys now, so I won't go off the rails or get taken out, as you aptly showed was easier than I had ever contemplated."

I didn't reply. There was nothing to say to that. Jimmy needed people around him who were paranoid because his was a trusting soul.

"We need a man of your talents for a job that we cannot do ourselves, but it's one that must be done."

"Are we being recorded?"

"I sure hope not," Jimmy replied with a smile. "What I'm asking for is less legal than what you'll do about it."

"Pragmatism trumps the law?"

"In the dark and cold of a basement doorway, someone told me that sometimes good men have to do bad things so the rest of the world can sleep peacefully. I'm not talking the slippery slope of political expediency, but there are some awful human beings in this world of ours. They need to not have contact with humanity ever again, and there's only one way to guarantee that. We need you to kill a man."

"Damn, Jimmy. You can't drop something like that on a peace-loving and law-abiding citizen like me." His face dropped. I leaned close and whispered, "Who?"

"His real name is David Corander, but he goes by David Quresh."

"Wasn't that the cult leader from Waco?"

"Our guy spells it differently, probably for trademark purposes. He's a real piece of work." Jimmy scowled and shook his head. "We need him to die in a way that doesn't implicate the federal government. We cannot have another Waco."

"You think I'm the one to help the government with this problem? Who has he hurt?"

"That is the right question." Jimmy gave an approving nod. "He's taken a virtual harem into his Idaho compound. Once they go inside, no one hears from them again. We're missing eighteen women and six children, all girls ages ten to thirteen."

I clenched my jaw so hard I couldn't speak. Jenny touched my arm, and I turned to see her eyes narrowed and a deep frown. She nodded one time to let me know she agreed.

"I can take care of that for you," I agreed. "But I'm in a

different position now. We run the organization that I used to work for."

"Even better," Jimmy said and returned behind his desk, where he flopped into his chair. "I wish this job was as straightforward as working with legislators to enact laws that make our country better rather than every day being a different exercise in damage control."

Jimmy checked his watch.

"Right on time. Let's go see the President."

"Let's go *what?*" I blurted.

Jimmy combed his hair with his fingers, popped out of his chair, and headed toward the door.

"I hope that I can help you so you can get back to what you're good at—convincing people to do the right thing."

"Nothing would make me happier, Ian."

As my stress level rose, I looked for my place of greatest refuge. Humor. "Please don't make me sleep in a doorway again," I told Jimmy.

He stopped and held out his hand. "As long as you make sure that I don't." We shook on our agreement.

We dutifully followed the Vice President through the halls, with his security detail on either side of us, until we reached a different part of the house that looked like a sitting room. We were ushered inside and the three of us left alone with the President. He pointed at a couch and we took seats, sitting stock upright.

We had expected to meet Jimmy in some dank back room, not with the President in a place of distinction.

"Call me Fin," the President said warmly, taking a wingback chair where he could see us as well as Jimmy.

"I don't think so, Mr. President," I said. "But I appreciate the offer. I'm Ian, and my wife is Jenny."

The President nodded politely. "Jimmy tells me you have special skills." I tried not to give away my surprise.

"He *knows*, Ian," Jimmy admitted, "that you were sent to kill me but refused."

"Good thing, otherwise this meeting would be more awkward than it already is," I quipped.

The President snorted and then laughed hard. "There isn't enough of that in this city. Everyone comes here somber and intimidated, even my own cabinet members. We have the full weight of the law on our side, but we can't exercise it as we'd like. There are some people who need to go away. David Quresh is one of those. We will make it worth your while."

"As I told Jimmy a few minutes ago, Jenny and I now run the organization that I worked for, the one that put the contract out on the future mayor of Seattle. We have a number of assets at our command and can probably relieve you of certain burdens. I'm sure you know that we have been doing jobs for the government for a number of years now, including the ATF, FBI, SEC, and CBP."

The President looked at Jimmy. "I did *not* know this."

"Why would the SEC hire assassins?" Jimmy asked.

"We're called 'operators.' The SEC hires operators to handle those people who are destroying lives through pyramid schemes and other reckless and illegal investment houses. If we can intervene early enough, it saves the government an expensive trial and the opportunity to recover some of the investors' money."

"The SEC is hiring *operators*?" The President looked shocked but turned it into a smile. "When a civil suit just won't do. This shouldn't be funny, but the government has two-point-one million employees and a budget of six-point-six trillion dollars. The numbers are so big that no one can get their arms around them or rein them in. I guess we have some enterprising folks who are trying to save money or shortcut justice. It's important that we know why someone is to be terminated. It will help me if we know there's another check and balance out there to make sure we don't slide down that slippery slope. We'll offer twenty million for this job, and then we'll assess for our other hard cases that you might be able to make go away. If you take care of us, we can turn a blind eye toward your other work as long as no innocents get hurt."

"That is what we're best at, Mr. President. Only the target."

"What is your company called, Mr. Bragg?"

"Does the name matter? It isn't in any public record," I dodged.

"It matters because that's what I'll pass on to my successor as people who will help keep the country moving forward when evil threatens to drag us down."

My mind churned to find a reason I shouldn't be straight with him. In the Marines, the oath I took was to defend the Constitution of the United States, not the President, but this man was the Commander in Chief, and I respected that. "We're called the Peace Archive. I have forty-one assets available for operations, which means we can handle a rather significant number of cases. I'll work with Jimmy to see if we can clear out some of your backlist, assuming we can come to an agreement."

Jenny gave my hand a gentle squeeze. I was doing the sales thing, and she approved.

"'The Peace Archive.' That's a name I won't forget. You accomplished all this in the United States, and your people haven't gotten caught?"

"Only one. Our people don't admit what they do or who they work for. It's bad for business. And we execute over a hundred contracts a year."

"A hundred murders a year, and your people don't get caught?"

That wasn't a term I would use, so I remained quiet.

"As a professional politician, I've gotten very good at reading people. I see the truth in you, Mr. Bragg. Tell me if I'm right by answering this question. Why do you do what you do?"

I didn't have to think about it. "I served in the Marines, and we had to do some things that didn't make sense to me. But then there were missions that were a perfect blend of extreme violence and compassion. I do what I do because others can't do it for themselves.

"People deserve to live in a peaceful world. All it takes is for someone like me to excise the cancers of our society. The challenge every single day is not changing the definition of cancer. Only the worst of the worst come before us. Jimmy's contract was an aberration. It should have never gone through, and that started the dominoes falling that put me in charge. All of our operators look with a critical eye at the contracts they're given. Like your David Quresh. If he is what he seems, then the sooner he's out of the picture, the better this world will be. No more Jonestown because the Peace Archive can stop it before it comes to something like that."

The President smiled. "A patriot who puts his life on the line for the greater good." He watched me with the practiced gaze of one who gave nothing away. "Leave no evidence behind, and we will funnel more work to you, probably more work than even your robust organization can handle. And no, we don't expect you to work for free, Mr. Bragg. I'm sure you have bills to pay."

"We have to pay a lot of bills. Secret lairs are expensive. I'll get my people on this one right away, and thank you, Mr. President." We stood, but the President was shaking his head.

"Not your people, Mr. Bragg. *You*. Jimmy trusts you,

which means I trust you, and you will set the standard for others to follow. Take care of this for us, and I will personally owe you a favor."

Washington, DC, the favor-trading capital of the world.

"An IOU from the President. I hope I never have to cash that in for both our sakes, but there's something you're not telling me. Whose daughter is in that compound, Mr. President? Who do you need me to rescue?"

The President's lip twitched at the start of a smile before he suppressed it. "Astute. I expected no less. The Senate Minority Leader's daughter is inside that compound. So there is a political side to this, but that doesn't change what is happening out there. David Quresh needs to go and will, one way or another. The quieter, the better. And the Minority Leader can owe me." He turned to Jimmy. "Make sure he gets Becky's picture. Even if we don't share with the good senator from Idaho, he deserves to have his daughter back. I don't wish losing a daughter on anyone."

Jimmy nodded, his eyes glassing briefly before he blinked it away. He had a daughter approaching the age of the children in the compound, but not as old as the college-aged Becky.

"Jenny. It was a pleasure having you here." The President stood and took her hand in both of his. "I wish more people brought their better halves into their business. I believe it strengthens relationships."

"Like you and the First Lady? You come across as a team, and that's who people like to deal with."

"Exactly. I hope you get to meet her someday." His words rang hollow. I didn't think there was any way Jenny and I could ever be seen in public with the President and the First Lady.

None of that mattered for this day. Jenny and I had to

go to Idaho to fix a problem because that was what we do. I had no idea how, but I expected we would figure it out. We had to. There was no choice to turn this contract down, just like the hit on Chaz's killer.

This train was racing down the tracks with Jenny and I hanging on for dear life.

CHAPTER FIFTEEN

"Simplicity is the ultimate sophistication." –Leonardo da Vinci

With the backing of the federal government, I became less worried about getting raided in the middle of the night and dragged off to prison. That meant we could prepare more deliberately.

We were dropped off at our hotel by the same gruff Secret Service agents. I never did manage to crack their façade, and it wasn't for lack of trying. I delivered my best jokes, but they remained stoic. I figured they were probably former Army. Marines would have thought them hilarious.

We returned to our room and sat there, looking at each other. We both wanted to talk about it but also not. We wanted to plan for Idaho but not right then.

"Call your sister. Maybe we can do dinner, as long as she's not cooking."

"I thought you'd want to get on the road to, you know, make the President not want to put us in jail."

"It's a secret compound in the woods. I need Marine stuff, and Quantico is less than an hour south. There have to be surplus stores."

"I know there's a massive outlet mall between here and there, too."

The smile slowly faded from my face.

Jenny cupped my cheek with her hand. "We met the President."

"I don't know what to say. I didn't expect that. At least the Archive is safe."

Jenny grunted. "The Archive? Ian, you are working directly for the President to deliver justice when the system is too cumbersome or slow. It's not quite Constitutional, but from what I've seen of you and what you do, it's putting the country in good hands. Isn't that what you wanted, to be responsible for keeping people safe?"

"It is everything I wanted from the second I joined the Marines. Deliver justice without the constraints that allow the guilty to go free. As long as I can be certain in my own mind that the contracts are sound, I'm happy to do this job. I hope the President knows that I will tell him no if things look off. He can sic the entirety of the Justice Department on someone if he wants as long as that someone isn't me, but he won't do that. We are linked to him and Jimmy. Still, I don't feel like I have as much leverage as I should."

"You have plenty of leverage. Take care of this problem, and the President owes you a favor. I like the sound of that." Jenny straddled my lap and positioned her breasts under my chin.

"Guys like me don't get to meet people like that," I continued.

"Jimmy talked about wasting time doing damage control. That tells me you're the kind of guy they want to meet with because you make problems go away. The quieter, the better."

"Which is why I want to go to the surplus store. I need a green ghillie suit, binoculars, and probably a fifty-cal sniper rifle, but there's no way I'd try to buy that in Virginia."

Jenny was instantly bored with the Marine talk. "Are we going to take a taxi all the way to Quantico?" Jenny was on to me.

"I thought we'd go to your sister's house and borrow a car."

"I'm not even going to ask her." Jenny tipped her chin back.

"Just a little ask." I kissed my way into her cleavage.

"You are incorrigible, Mr. Bragg."

"Very much so. I think Brazilian for dinner sounds good."

"And this time, please don't chant 'Meat, meat, meat.' That was embarrassing."

"I can only promise that I'll try. It's like a playground for men in there."

"Everything is a playground for men in your world."

It was hard to argue with that while my face was buried where it was. I came up for air. "The dickens you say!"

Jenny laughed until she stopped with a smile, and her green eyes watching me.

"No matter what else happens, we won today because of what we did a year and a half ago."

"*We* meaning *you*. I'll give my sister a call and see what we can set up. It's the weekend, so they should be around, but it's the weekend, so we may not get our first choice of places to eat. We might even get my brother to join us."

"He's such a tosser."

"Watching too many British crime thrillers?" Jenny asked.

"Harry Potter. I hear he's a tosser, too."

Jenny closed her eyes. "What am I going to do with you?"

"Breakfast would be good. It's still morning, isn't it?"

Jenny pushed me away and stood. "I guess the honeymoon *is* over." She stood defiantly, feet shoulder-width apart and fists drilled into her hips.

"I suspect I did something, but I have no idea what. This is the part of our relationship where you have to help me understand." I listened intently. Rush's *Circumstances* played in the background of my mind.

"You were making your move and I was showing the goods, and all of a sudden, you hit me with, 'I'm hungry.'"

"For woman-flesh," I tried. My attempt was weak, and she knew it. She glared at me.

I maneuvered to the door and put out the Do Not Disturb sign, then locked and chained the door.

"We're going to settle this before we leave this room." My stomach growled. It was a most inopportune moment. She charged, and I wasn't ready. Jenny dug her fingernails into my side while pushing me back into the wall. I shredded the buttons on her shirt. I saw her mouth heading for my neck. It felt like I was about to be attacked by a vampire. I pulled her tight against me so I could reach behind her to undo the clasp on her bra.

We awoke after noon to find our destroyed clothes and the room a shambles.

"Oops." Jenny put a finger to her cheek and tried to look innocent. There was a rather significant bite mark on her neck. I pointed to it without saying anything. She hopped up, still naked, and strolled to the bathroom.

"Ian!"

I joined her, only to find that we shouldn't go to the pool anytime soon lest someone call the police on us for domestic abuse.

She hugged me. "I guess the honeymoon isn't over. I'm hungry. We should probably grab something and then start making phone calls."

"Interesting."

Jenny raised her eyebrows.

"When I say I'm hungry, I get attacked. When you say *you're* hungry…"

"And?" Jenny wondered.

"And nothing. I'm still hungry from before because we still haven't eaten, but we should put on our adult clothes and figure out what we need to do to satisfy this contract."

"We'll have to consider the damsels in distress, too. If he doesn't have any other men in the compound, who is preventing them from leaving?" she asked.

"Exactly. We're going to have hostiles who we might think are captives, and all of them are victims, but we probably shouldn't turn our backs on them."

"Which means I need a ghillie suit, too."

We had told the President we were a team. My long hesitation told Jenny that I had not intended to take her to the compound with me. "Of course," I conceded. "I better check the information they gave us and see where we're going and what we might need to do."

We took the hotel shuttle to the airport and rented a car rather than impose on Jasmine, her big sister. Jenny worked the phone to get us reservations at the Brazilian place. It would be just us, Jazz, and her kids. Jack and Kate, her big brother and his wife, had another event they had already committed to but insisted we stop by first thing in the morning on our way to the airport.

I didn't want to. Neither did Jenny, so we told them we'd be able to come for a few minutes.

The surplus store had only one ghillie suit that would fit Jenny. Everything my size was in a desert color scheme. I bought it but wasn't sure I'd use it. I picked up a set of woodland camouflaged utilities, too. Marine Corps-style, but in a new pattern that hadn't been available when I served. We bought enough tactical equipment to outfit us both for a week in the woods. We bought two duffel bags to squeeze it all into.

The only thing remaining was weapons. A quick internet search showed us that Wyoming was the place to get a weapon without any waiting period. It also showed that I could buy a fifty-caliber Barrett at a gun store in Cheyenne. "We need to go to Wyoming and then drive to Idaho Falls." Another map search. "About a nine-hour drive."

"Roundabout approach to get where we want to be," Jenny observed. She knew why. "And then what's left after that? A twenty-five-mile hike through the mountains?"

"A minor stretch of the legs, but it's the only way to come in on the far side of the compound. They'll have eyes and ears up and down the approaching road. They won't be watching the more rugged terrain on the eastern side, or if they are, it won't be to the degree they'll be watching the southwestern approach."

"Because the FBI is lazy?" Jenny asked.

"It's just how people think. They assume their enemies will take the path of least resistance. That may work for electricity and water, but military tactics? Be where they can't believe you would be."

Jenny's lips turned white as she drew them tight against

her teeth. I'd be taking her into a world she didn't know.

"Are you sure you want to come along?"

"I have to. I'm not leaving you out there all alone. You take care of the job, and I'll watch your back."

"Deal," I agreed.

We left everything in the trunk when we arrived at Jasmine's house. Her husband Dylan was on another gig as an interpreter, so I had yet to meet him.

Jazz ran out the front door in her usual ebullient display. I stayed out of the impact area as the sisters did their thing. I could only think about the job.

A sniper shot or up close and personal? I couldn't take on all the women. I wouldn't fight them, but if they were devout adherents, maybe I'd have to. And Becky, the senator's daughter. It was a complete mess. No wonder the government wanted it handled outside the boundaries of the media. Make the bad man go away. It was what I excelled at.

The sisters caught me staring and surprised me by each grabbing an arm and dragging me toward the big colonial home.

Jasmine worked as a wedding planner. Since it was Saturday, it surprised me that she was home. I had hoped— which I would never tell Miss Jenny—that they weren't available so I could monopolize my wife's time. I liked being alone with her despite the bites and scratches currently marring my body.

And hers. We had no idea what brought that about, but it worked for us.

We'd met the President, but we couldn't tell anyone about it. I expected Jenny was dying to tell her sister, but she wouldn't.

"New contract," I blurted.

"What?" Jenny and Jasmine said at the same time.

"That's why we're here. We'll probably be here fairly often nowadays because of some new work while staying on the down-low."

"That's great news! We'll clean out the spare bedroom, and you must always stay here."

I tipped my head down to look at her.

"Always," she said in a low and firm voice.

"I feel like I missed part of a conversation."

"You missed the entire conversation, my dear," Jenny said, hugging me before we took our places at the dinner table to chat and kill time before our reservation. As soon as Jasmine's butt touched the chair, the phone rang. She popped back up and hurried to the kitchen to answer it.

"Jack! The play was canceled, so you can make it. Sure. We can fit you in. See you in an hour."

"Joy," I grumbled.

"After your last visit," Jazz offered, casually leaning against the doorjamb, "he has made a night-and-day change. I don't think he ever contemplated that there would be someone in the family he couldn't bully. He's a changed man."

"We can only hope," Jenny said softly, playing with my hair. I looked at her. "It's getting long. I can't believe you saw the Pre..." She caught herself before finishing the word. "While looking like a ragamuffin."

"It's my best look. Chicks dig it."

"Out with it," Jasmine ordered while putting glasses of iced tea on the table for the three of us.

"We met with the president of the company Ian works for today. It was a good meeting. We'll be busier than ever. More travel."

"I didn't talk with you for months, and all of a sudden, you show up here. What is going on?"

"We took an around-the-world cruise. It was four

months long. And then we had to move to Chicago. Ian now manages an international jetsetter's club. We also bought a house there."

"Chicago is nothing like Vegas."

I nodded while frowning.

"But it sounds like a good position. An around-the-world cruise?"

"Call it a signing bonus," I interjected. I didn't want to talk about me or us. "What have you been up to? People have to be getting married at the cyclic rate."

"I suspect that means at a high rate of speed and in that case, I know, right?" Her shoulders slumped. "But they aren't. Too many hippies out there."

Jenny laughed. "They're not hippies! Why don't you start a partnering ceremony? Looks just like a wedding but freer, with no bureaucracy. I bet people would spend the same on something like that."

"You might be right, Sis. It's all about the marketing. *Celebrate your free partnership.* I can see it now. *Special package, only nine thousand nine hundred and ninety-nine dollars...*"

"Is that what you charge?" I had never contemplated a normal wedding and the people and costs involved.

"That's a cheap one, honey. I've charged up to fifty grand for a single event."

Jenny and I looked at the table. "I gave Elvis an extra hundred for his troubles," I mumbled.

"We eloped."

"It's not because we weren't willing to spend a fortune on a wedding!" I declared with a firm fist-pound into my hand. "It's just that we don't know anyone or like them enough to invite to our wedding."

This drew the ire of both women.

"I'll shut up now." I sipped my tea. Too sweet for my

taste, but I'd finish it because I didn't want to insult our host.

"You could have a second event here. I'll make it spectacular, even if only the nine of us join you. It won't cost you anything, so Mr. No-Friends Cheapskate won't be put out."

The Lawless sisters stared at me.

"I'm not as offended as you might think. Actually, I'm not offended at all."

Jenny smiled. "Ian has friends, but he never imposes on them. And you'll have to take my word that they are very good friends, people who would die for him."

I returned to staring at the table. I knew Jenny was proud of me, but bragging to her sister was something different. She pulled my face up to share a moment before her sister gasped. We were wrenched away from each other's eyes.

Jazz pointed as if she saw a spider. "What happened to your neck?"

"Passionate lovemaking. I see you bear no marks. What a shame to give up on life so early into it," Jenny smoothly explained.

I checked to make sure my shirt covered the worst of the other marks. "I saw that. Lift it, mister."

I thought about complying and decided it was better to sit there without moving. "No."

"That bad, huh? What happened to you, little sister?" Jasmine sounded concerned.

"Passion for life. We have no problems in our relationship. We aren't beating each other up. This morning was an incredible meeting that was a once-in-a-lifetime thing, and I got to be a part of it. A nobody from Bumfudge, Washington."

"Two nobodies," I added. "Two nobodies who are doing

right by this great country of ours. We can't explain further, so don't press, but understand that today was a very good day."

"I guess I'll take your word on that." Jasmine stared at the mark on Jenny's neck. "Is that a bite?"

"Oh, yeah," Jenny purred.

"Aren't you a little old for hickeys?"

We looked at each other and shook our heads in unison. Jenny answered, "No."

"Look at the time!" I stood up and collected the glasses to take them to the kitchen.

"Uh-huh." Jasmine eyed us skeptically while Jenny giggled.

"I'm going to hit the head, too." I knew they wanted to engage in sister talk unimpeded by a third wheel, and I fully concurred. I had no desire to listen in. The good news was that I was plenty hungry. Breakfast had been insubstantial because it looked like a quick lunch.

We hadn't checked in with Vinny about the meeting. He would be wondering. After a quick trip to the restroom, I waved my phone at Jenny as I headed outside to dial Vinny's number.

The line connected, and I spoke right away. "Vinny, it's Ian."

"I wondered when you were going to call," he answered.

"I have to personally do a gig, and it's not for Jimmy. It's for this guy called Fin."

"Well now. That's unexpectedly good news."

"I think we'll get as much work as we can do as long as Jenny and I take care of this little burr under their saddle. I won't tell you where we're going or how long we'll be there, but we'll be back when we've taken care of business."

"Nothing short of perfection, Ian."

"Sounds like what our employer said. It's for twenty big

ones, in case you were wondering if they were serious or it might have been a setup. I am confident it is not. Their necks are out a lot farther than ours."

"I'm pleased, Ian. I'll take care of things here, consolidating into three directorates and getting the pending contracts going to keep our people earning their keep."

"Everything but Segway's. We kicked that back. It was a bad one."

"I know, Ian. I've already refunded his money and told him to live up to the standard we expect. Market share is not an issue we'll address. It's not a problem that we fix."

I strolled back and forth on the short sidewalk between the front door and the driveway. "I'm glad we're on the same page, Vinny. Our new clients aren't keen on contracts where an innocent might be involved. Not too keen at all. We have to make sure that no one is involved who shouldn't be."

"That is what we've always strived for, Ian. When you get back, you'll make the determination on each one. I hope you don't let it get to you or start slipping. You are what we all aspire to be. See you when you get back. We'll be ready to go, so try not to keep us waiting too long."

I turned the phone off and stuffed it into my pocket. It was a middle-class neighborhood in upscale Woodbridge. It would have been upper-class in nearly all of the rest of the country. Fifty grand for the organizer's fee. I was sure it was spectacular, but it wasn't my idea of something anyone needed to do. Have a buffet at the golf course. Squeeze in a few holes. Enjoy a nice day. Too much ceremony ruined everything.

Jenny and I did not have to put on airs for anyone. We could be who we were. The air was humid, and the rank scent of a nearby salt marsh sharpened the smell. From the grass to the tops of the trees, summer green was on full display. I ran my hand over the grass of the front yard. Rough, more for show than playing on. It was immaculate, as if it had been groomed.

It would have been good for archery if the neighbors didn't mind their house being used as a backstop. Or horseshoes. Something to do while steaks grilled. *Is there a grill at the house in Chicago?* I wondered. If there wasn't, I'd buy one. *Have to get rid of those race cars, though.*

The door opened, and the sisters walked out with two tall children. I think they were eleven and thirteen, but I wouldn't ask to clarify. Jenny would know.

"We're driving," Jenny said before opening the doors to let everyone in. She climbed into the passenger seat. "You know the way. Chop-chop."

Wearing a big grin, I glanced in the rearview mirror at Jasmine.

"You two plotting against innocent ol' me. I shall chauffeur the princesses and their spawn to the place of food worship, where I shall see that the finest bits are delivered to your plates first. And then I shall embrace the bill as is my duty to the fair one who shares my bed."

"There are children in the car," Jazz deadpanned from the backseat.

"Mom!"

"One bed for your aunt and me because we're lovers."

"Mom!"

I could see Jenny roll her eyes without looking. The drive took the usual five minutes. We headed for the door with one minute to spare. Jack and Kate were already there and waiting. Jack approached but was on guard to prevent his sister from bruising more than his ego. She hugged him to keep him off-guard.

"Jack," I said evenly.

"Ian," he replied before taking his wife's hand and heading inside.

Jenny tried not to laugh while she whispered to Jasmine, "Men."

"And you got yourself a good one. I've never seen you happier," Jazz whispered in reply.

The table was unsurprisingly the same they'd had for their previous family get together. It was either the group table or those they didn't want any other customers to see. It was also at the far end of the meat delivery circuit. I wasn't afraid. Our flight didn't leave until mid-morning. I'd wait them out to get the choice bits.

"What brings you to DC?" Jack asked, looking at me.

"A business trip. New clients, new contracts, big promotion, and now we're busy. We leave tomorrow and will be on the road quite a bit."

"But…" Jack looked around. "What about that other thing? You're supposed to be lying low, right?"

"That resolved itself in a way where we are no longer in that program. We can live like normal people, somewhat."

"That's good to hear." Everyone was watching him. "If your company has contacts here, you'll be coming this way more often?"

"That's twice now and you're still at zero to visit us, but you don't have to come to Vegas anymore. It's okay."

"No, no. We are looking for a good time when our schedules match up, but we are coming to visit you."

Jenny took my cue and answered, "Then you better not go to Vegas. We don't live there anymore. We have a house in Chicago. It's pretty nice. You are always welcome to stay in the guesthouse on the property."

"Guesthouse? What kind of money do you make?"

I delivered a perfect harumph. "And to think you accused me of being after Jenny's money. Shame on you,

Jack. We do well enough that we have a nice house on a golf course. If you come to visit, make sure you bring a coat and tie. There are standards at our club." I instantly felt bad. It had been given to us, just like the house. Damn siblings. "I'm sorry. We're being jerks. We've moved, and you are welcome to visit. You don't have to travel anywhere nearly as far to visit us—whenever we're home, that is. I see a fair bit of travel in our future, two to three weeks out of the month."

"That's harsh," Jack replied. "But congratulations. It's nice to join humanity again, isn't it?"

"That is most astute. It is nice to be able to travel, to breathe fresh air. It's nice to be married to Jenny. And I'm okay with you, too, Jack."

"Thanks. I'm glad you don't want to beat me up because I'm sure you could take me."

"I can take you," Jenny said, making a fist for emphasis.

"Down, Fido." Jack pointed at the table.

"Hey, look at that meat!" Jazz stated. Two servers deftly stroked chicken from their skewers onto everyone's plate.

I stopped the server and slipped him a twenty. "Filet, my man."

"That's next," he said, sliding the bill into his pocket.

Jenny looked at me.

"We have standards when it comes to steak, my dear. We're going to need that protein."

She nodded. Starting tomorrow, we were on the job to deliver justice on behalf of the federal government without anyone ever knowing that it was them. Sounded like business as usual, putting me back into the shoes of an operator. We both tried to get into the spirit of the evening, but the job loomed large.

Twenty million, to be exact, and the future of the Peace Archive.

CHAPTER SIXTEEN

"What worries you, masters you." –John Locke

We connected through Denver to get to Cheyenne, Wyoming, where the tiny airport was able to put us into a compact rental car. It was late spring and we wouldn't be doing any off-roading, so it would do. I tried not to frown, but it was less obvious than a nicer car. I had to tamp down my appreciation of the finer things in life.

The trunk was big enough for all our stuff, two duffels and a Barrett Model 95, which sported a twenty-nine-inch barrel. It was a bullpup design, putting the bolt assembly and magazine feed behind the trigger assembly, which shortened the weapon's overall length to forty-five inches even with the three-port muzzle break and adjustable shoulder pad.

There were a number of gun shops in town. For a Marine like me, weapons were just another part of life. I appreciated the opportunity to stop by, purchase a weapon and ammunition, and leave without any hassle. In this case, I was buying a gun for a purpose that wasn't condoned. The laws couldn't protect people from me, as I had shown on multiple occasions, since I would always find a way to make a hit. I didn't need a gun.

But when I saw the Sig Sauer P250, a compact .45, I bought it, too. I asked for twelve rounds of ammunition for the big rifle and a box of fifty shells for the Sig.

"Twelve?" the clerk asked. "How about twenty since they come in ten-packs?"

"But you charge by the round," I countered.

"But they come in packs of ten."

"You drive a hard bargain." We shook hands, and I bought the rifle, the pistol, the ammunition, and a Millett 6-25X56 LRS-1 scope. It was the best they had for long-range and low-light shooting. I didn't know when I would be able to take a shot, so I needed to be ready for anything. I added a sling, a holster, and a soft-sided case for the rifle.

It took an hour in the gun store. Jenny tried to be patient, but it wasn't her thing. I was in my element, as was the clerk when we talked about taking hard shots. He had been in the Army so I tried not to give him too hard of a time, especially since he loved shooting and was plenty knowledgeable. I told him I'd received a big tax refund and there was nothing I wanted to spend it on more than upgrading my range-ready firepower.

We wished each other well, and Jenny and I went on our way. We started driving but had only made it to Laramie fifty miles away when we decided to stop and settle into a hotel. Tomorrow would be a travel day, and then we'd start our overland jaunt.

We ate dinner at a local greasy spoon in silence, where I devoured one of the best burgers I've ever had, and called it an early night. I checked my computer, but there was nothing of interest in the documents Vinny was working on. I closed out, turned on the TV, and hugged my wife while we watched mindless reruns, neither interested in anything more. We were on a mission and our attention was focused there, even though we could do nothing about it until we saw what we were up against. Still, it occupied our minds, and when we talked, it was about eighteen women and six girls. Twenty-four souls in a captivity probably not of their choosing.

I couldn't abide that. Neither could Jenny.

We skipped past Idaho Falls and drove to the center of the state, to the edge of the Salmon-Challis National Forest. The Quresh compound wasn't far from the nearest town, Challis, but I wanted to approach the compound from the far side. That meant a long hike to stay out of the sight of any prying eyes, human or camera.

Hiding the car would be impossible. Someone would know about the strangers who came to town and disappeared into the mountains.

Any action at the compound would happen before we returned.

We opted for hiding in plain sight by being so obvious that people wouldn't think twice about us. That also meant time. There was one bed and breakfast in town. We were able to snag a room for two weeks before the rooms were committed to a tourist group. We set ourselves up, only bringing our small bags into the room, not any of our other gear.

This part of the operation was to establish a local

presence being the happy young couple who loved to hike. Jenny purchased t-shirts for us at the local convenience store, the only shop in town. We settled in with a map of the National Forest's hiking trails.

That was for public consumption. I had a GPS that I picked up outside Quantico and the coordinates of where we wanted to go. We weren't going to guess. The less we left to chance, the better the setup for a clean kill would be. Jenny's trepidation grew with her silence. Worry lines crept into the corners of her eyes, but she insisted she was fine.

In the Marines, we found the bush to be the great equalizer. The bush. The field, whether jungle or forest. The confines of the great outdoors. The wilds of nature would close in on us until we showed it that we were not afraid. Until we mastered it.

The next morning, we put on a good show of enjoying our breakfast and banter with the owners before heading out on a day hike. We left town in full sight of anyone watching to take the main trailhead.

I was surprised to find it wasn't heavily used. "Rugged camping isn't as popular as it used to be."

Jenny took four more steps, head down, watching where she placed each foot. "I can't imagine why."

We forged our way forward. The trail through the sparse, desert-like hills disappeared by the second mile. We stopped for a short break. I used my GPS to see where we were in relation to the compound and noted our location on the map.

"I was wrong. We only need to cover about ten miles from here to get to the back side of the compound. We could get there today if we wanted, but we might not be able to get back, and we don't have our gear."

Jenny nodded.

"Please talk to me," I begged.

"I can't abandon you, but I know I'll hold you back." She pointed at the trees and mountains ahead of us. "This is not me. I don't hike for fun or any other reason, so with each step, I move that much closer to failing you."

"That's deep. I thought you were going to talk about how much you hate bugs."

"That too," Jenny admitted. "I have a different idea for a plan."

"And that is?" I wanted to hear what she had to say. It was usually just me. I wished she gave her input more often, but I did most of my work while she was still asleep.

"I go in undercover."

"Absolutely not!" A million ways the hit could go sideways flashed through my mind if Jenny was alone on the inside.

"That's why I didn't bring it up. Think about it for a minute, and you'll know it's the best way to make sure the hit is clean."

I stood up and faced a barren hillside. I tried to focus on my breathing, but it was coming in ragged gasps. My stomach started to hurt. "I can't tell you how dangerous it will be in there."

"What is he doing with the women? You may be walking into a deathtrap."

"Then let's get to where we can see and take a look. Like you said, it's only ten miles."

"I don't have the scope with me. With the rifle, we'll be able to observe from as far away as we can be. Plus, I need to zero it in. That'll be five shots at least one range and valley over. There's a lot of work to do just to get to where we know enough to develop a plan."

"Your special phone is a satellite phone, isn't it?"

I took it out of my pocket and dialed Jenny's number. It immediately went to voice mail since there was no signal, but I could call out.

"It's settled. You go in tomorrow and observe. I'll be at the B and B. Call me when you have an idea. I'll walk to the compound from town."

I stared at the mountains, demanding they offer a better alternative, but they remained silent. "We can do this from the outside."

"You know we can't. You know *I* can't."

"I *don't* know that, Miss Jenny."

"The decision is made. You go at it from one side. I'll attack it from the other. We'll meet in the middle. We need to free those people once you've determined that they are indeed being held against their will, but I don't think you'll be able to make that call with what you see through the scope. I'll be able to figure it out once I'm inside."

"I don't want you to go in there."

"I don't either, but we have a job to do, Ian. A job that the President of the United States gave us. I was raised to respect that office, and I believe that predators and self-styled demi-gods can't be allowed to turn this world into their personal playground, the rest of the people be damned. You taught me well. I can fight. They won't be as suspicious of me because I'm a pretty girl, aren't I?"

"I feel like I've been kicked in the nuts."

"You feel like you can't protect the woman you love," Jenny clarified.

I finally faced her. "It's the same feeling."

"You are such a man. Call the room when you're in position, and we'll make this thing happen. As long as you're watching over the compound, I'll be fine. I'm leaving my phone and everything else behind. I won't have anything with me besides the clothes I'm wearing. The ten-mile jaunt will be a little easy without hauling my usual pile of garbage."

"That'll be best. Give them nothing, maybe a couple hundred dollars in cash. Offer it to them as the last of all that you have."

"Good idea. What do you say we head back?" Jenny stood up from the rock she'd been sitting on, wiping the dirt off her jeans.

"Bugs getting to you, Miss Jenny?"

She chuckled lightly. "Something like that. Maybe we can spar, just to sharpen the blades one last time. I expect I'm going to have to fight someone."

I zeroed in like a laser. "You have to be ready. I think you know what this guy does to women."

"And he'll be sorry if he tries it on me. You've taught me well, Ian. I will fight him with every ounce of my being. I won't let him touch me."

"I will be as close as I can get and will be there in no time if I see any sign of a throwdown. There is one thing I think we can guarantee. The fence won't be electrified." I planned to get inside the fence the second Jenny arrived if I could. I wouldn't share that detail with her.

"Not unless he has some evil-lair business going on, but I don't think so. We've looked at the info Jimmy gave us. Two main buildings, no electricity, and four small outbuildings, little more than sheds, but are they? I'll confirm as much as I can before I call." I picked up my pack and balanced it on my back, bouncing to make sure it was settled.

"You know this is the right way to do this. If I find anything out, I'll escape to the northwest in your direction. Then we'll decide what we need to do from there to finish the job."

"So we can declare victory and go home," I added. Jenny took the lead. She turned quickly to catch me looking at her butt. "I'm not sorry."

"I'm glad," she replied before turning her attention to setting a record pace out of the rugged hills.

CHAPTER SEVENTEEN

"Get busy living, or get busy dying." –Stephen King

I tiptoed out of the bed and breakfast at three-thirty in the morning. Jenny followed. Outside, dark windows greeted us. I took the duffel bag and rifle bag out of the trunk and threw the duffel's straps over my shoulders while cradling the rifle bag in front of my chest.

Jenny watched me closely. Once I'd closed the trunk and the light was out, I pressed the keys into her hand. "I'll be in position and will start collecting information today."

My duffel was light, even with three canteens of water. I'd refill from mountain streams, where I expected the water to taste better, even if it did make me sick without a filter straw. The heaviest thing I carried was the rifle, at just over twenty-three pounds plus the weight of the filled five-round magazine.

The desert ghillie would have to blend into the variety of mountain foliage. I had no choice but to trust it. I'd cross that bridge when I came to it. In between, I needed to zero the rifle and pistol since I preferred to hit what I aimed at.

After one final kiss, I hurried through the open area toward the trailhead. Once on the trail, I disappeared into the darkness. I went slowly at first since the trunk light had torched most of my night vision. Because I'd lost my focus and failed to foresee the light, it would cost me time.

I frequently stopped to listen, and after a solid thirty minutes, the cool of pre-dawn settled, delivering the darkest time of the day. I continued to move slowly as far through the open area as I needed to go. After an hour, I found a place to wait for the sun to rise. I'd make up any lost ground once I could see clearly. All I wanted to do was get far enough away from town to avoid being seen.

The water was cool, but I drank sparingly until I was sure I could refill the canteen. As we had confirmed in Arizona, a stream on a map might not have water.

As the first tendrils of dawn highlighted the branches of distant trees, I redoubled my efforts and reached the trees before the sun poked its head above the horizon. I pointed my feet toward Corkscrew Mountain and hurried almost to the point of running. I cleared one range of hills and headed downward, slowing since it was easy to get hurt while descending.

When I reached the bottom of the valley on my way to the other side, I found a rough road—little more than wheel tracks, but there was a sign: Rough Road Ahead.

I walked on the hard ground to avoid leaving tracks, wondering who would drive on such a dog track, but people lived out here. Forest rangers worked out here, and game wardens, too.

The next range was a rougher ascent, and I had to zigzag across the face to gain altitude. Once I passed over a saddle, I found what I was looking for. I could shoot from this hillside over the neighboring lower hills into a rock face on the far side. I figured it was a mile and a half. A shorter shot at the neighboring hill was only four to five hundred yards. I wanted to be comfortable at both ranges.

I took the rifle out of the bag and stuffed the bag into the duffel. The only things outside were the rifle, ten rounds, and the adjustment tool for the scope. I checked the rifle to make sure there were no obstructions in the barrel.

The best I could do with the scope was boresight it, looking down the barrel and then through the scope and estimating they were in the same vicinity. I steadied the rifle on my duffel bag as I picked out both near and far targets and prepared for a rapid zeroing. Five rounds would be best, but I was prepared to fire ten. Then I'd run over the hill in the direction from which I'd come and work my way south before turning east to approach the Quresh compound from the far side.

That was the plan.

I aimed and slowly squeezed the trigger. The rifle slammed into my shoulder, even though I had pulled it in tight. I looked through the scope to see a wisp of a dust cloud low and far to the left. I estimated it was nearly ten feet to the left and two feet low at six hundred yards.

That meant at a mile and a half, I might as well be trying to hit a target the size of a barn.

I cranked the adjustment screw so much I saw the scope move. I took it easier as I adjusted it upward.

I lined up and fired again. This shot was one foot right and six inches high. I adjusted a click down and two clicks left.

The third round hit within the body mass of a man.

Good enough for government work. If a bullet of this caliber hit someone, it would rip off a limb or tear out a big enough hunk of flesh that no one would survive. At least not be able to walk away before a second half-inch round finished them.

On the distant hillside, the fourth shot through the rifle impacted a good six feet low but right on from left to right. I cycled the bolt and chambered the next round without adjusting the scope. I aimed one man-height high, and the round impacted exactly on target.

I pulled out the pistol and snapped off three shots. I adjusted my aiming point and fired three more times. I needed to aim at two o'clock high. Good enough. I holstered the pistol.

I reloaded both magazines, slapped them into place, and stuffed the hot brass into my pocket.

With the duffel bag over my shoulders and cradling the rifle, I scuffed up where I'd been lying and headed over the hill.

I stayed within the treeline as I moved, checking the GPS every thirty minutes. I had every bit of eight miles remaining, even though I'd already traveled five but out of the way since I didn't want to shoot anywhere near the target.

"Jenny, if I didn't love you, I would love this big gun. What I could have done with this monster in the desert! No one would have been able to get close to us. What a shame I'm going to have to dump you, lovely rifle that I shall call Betsy Ross. This could have been a magical love affair."

I moved consistently through the shadows of the tree line until I transitioned to movement to contact. I parked myself between three close-growing trees and put on the ghillie suit, which blended better with the terrain than the woodland camouflage would have. Sometimes nothing could beat pure dumb luck.

Counting on that wasn't my first option. I hid the duffel bag under a deadfall and kicked enough pine needles over it to break up the dark green and keep it hidden, then used a branch to brush the area to make it look like I had never been there. With Betsy Ross pulled tight to my chest with my ghillie sleeves covering most of it, I moved slowly through the open area and into the woods on the opposite side of the valley. I started climbing a shallow incline that grew steeper toward the ridge.

I found the best place to cross and slid slowly over the top, not giving anyone a quick movement to spot or a skylined figure. I maneuvered into the trees to take advantage of the shadows. A small hill that stood alone blocked my view. The lake that was within the property was visible, but not the buildings. I turned south until I could see the compound.

That was where I set up. With the scope, I estimated the range at one mile. I got comfortable and started to scan the compound clinically from one side to the other, noting the details to better see when something changed. Doors closed. Curtains drawn. No one outside. A substantial-size garden with new growth. Two trucks.

I contemplated the meaning of two trucks. Who took them to town to get supplies? And who watched over the compound when the driver was gone?

We knew there would have to be more trusted insiders than just Quresh. Did he have the magnetic charisma of other cultists? That was the question, and we had to assume he did.

The compound was enclosed by a double-height chain-link fence with twin strings of barbed wire on top. All the buildings and the garden were contained within the fence. Well-trimmed grass surrounded the buildings. Outside the fence, at least two hundred feet of cleared area served as a moat between the compound and the nearest trees. I couldn't see any blind spots where it would be easy to cut the fence.

An hour went by, then two. I watched over top of the scope to see more of the compound. At three in the afternoon, a dust cloud on the road beyond signaled an approaching vehicle. A truck appeared, driving slowly and stopping at the closed gate. I checked through the scope. The woman wore a Post Office uniform. She opened the passenger door and pulled out a bundle of mail and two packages, carried them to the gate, and waited.

I scanned the area until I saw the movement of a door opening. Two women stepped out with two of the girls. The pre-teens ran to the gate, waving at the delivery person.

They didn't open the gate but took the packages through an opening. The exchange was brief. The postal employee hopped back in her truck, backed up to turn around, and slowly drove off.

The two women let the girls carry the packages as the four retreated into the house. A curtain moved. Someone had been watching. The door closed, and that was it—the totality of all afternoon activity in the course of two minutes.

"It's a beautiful day. You should come outside and play," I muttered.

It took another hour before they complied with my request. The doors were flung open and bodies filed into the yard. I counted them carefully three times. I came up with sixteen adults and six young girls, without any sign of Mr. David Quresh.

I scanned from face to face, looking for the Minority Leader's daughter, but no one looked like her. I tried to interpret what she would look like without makeup and hair pulled back versus fresh from the hairdresser. Still, none fit the bill.

"Why you gotta make this hard, Davey boy?"

I studied the body language of those in the garden, weeding by hand—subdued, except for two women walking around the outside of the group. I looked over the top of the scope, and it was obvious that they weren't helping. They were acting as foremen. I dialed the magnification up as high as it would go to help me burn their faces into my memory so I could describe them to Jenny. *Don't turn your back on those two.*

They weeded the garden before walking around the compound as a group, picking things up off the ground that I couldn't see, and depositing them into a bucket one of the women in charge carried. Once they were finished, they broke into separate groups of two or three and huddled together under the watchful eyes of their overseers.

The foremen talked until one checked her watch and shouted something. I couldn't hear it from where I was. The women trudged through the open door, and that was the last I saw of them that day.

CHAPTER EIGHTEEN

"You are what you believe yourself to be." –Paulo Coelho

After the sun set, faint lights flickered within the buildings. Candles.

I took a small drink from my canteen and left it in my hidey-hole. I carried my rifle with me and moved out, carefully stalking toward the compound, using the trees to block the direct view from the windows facing west. I moved slowly, letting the ghillie suit break up my outline and become its own shadow.

An hour. Two. The lights went out. I made it to the edge of the compound. If I only had night-vision goggles, but I didn't. The good stuff was hard to find if you didn't order online.

I circled the entire compound.

Slowly.

Studying the chain-link, looking for a way in or a place I could create a breach.

The main gate was secured by a heavy chain and a

coffee can-sized lock. I refrained from touching anything. From ground to sky, the fence had been built to keep people out, but it would be equally effective at keeping people in. I returned to the main gate. It was a single panel that bent slightly under its own weight.

Two hinges allowed it to swing in or out. I checked the size of the hinge pins by holding my finger up next to one. Two well-aimed rounds from Betsy Ross would take the gate off at the hinges. Access in five seconds or less, and the sound of the cannon breaching their front gate would convince them to keep their heads down.

I hadn't seen any weapons and didn't expect they'd have any. Living with your captives suggested making weapons available wasn't the best idea for long-term success. I heard snoring from within a building. I couldn't tell if it was a man or a woman. Another drawback of communal living. In the Marines, those guys who snored would get pummeled in the middle of the night until they learned to sleep on their stomachs.

On the lake-side of the compound, there was a pedestrian gate secured by a hasp and a clasp. It seemed as robust as the chain and lock used on the front gate.

I skulked away as silently and slowly as I had come. Nothing for anyone to see. It was time to get some sleep to be awake for when the compound rose. What was their morning routine?

That was the next question that needed to be answered.

I returned to my observation point, and my canteen confirmed I was in the right place. I settled in to sleep under the stars of a mild Idaho spring, hoping I wouldn't wake up with a rattlesnake sunning itself on me. I made sure my pocket knife was easily accessible just in case.

The discomfort of sleeping on the ground in a ghillie suit meant I slept the minimum necessary to be functional and not a second more. It was still pitch-black outside. I uncovered my watch and checked the time—three in the morning.

I tried to rest more, but it was fitful and less than invigorating. By four-thirty, I gave up and resumed my watch position. By five-thirty, the pre-dawn light showed a hill that I had looked at yesterday but discounted for being too close. After walking to the compound last night, I knew I wanted to be closer.

I left my position and moved like a shadow among the trees, embracing the darkness of the pines to cover ground quickly and find a place near the top of a rocky escarpment. Nothing grew among the rocks. I squeezed into place, letting my ghillie suit break up my outline and hide me.

Two of the five protein bars I had brought with me were gone. I'd shepherd the remainder over the next two days. Eating too much in the field meant relieving oneself more times, and that meant the potential for being discovered.

Reduce the risk to increase the probability of mission success. Little things added up to be big things.

I missed Jenny. We'd talk about how it all worked. I'd be excited to share how I saw it, and she would ask questions, sometimes to help me see better or for me to learn. She often feigned not knowing something so I could be excited about explaining it. She made me better when I took the time to listen.

With the sunrise, I was trapped on the rock all day, but I had a much better vantage point. I was close, a half-mile from the nearest building.

At six-thirty, the doors opened and the group filed out.

I looked through the scope, expanding the field of view to take in more than individual faces. I was close enough to see all the details now.

That worked for me. Eighteen and six. All the women were accounted for, and David Quresh followed them out. One of the women I had identified as a foreman unlocked the pedestrian gate. They walked out to the dock, where they dropped the towels they'd been wearing to reveal their naked bodies for a brief moment before they leapt into the water.

The two women watching remained clothed on the dock with Quresh. He stood there with arms crossed and watched the naked women swim while washing themselves with soap that had been stored in a basket attached to the dock.

Quresh said something to the foremen before stripping off his clothes and jumping in. I wanted to shoot him right there as it became crystal-clear in my mind how the compound worked. There were three of them in charge, and all the rest suffered under their control. With my pistol, I could run down there right now and end it.

What would they do to the others? Quresh swam toward Becky. She tried to move away, but he caught her and tried to pull her close.

The others swam in a tight circle around them and started splashing and yelling. Becky worked her way free and joined the splashers. Quresh found himself splashing back. I dialed in to just his face; he wore a plastic smile, but his eyes kept darting to the senator's daughter.

I pulled the rifle into my shoulder and slowed my breathing as I took aim, mentally calculating the range to determine where my best aim point would be. High at half a mile, but only a few inches as the bullet came out of the barrel low and rose above the line of sight to then drop back down at range. At closer range, the drop was only an inch or two, but at a distance, the drop could be significantly more.

Thinking back to my test shots, I doubted I could hold the bullet to a face-sized impact area. I needed a body shot with a clean background. I should have blasted those three when they were standing on the dock together. I could have gotten two with one shot and nailed the third when she started to run.

When they see a body explode next to them, they always run.

I'd missed my chance. They climbed out of the lake as a group, Quresh blocking them from getting their towels, making them pass one by one to get back to the dock.

Power. It had gone on too long and needed to end. They managed to get under the towels and troop back to the buildings under the watchful eye of the foremen. Eighteen and six disappeared back inside.

I relaxed the rifle and pulled out my phone to call the bed and breakfast. Jenny answered on the second ring.

"What time is it?" she mumbled. I envisioned her messy hair and pillow lines across her face. Naked and warm.

"I don't know. Seven, maybe? This guy needs to go, and he needs to go today. How long will it take you to get into character and get out here?"

"Walking six or eight miles? Three or four hours if I leave right away."

"Shoot to be here by noon. I think we can have this wrapped up tonight, all things being equal."

"That soon?"

"Suffice it to say, I hate this guy and his dominatrices." I described the two in case they tried to play a game with Jenny. She needed to know who the insiders were, the ones facilitating David Quresh's compound, and now she did. "Be wary of all, and if he tries anything, beat him to a pulp."

"You know I will. I miss you, Ian."

"Me, too. I couldn't stop thinking about you last night. I've scoped the compound to find a way in, and hopefully, we'll take care of this thing today. Getting the keys to the gate would help me, but I can get in without them. Take care of yourself first, and know that I'll only be a couple hundred yards away. Just scream as loud as you can if anything goes wildly wrong. Within a heartbeat, you'll know I'm coming. Everyone inside that place will know I'm on my way."

"I'll count on it."

I needed to maneuver closer, as close as humanly possible, and then wait. The morning sun was bright but cast long shadows.

Unfortunately, it was right in my face, too. I backed out of my rocky observation point, relieved myself on the far side of the rocks, and then edged out beyond the stone to hit the ground and start crawling. Three or four hours to cover less than five hundred yards seemed about right. I moved at a snail's pace, sticking to the shadows as much as possible while powering forward.

Inch by inch.

Jenny walked fast along the road to the cult's area. She carried nothing but a bottle of water and three hundred dollars. She'd left the keys with the B and B manager so she wouldn't lose them while she was out for a hike.

She had told them that her husband went out early to catch the sunrise from a distant peak.

They thought that was a worthy endeavor, but not for everyone.

Five miles along the road, Jenny realized she looked too clean. She strolled off the dirt road and rolled into the ditch, avoiding as many of the rocks as she could, then crawled on her hands and knees up the embankment to get on the road. The knees on her jeans had ripped, and blood trickled from the scratches.

Jenny rubbed some dirt into her hair and then tried to comb it with her fingers. She drank most of the water and kept going. She sped up to get a good sweat going. After one last corner, the area opened up before her. Two main buildings. Four smaller buildings. A tall fence with barbed wire on top.

A locked front gate.

For Jenny, the curtains had opened and the show had begun. She was on the biggest stage of her life, and if she didn't play her part well, she would suffer at the hands of those watching her act. She fell to her knees and started to cry. The pain of hitting the ground made it easy for the tears to come.

When she stood, her knee screamed in agony. *That isn't good,* she thought. She took a few tentative steps and settled for a heavy limp. It was her right knee. She kicked better with the right leg, but Ian had been merciless in training her to kick, punch, and block equally with both sides.

"Fear the woman who has practiced one kick ten thousand times," she mumbled to herself. She started to run, trying to loosen up her knee and increase her look of desperation. She managed a rambling gait. She kept her head pointed toward the compound while using her eyes to scan the nearby trees, looking for where Ian might be hiding.

She didn't know but hoped he had seen her. She reached the fence and started yelling.

"Help me! Help me!" She rattled the gate, shaking it as loud as she could. The chain clashed and clanged. Jenny didn't see how Ian would get it open as he'd said. She spotted the small gate at the back of the compound. Maybe he'd meant that one.

"Please." She let her last call taper off as she sank to the ground and leaned against the fence desperately, like one who was about to give up on life. She had a couple swallows of water left. She let the bottle drop from her hand and spill on the ground.

Like one might do who had nothing left to live for. She bowed her head and stayed that way, struggling to summon the patience to wait.

She had no choice. Sit there and be pitiful for as long as it took. The women inside those buildings were counting on her, and they didn't know she existed. She chuckled briefly at the irony.

That was how Ian lived his life. People didn't know how much they needed him to do what he did. Jenny, too.

The Peace Archive. Hitmen killing bad people.

Her mind raced through the twists and turns of her life. She'd met the President, all because of doing a job that no one needed to know was being done. The heat of the midday sun beat down on her.

Ten miles. Too little sleep. Her chin tucked to her chest as the adrenaline rush faded. She whispered his name and reached for a hand that wasn't there. "Ian."

CHAPTER NINETEEN

"Wisely, and slow. They stumble that run fast." –William Shakespeare

I spotted Jenny when she appeared at the corner. Damn! I wasn't in position yet, so I maneuvered to where I could at least see her. If I had to act, I was still in a better place than I had been. I could be at the gate in thirty seconds. Not optimal, but it was the best I could do at that point in time.

Hoping to get there faster was immaterial. I had to deal with truths, which meant I needed to get closer incrementally. I couldn't alert them to my presence. Seeing people approach from two directions would alert them. Jenny reached the front gate and called for help. I could hear her.

One can grow used to hearing a voice and it provides comfort, but when that voice called for help, it set my teeth on edge. No one came for her. She collapsed on the ground and leaned heavily against the gate.

No one came for her.

I started to move slowly and steadily, glimpsing Jenny when a gap allowed. She was there for nearly an hour before the door opened and one of the foremen came out and strolled to the gate. I raised my scope and agonizingly slowly moved my hand toward it to reduce the magnification. By the time I could see the gate, the woman had reached Jenny.

A hand touched Jenny's shoulder. Startled, she fell away from the gate.

"Am I in the right place?" Jenny finally managed.

"It depends what you're looking for. You are at a place we simply call 'the Q.'"

"I'm looking for a place where my ex-boyfriend can't find me, a place where I'm free to be me while helping others. I want to live off the grid."

"Your phone, lass. It's the first thing we give up here."

Jenny used the fence to pull herself upright. The woman had not opened the gate and spoke through the fence, trying to appear welcoming. She was one of the two Ian had described in great detail. She was not to be trusted.

Jenny turned out her pockets. "I have a little money and that's it. I don't have my wallet, a phone, or anything. I had to get out of there before my ex killed me."

"We share your pain here, but you have no need of money." She held out her hand, and Jenny stuffed the twenties, appropriately crumpled from being in her pocket, along with smaller bills and some coins, into it. Jenny thought it was a nice touch as opposed to looking like she just came from an ATM.

The woman had to cup her hands to take it, then nodded and walked away.

"Can you help me?" Jenny pleaded.

"I must discuss you with our guru David. He will decide, as he decides all things that affect our lives."

She continued to the closest building and went inside, closing the door behind her.

Creepy, Jenny thought. She held the metal gate with both hands, comfortable that she wouldn't be shocked by an electric fence. There were no wires and no generator. There was no artificial sound at all. Jenny turned her face to the sky and took in the silence. She could see the allure of serenity.

Contrails from high-flying airliners marred the otherwise-perfect blue sky. There was no breeze to rustle the pines. She clung to the fence and begged for patience, trying to get her heart to slow down. Only ten minutes passed before the door popped open and the woman walked out. David Quresh followed her. He wore a flowing robe with nothing underneath as if it were a toga at a college frat party.

Jenny fought the visceral hatred. How such a man drew women in was lost on her, but not everyone enjoyed a relationship like the one she was part of. She smiled, closed her eyes, and nodded her head as if she were praying in thanks.

She opened her eyes and stepped back as he reached for her arm.

"Come, child. Let us see you."

She was three feet from him. He could see her just fine.

"I have escaped from the abuse of another. I shy from touch, but feel that in time, I will be able to once again be okay with someone touching me."

"Let your healing start now. Please." He waited. The brown of his eyes was overly large, leaving little white in his eyes. It gave him a cartoony look. "Please." He gestured, and Jenny moved closer.

He took her hand and held it in his warm and soft one. He traced a line down her forearm with the middle finger of his other hand, never taking his eyes from hers. Goosebumps appeared against her wishes and outside her control. He smiled easily. "You shall recover quickly as part of the Q, and you shall become one with us."

"In time, yes. That would be best." Jenny nodded and put her other hand over his for a moment before pulling away. "I'm sorry, but that time is not now."

She let her arms drop as she stepped back. She bowed her head and looked at the ground, shoulders hunched in defeat. She wondered if Ian had the man centered in the reticle. She wasn't sure what a fifty-caliber bullet fired at close range would do to a human body but figured she was too close for Ian to take the shot, especially since the gate was still locked and only two of the three targets were in sight.

Quresh nodded at the woman, and she produced a key to undo the padlock.

She pulled the gate toward her and freed it from the chain.

"Come, child," Quresh repeated in a soft voice. He clasped his hands behind his back and waited until Jenny had entered. The woman closed the gate and wrestled with the heavy chain while Quresh guided her toward the garden. "We grow most of our food, and we prepare everything ourselves. Right now, all are studying within. What are you good at, Ms., Ms...."

"Just call me Jenny." She wondered at the question. She was trying not to limp too badly, but her knee had stiffened while she leaned against the gate. "I'm a good teacher. Middle school."

Quresh drew up short. "How interesting. God works in mysterious ways and grants answers to wishes we don't make. We have some young ladies in need of a more formal education, although their spiritual and physical needs are well-serviced. Still, there is more to this world, isn't there?"

"Body, mind, and soul. The holy trinity."

"I agree fully." He laughed lightly, keeping his hands behind his back. The woman stood in the middle of the compound and watched them like an eagle watching a rabbit running across an open field. Quresh wasn't heavy-handed, unlike the woman, but without her, would he have the same authority?

It's not the person but who surrounds them that brings the power. No dictator ever got to the top on their own.

Jenny followed Quresh around the compound, listening carefully and nodding appropriately as he pointed details. "We bathe as one, letting the lake water cleanse our minds and free our souls."

"Of course. There should be no other way," Jenny agreed. They walked toward the door to the main building. Quresh opened it and they walked inside, Jenny climbing the three steps one at a time because of the pain in her knee. The woman followed them in and secured the door behind her with a complex lock that suggested Jenny was not free to leave.

The blood pounded in my ears as I kept the crosshairs on his chest, but he kept his hands off Miss Jenny, walking casually and talking. Jenny showed the appropriate interest as she tried to earn his trust.

No one had offered to clean her up or help her with a limp that looked real. I should have met her on the road to talk to her one last time, make sure we were on the same page.

But no, in case the road was monitored. They didn't use electricity like normal people, but that didn't mean they didn't have low-power cameras hidden in the trees. If they did on this side of the lake, they still might not have registered my passing.

A good sniper could pass before their eyes and they would never know. It was what made good snipers great, being able to hide in plain sight.

Where would that takedown happen? The only option where all three would show up. The lake. Bath time.

He'd see Jenny naked, but it would be the last thing he'd ever see as I brought his life to a quick and unceremonious end.

I needed Jenny's intel before I pulled the trigger to make sure it was a clean kill. I intended to do the big three, Quresh and his female foremen. Waiting wasn't my strong suit when Jenny was inside that building where I couldn't see or hear what was going on. I eased my hand down my side until I could touch the Sig on my hip.

Primary and backup plans had been swirling in my mind since I'd first laid eyes on the compound. They started to solidify in my mind. Violent action performed at a high rate of speed under the watchful eyes of all the women. They'd see a running bush, nothing more.

Then Jenny and I would fade into the woods, leaving the women to find their own way out.

That wouldn't work. The women would need help. I'd call the sheriff using my untraceable phone, and we'd disappear once the authorities showed up to get the captives the help they needed. If I was going to call the authorities, I couldn't be anywhere nearby. Despite this death sentence being issued by the President of the

United States, the local sheriff would be looking for a murderer.

He'd be looking for me. The deaths had to happen in a way where no one saw me.

I held Betsy Ross in my hands, my fifty-caliber rifle. At this range, the target would be dead before the roar of the round firing would shock their consciences.

I looked through the scope at the windows. Curtains blocked my view, revealing nothing that happened within. I listened with every fiber of my being. I doubted Jenny would get more than one scream out before getting muffled.

Still, I couldn't come up with a better plan to make sure we hit the right targets.

I turned slightly to block my hand from sight as I took out a protein bar, then settled in to watch and listen.

CHAPTER TWENTY

"Mankind is not likely to salvage civilization unless he can evolve a system of good and evil which is independent of heaven and hell." –George Orwell

The first thing Jenny noticed was the smell, a rank odor of outhouse combined with the taint of bleach. Dust filled the light rays that beamed through the thin curtains. At one end of the large room, chairs surrounded an old-fashioned chalkboard. Six young girls sat in the first row and half of the adults sat behind them, while the other foreman faced them.

All eyes had turned to Jenny. She tried to keep her wits about her by counting heads. Six girls, Quresh, two women in charge, and she needed sixteen more women. The second row held six. Ten adult women were missing, but Jenny's eyes had not yet adjusted. She blinked to try to clear them.

"This way," the woman with Quresh said abruptly. They walked past the class to a door with a walkway that led to the second building, where the other women lounged in various stages of undress. Sunken eyes looked vacantly into space. Jenny tried not to fixate on them, but she couldn't help it. She stopped to move a woman's leg that hung off back onto the bed.

"Come."

Jenny apologized and looked down instead of meeting the gruff woman's gaze.

"You need to cleanse your mind and your soul before you can interact with the Q collective. We are here for a single purpose. Master Quresh is too proud to say it, but I will. We all serve his pleasure, and he brings us enlightenment in all ways."

"I don't know what that means," Jenny said, avoiding a sarcastic response that would give her away. Unlike Quresh, who put on an act of kindness, this woman didn't bother. She was the brute force to Quresh's indirect approach.

"In," the woman commanded. A small closet stood open. It was wood-lined, without a chair or a pillow or a blanket.

"I haven't eaten in days," Jenny lied, trying to find a way to avoid being locked in the closet.

"You're thicker than what he likes, so you'll need to trim down a bit. Now get in there. I'll come and get you when it's time to bathe—if you've been good, that is. You make one sound, and it'll be tomorrow before you come out of there."

"I don't want to be trouble. I have nowhere else to go." Jenny backed into the small space. The door shut and two deadbolts slid home, one high and one low. The space was too small to get any leverage if she wanted to try to kick the door off its hinges. She squeezed her way down until she was sitting with her knees braced against the far wall.

Ian, why didn't I let you talk me out of this?

Jenny listened carefully as she tried to relax. She finally stood and found that to be the most comfortable position, except for her throbbing knee. She cursed herself for her exuberance in trying to look appropriately weathered. She thought she had been convincing. The first rule in taking a captive was to break them down to the point that they would give up and be more responsive to suggestion.

The sounds from the room beyond were muffled and faint. Those living there were shells of their former selves unless they were weaning off drugs. Possibly. Maybe. They looked bad. Jenny tried to relax, but the aura of the place was dark. She wanted to get out and run away from it.

Leaning one way and then the other, she exercised her knee as much as she could, but it needed ice. There wouldn't be any ice. Maybe the lake water was cool. She pinned her hopes on that potential respite.

She lost track of time, not that she knew what time it was since she'd left everything at the bed and breakfast. A soft bed waited for her. *I hope you're right, Ian,* she thought, *and we can end this thing tonight.*

Time dragged while Jenny was unable to get comfortable. She wasn't claustrophobic, but the small space was starting to wear her down. She froze at the sound of footsteps. They came straight to the door. The first deadbolt was released. She faced the door, ready to leave.

When it opened, Quresh stood there. He forced his way in, and someone shut the door behind him. Jenny was pressed against the back wall, his face inches from hers as they shared a space that was too small for one.

"I want to talk with you about cleansing your soul," he started.

Jenny saw no way out. She had lifted her arms to

protect herself, so her hands were up but wedged between the two bodies. She couldn't move. "I'm not good with tight spaces."

"Space is ephemeral. Your mind can convince you that you are in an open field. Close your eyes."

Jenny complied but clenched her jaw, ready to bite his lips off as a start. She thought she might be able to get a knee into his groin. With her eyes closed, she planned the ways she could hurt him until his senseless body fell out when the door reopened. She flexed her fingers and prepared to gouge his eyes.

"The sky is blue and clouds look unreal hanging above the ground, littered with pine scrub across a rocky desertscape. The lake stands outside the compound, clean and clear. The sun sparks off its shimmering surface."

Jenny flexed and tightened her muscles as if defending herself against an impending strike.

"My, you take up more space in here than the others," he said as part of his stream of consciousness. "When the wind blows, it sings through the branches, calling to us. Let the wind embrace you."

His hands crept up her sides. She clamped her elbows on his fingers until he grunted and tried to pull them away. He had no leverage either.

"I said I'm not ready to be touched. I expect you to respect that. This place was supposed to bring peace, not another abuser. Is that what you are?" Jenny had to set the boundaries, even while trying to play a role.

He turned his head to the side. "Belle, open the door, please."

The bolts instantly slid away since the woman hadn't moved from outside the door. Quresh backed out, and Jenny followed closely. She had no intention of returning to the closet. She stretched as much as she could, ready to take both of them down.

They had no idea who stood in front of them. She was ready to deliver a deadly surprise.

"She has no need for further contemplation. She will come about in time. Whatever class was your favorite, my dear, please. Your students are waiting.

Jenny deflated, almost toppling as her muscles were denied their chance to act. Her knee welcomed the respite.

"I would love to," Jenny managed to say. They walked in front of her, leaving her unobserved to look around. She counted eight more bodies in the beds. Still missing two unless they had moved from this building to the other while she was secured in the closet.

With their backs to her, she realized they had already given her a position of trust. Her ruse was working. Playing a role while also being a part of herself. She shivered, remembering being trapped in the small space with Quresh.

Thinking critically, trying to put herself in Ian's shoes, Quresh was creepy and ego-driven, but did he deserve a death sentence? She only knew about thirty minutes when there was a much bigger picture.

Like the women trapped inside that god-awful-smelling building and the vacant looks on their faces. She'd get her chance to interact and watch for more clues. What about the young girls? Was Quresh a child rapist?

That was the death sentence if it proved true, and she'd kill him herself. The rage that had seized her when Jack tried to kill her was there, simmering in the background. Quresh walked behind the first row of children, dragging his hand across their narrow shoulders as he passed, and he touched the faces of the women in the second row.

Guru.

The young girls stayed rock-still. A couple of the older women were entranced, beatific smiles on their faces as they gazed upon the visage of their one and only master. Jenny studied them. They would have a different reaction to whatever Ian and Jenny ended up doing.

Jenny's plan remained no more solid than morning fog. She wasn't sure what Ian planned, but the true believers needed to be kept out of the way. They'd protect him with their bodies. She wished she could talk to Ian because he would be able to provide insight into their behavior and guide her on how to minimize their interference.

She'd keep an eye on them for the time being. The woman acting as foreman and handler for David Quresh motioned with her head for Jenny to take the stage and begin teaching.

As if it were a switch one turned on and off. Jenny took a quick count under the guise of tallying the number of students, pointing and counting out loud.

She was still one short: the second woman in charge. Now she had eyes on Becky, who sat in the back row, staring at the floor. Quresh stopped at her and kneeled before her. He lifted her chin to face him.

"I'm sorry," she cried softly. "I won't let it happen again, master." Her eyes glistened but radiated. She caressed the side of his face.

This is going to be a problem, Jenny thought.

"My name is Jenny, and I am happy to be here. I taught middle school for a decade before an abusive relationship drove me away. I find myself among friends, probably with a similar story to tell…" The foreman's glare suggested Jenny was walking into a minefield. "…but none of that matters. We're here now, and there is no better day than today and no time like the present.

"I'm to give you a class. My favorite class involved

communication. How do we get the most from our words? How can we help others to better understand us?"

Quresh stood next to Becky, his hand on her shoulder. "I am curious to hear your guidance on this. I myself have never had a problem being understood."

Jenny smiled and nodded. "There has never been anyone like you before, and there won't be again. The rest of us have to work at what comes to you naturally."

"It's a divine gift. There's nothing natural about it." His voice turned cold.

Jenny glanced at the others. Bowed heads. One didn't argue with the master. Jenny mirrored their body language and bowed her head. "I meant no disrespect. Can you find it in your heart to forgive me as I learn from you?"

He tipped his head back. "Yes. Forgiveness is always in my heart. I apologize to you for being so short. You don't know our ways. In time, you'll come to learn them well. You can recite the codex posted on the wall of the study chamber while you're in the daily time of individual reflection.

Back into the closet? Screw that, anyone who tries to put me in there is going to get their face kicked in. Jenny looked up and forced herself to smile. "Of course, I look forward to it. As a career educator, learning must be one's lifelong journey. No matter how much I think I know, there is more to learn, to the point that I realize I know nothing."

Quresh clapped and gestured for Jenny to continue.

Her mind raced as she worked through the problem of freeing herself and the others before she took another trip into the closet, where she would lose any ability to act. What was Ian doing? What time was it? Jenny hadn't realized how disoriented she was. She cleared her throat before facing the chalkboard. She took the small nub of chalk and started with a basic element of communication.

"I could talk on this all day," she blurted before she wrote on the board.

"How do you intend to make the listener feel?" She put the chalk down and faced the group. "As humans, evoking an emotional response is most of the communication that occurs. Adding intentionality to that element heightens your engagement and awareness but as both speaker and listener. Shaping a conversation to be open or closed." She looked at the oldest of the young girls. "How does that comfortable chair help you learn?"

The girl cocked her head sideways like a dog might. "I don't understand."

"A comfortable chair makes it easy to focus on the teacher's message. Does this sound like how you feel?"

Her eyes darted to the side while her head faced front. "Yes. I learn better in this comfortable chair."

The chairs were wood, and the girls fidgeted and shifted. They were young and still questioned what they were told. Jenny smiled, not at the contrived answer, but at the hope she felt for them. One of the worshippers from the back row raised her hand. Jenny pointed at her.

"I think this is the most comfortable chair I have ever had the pleasure of sitting on." She grinned and turned her head toward Quresh. He nodded at her. She beamed at Jenny.

Rush popped into her head and played *Subdivisions*. Her lip twitched upward as she felt the connection to her husband, and the song was right. *Conform.* It was also her cue to solidify a plan that didn't include Ian in case the only opportunity arose within the house. *I can do it,* she told herself.

She continued her lecture. "And you are learning so much better because of it. Making you feel good about something is part of persuasion. You know what? I want to sit down now because I like comfortable chairs."

Quresh's gaze turned into a glare. He withdrew farther into the room, and the foreman joined him. They had a private whispered conversation.

CHAPTER TWENTY-ONE

"Inaction breeds doubt and fear. Action breeds confidence and courage. If you want to conquer fear, do not sit home and think about it. Go out and get busy." –Dale Carnegie

It had been two hours since one of the two women had left in the truck. The gate was opened for only the time the truck needed to drive through. It bounced up the road on tortured shocks and disappeared around the corner. The second foreman secured the gate and returned inside.

Then nothing happened for so long that I wondered if the woman was coming back or if the truck had broken down. In my narrow view of this contract, that meant one less antagonist to deal with, but would she return in the middle of the action?

I started to fade and eased sideways to get more fully behind a tree trunk, then removed a canteen that I'd filled in the lake the night before and took a long drink, expecting to taste soap but not doing so. It was already past the time when the group had come into the yard to tend the garden.

The problem with observing for only one day was that if the routine wasn't daily, one worked on misassumptions. Did they bathe every day? I expected that was a daily thing since Quresh had liked seeing his harem naked.

What about the foremen? When did those two women clean themselves? In twenty-four hours, everyone else had taken a dip. Separate the overlords from the master as part of a divide and conquer strategy. I knew Jenny could handle him if it were just the two of them.

She wasn't equipped to fight multiple assailants. She had previously, but only when knocking out the first attacker. Leaving her to focus on just one.

That was how I fought, too. Hurt each one badly enough that they don't return to the battle. If I have to hit someone, I want to hit them hard enough to take them out. I don't like fighting the same person twice.

And Marine rules applied. If it's worth fighting for, it's worth fighting dirty for.

It grated on my soul that I couldn't see Jenny on the inside. I was used to dealing with less-than-perfect intelligence about a target, but not with knowing almost nothing. The intel was inside that building in Jenny's possession.

Was she good enough to be an operator?

Only she could answer that question. I wouldn't have agreed if I didn't think she was capable, but was she in the right frame of mind? Where did that limp come from? I had nothing but time, an unlimited number of questions, and no answers.

My mood remained dour. I checked Betsy Ross' breech to make sure it was clean and would cycle when I needed her. I hugged my rifle to me. The pick-me-up I needed was Rush, but I'd have to play them in my mind. I chose *The Camera's Eye* and realized I sucked at remembering lyrics. I did the best I could while listening to the rhythm.

Mystic Rhythms followed as I tried to get my head on straight. I'd probably only get one shot. I stopped goofing off and got back into position, peering over the scope to take in the entirety of the compound.

I hadn't scanned the area fully before the door flew open, and I centered the door in the scope's field of view. The foreman walked out and stopped. She checked the gate before looking through the trees from her left to right, incrementally, intentionally. She stopped and stared right at me. I was confident she couldn't see me, but my heart skipped a beat. Range to her was less than a hundred yards. *If I pulled the trigger, a major part of her body would be vaporized and the round would continue into the building beyond.*

The woman walked slowly up the three steps and inside. The door closed, and I was none the wiser about anything going on within the home. The second woman still being gone, they probably would keep everyone inside until she returned.

I wasn't in a position to intercept the truck and create an accident that killed the driver. That would be my first choice if it were an option. Divide and conquer, but there was nothing I could do about it now.

And nothing I needed to do. They'd come out, or Jenny would scream for help and I'd go in. Either way, the longer Quresh and his people dragged this out, the uglier it was going to be for them.

Prey should know its place in the predator hierarchy. They weren't going to make it easy, but the end was inevitable. I had no choice but to complete the mission.

Would they hurt Jenny first? That was the only clock ticking in my mind.

I spooled up *2112* in my mind and listened carefully, creating my own space fantasy as it played. I waited, watched, and strained my ears to listen for any sound from inside the buildings.

Jenny finished the lesson and bowed her head to the students. She tried to have better interaction during the class since lectures were the least-effective teaching method. She wanted interaction and practice, but the students were mostly numb to personal initiative. They answered questions when asked with the least amount of information possible.

That was a learned behavior. When students were belittled for the questions or answers, they grew silent. Never volunteer. Having punishment disappear was the reward for not speaking up.

The signs were there. Someone was giving these people grief and probably abusing them, but Jenny didn't see that directly. The warning signs were there, as she had tried to put on display, but her act was nowhere near the real thing. She spoke with confidence. She showed no fear of the commune's leadership, at least not a realistic level of fear.

She stood at the front with her head bowed, waiting to be told she could sit or go away or do something other than stand there. The woman went outside while Quresh stood and watched, his hands clasped easily before him. He made no move to give an order. Jenny kept glancing up but stayed rooted to the floor.

The woman returned after a short time, shaking her head when Quresh looked at her.

"One more lesson. This time on the sordid history of the United States."

"Yes. I can do that. Where do you want me to start?"

"At the beginning, of course."

"The beginning of the United States. In order to form a more perfect union…" she started, deciding 1776 was a good year. She liked the topic and had taught it for most of her years. She jumped into the forming of the union and what it meant, who the key players were, and how they thought, at least as much as modern historians could figure.

A vehicle's horn sounded outside. All eyes turned toward the door. The woman looked outside, waved at someone, and returned to clap her hands. "Be ready to help unload provisions."

The woman went outside while Quresh looked down on the group, legs spread wide under his toga and arms crossed. One of the sycophants rushed down the hall to the next building and encouraged those in their bunks to get up and join the work party. Six followed her back. The others had gotten into a line and stood like schoolchildren waiting for recess.

The foreman came inside and held the door as the women filed out. Jenny made sure not to look at her while staying close to the senator's daughter. One of the compound's two trucks had backed up to an outbuilding. The women stood shoulder to shoulder to move heavy foodstuffs like rice, flour, and sugar into storage.

Jenny had been there since what she estimated was noon and had yet to see anyone eat anything or smell anything cooking. With everyone accounted for, who cooked what and when? Who cut the firewood?

Too many questions that appeared to suggest they didn't eat often. Jenny was thicker than the other girls.

Half-starved and rail-thin because of it. Jenny had no intention of spending one more minute than she had to in that place. They weren't going to starve her into submission.

Where are you? she asked herself, glancing into the nearest trees, looking for Ian.

I was pleased to see Jenny conspicuously with Becky in the unloading line. The two acting as foremen were outside, but Quresh was nowhere to be seen.

It's like herding cats, I thought. I counted the heads. *And missing a couple of the adult women, too.*

At least I could watch Miss Jenny working, although at this range, I could see what a mess she was. The knees of her jeans were ripped and the skin bloodied. Her hair was a mess and was off-color because it was so dirty, like her face and arms.

She had put on the best show she could for David Quresh. It looked like they'd bought it since she was in the middle of the women, working as they worked, standing as they stood. She kept glancing at the trees, everywhere but where I was. I wouldn't give up my position to make contact. It could get ugly for her if someone else saw me.

I remained still and watched. They unloaded the truck quickly, then all the servant women but two went back inside. Jenny and Becky waited under the prison guard-like watch of the women in charge. She took them into the storage building, where they stayed out of sight for a few minutes. At the end, they carried supplies toward the house. Why didn't the foreman break it up and split it among the larger group?

Because then she couldn't give grief to Jenny and the

CRAIG MARTELLE

senator's daughter. Jenny hauled at least a fifty-pound bag of flour. She hoisted it over one shoulder and carried a bag of onions in the other hand, maybe another ten pounds. "That's my girl," I whispered. She took small steps with a pronounced limp, but she didn't let that deter her. Becky was in trouble. Even with a lighter load, she struggled. Jenny added another bag to her own load.

She carried herself upright, with the big bag on one shoulder and two bags of vegetables in her off-hand. Jenny wasn't done helping Becky. She encouraged the young woman to keep going because the foreman wasn't lifting a hand. They'd have to make it.

I expected there would be harsh punishment for failure. I put the crosshairs on the chest of the woman I'd named Battleaxe One. The building was behind her, and I was missing two of the targets. It was a nice thought to blow her away, though.

They were right.

It gets easier to kill people after you've already done it. I eased the barrel down and watched Jenny and Becky climb the short steps and enter the house. Battleaxe One went inside. Silence returned. It was early evening. In my mind, it was bath time.

But the only thing that came was the darkness.

I eased upright, put the rifle across my back, and walked slowly toward the compound.

CHAPTER TWENTY-TWO

"Patience is a bitter cup from which only the strong may drink."
–Anonymous

Jenny heard the door close. Beside her, Becky's breath was ragged and raspy while they waited for someone to direct them. None of the other women or girls offered to help.

A rite of passage, Jenny thought. *We'll stand with our burdens until we submit.*

Becky lasted five minutes. As soon as Quresh and one of the women strolled in front of them, she collapsed and started to cry. Jenny leaned over to put down the two bags in her hand, but Quresh stopped her.

"Please help her," Jenny asked.

"We will when the time is right." The other women stood with their heads bowed. Jenny looked from one face to the next, counting as she went. Seventeen plus six. Only one of the women in charge.

She expected the other was behind her. She turned her head quickly back and forth as if trying to stretch her neck.

There she was, close to the door. *Got you.*

"I don't understand," Jenny said, looking at the floor rather than Quresh.

"Patience," the man said and took a seat.

Jenny adjusted her fingers where she gripped the two bags since they were starting to go numb, but she refused to drop her burden. Time slowed and forever came and went, then the clock started again.

The women waited, shifting their feet as they, too, were forced to stand, even though no one had told them to do so.

With each passing tick of the clock in her mind, she knew she was becoming a greater enemy to David Quresh. All she had to do was call for Ian and he'd help her end it, but there would be too great a time lag. How long would it take him to get to her? A minute? Ten seconds? Both would be too long. How much damage could the foremen and Quresh do in that short a time?

Who would they grab as a hostage?

Sweat poured down Jenny's head since her body was in a constant state of micro-movements to keep her muscles from freezing up. She breathed heavily through her mouth, and for once, she was not inundated by the stench that permeated the building. She fought the desire to quit.

Outside, the darkness mirrored the soul-crushing aura within.

Quresh stood and clapped. One of the foremen stood next to him as he approached Jenny.

"The power of resistance must be purged through sacrifice. We will not start preparing our meal until after you have surrendered to the inevitability of it all."

"Dinner sounds good right about now. I seem to have missed breakfast and lunch."

"Not that often, by the look of you," Quresh replied.

"But no, you missed nothing here. We eat only once every two days. It's good to purge your body of the toxins hidden in today's food."

"We grow our own," Jenny countered, now better understanding why the women and girls were waif-like in their shapes. All of them were half-starved.

"It's a small garden, and we have grown because the allure of this way of life is strong, drawing many to us."

Jenny didn't bother telling him to expand the garden. He wasn't starving, and neither were the two women he used as his enforcers. "I'm getting tired."

"Surrender is inevitable," Quresh stated.

Jenny gauged the distance. She flexed the fingers holding the bags. She let the bag of flour slip forward a touch.

"I'm ready," she whispered and dropped the two bags as she heaved the fifty-pound bag of flour at the woman at Quresh's side.

Jenny dropped and delivered a vicious uppercut into Quresh's groin. She screamed her greatest war cry as she picked up the bag of onions and twirled like a discus thrower, stepping over Becky to fling the bag at the woman by the door.

With Jenny's scream, I vaulted up the chain-link, climbed, and threw myself on the barbed wire across the top, counting on the ghillie suit to provide a cushion. Betsy Ross bounced over my head, and the sling caught on my arm before I dropped to the other side. I let the rifle fall when I hit and rolled, pulling my pistol out when I came to my feet and sprinted.

I vaulted up the three steps to hit the door with both feet, bursting it at its lock.

The door slammed into someone on the other side and bounced back, stopping my momentum. I hit and rolled down the steps to the ground.

I popped back to my feet and ran up the steps, hitting the door with my shoulder. It caught a body on the other side, sliding it open enough for me to enter.

Jenny was straddling another woman and delivering a series of punches into her face. Quresh was on the floor, groaning.

I grabbed Battleaxe Two by the head and twisted it until her neck broke. I took one step, and the room descended into a fanatical melee.

The smell struck me before I could go any farther. Two candles provided light for the *danse macabre*.

Women fought women, pulling hair and screaming unintelligibly. Defenders of Quresh against those who were not about to give up their newfound freedom.

Jenny beat Battleaxe One to a pulp. I moved to her side but didn't say anything. She breathed quickly, almost to the point of hyperventilating. Becky was on the floor in the fetal position. Quresh struggled to move. I grabbed him and pulled him to his feet. He tried to push me but was weak.

I spun him around and wrapped an arm around his throat. No one would care if the life was choked out of him, but people would get upset if an unknown gunman started dropping people. It was time for the contract to be carried out.

It was time for Quresh to die.

Not before he suffered a little bit more. Jenny delivered a finger strike to his solar plexus. He choked and gasped. She hit him in the face with the palm of her hand to drive his nose bones into his brain, but the angle was bad. His nose splattered, sending a spray of blood around me. I yanked him backward, and he passed out.

I kept the pressure on his throat for another minute while Jenny waded into the women, pushing them apart.

Quresh was finished. I tossed his body to the side. He landed with a loud thump.

"He's gone!" Jenny yelled, pointing at him. "You are free from his abuse. You are free from living under his dictates. And by all that's holy, open the windows!"

No one moved. Jenny took a wooden chair and smashed it through the curtains, shattering the glass. She moved to the other side to permanently open another window, then walked through the women, eyeing them one by one.

Compared to Jenny, they were nothing more than skin and bone, barely strong enough to carry themselves upright. Four of the women cried. One of them stopped Jenny and pulled her close for a hug. Others piled in.

I picked Becky up and moved closer to the door. I wanted the key to the gate, and while I was at it, one of the trucks. I wasn't up for a ten-mile hike in the middle of the night. I'd do what I had to, but a tenet of the Marines was to only walk if you had to.

No one would be able to identify me in the darkness and the cover of the ghillie suit, so I would have to change at some point before we made it back into the public eye. Becky had enough energy to pull away from me. I let go of her. She walked across the room with her head held high and kicked Quresh's body. She moved to Battleaxe One and kicked her in the face.

Then a second time. The others left Jenny's group hug and joined in.

I waved for her to join me. She came for a hug, and I

pulled her close. "Keys," I whispered. She nodded before checking the pockets of the woman by the door. She found the truck keys. She had to elbow her way to the other woman, whose breath bubbled with foam. It was too dark to see if it was red, but it probably was as a result of broken ribs ripping apart her lungs.

Jenny came back with the gate key. She took Becky by the arm and pulled her toward the door. Becky's eyes rolled back in her head, and she passed out. Jenny caught her. I moved in and tossed the woman over my shoulder.

"You get the gate. I'll get the truck."

Down the steps and across the yard to where I'd dropped Betsy Ross. She was coming with me. I had to dip carefully to pick the fifty-cal off the ground. The chain rattled as it came free of the gate. Jenny opened it and used the chain to block it open. I hurried to the truck and carefully slid Becky into the middle of the bench seat. Jenny squeezed in the passenger side. I turned the key, and the starter churned and churned before the engine caught.

Maintenance hadn't been important to Quresh, but this truck only needed to cover ten miles. Then I didn't care what happened to it. We'd be long gone.

I eased the truck through the gate and breathed easily as we left the compound behind.

We rounded the first corner. I took it easy, not wanting to break anything on our run to freedom. My clothes and duffel bag were out there in the hills. Like a dozen times before, none of it mattered. It could all be replaced, and would.

What the others in the compound did was up to them. They were too dazed and confused to be of any use to the police whenever they might be summoned. Maybe the next day, maybe longer.

"I missed you," I said over Becky's head.

"Me too, Ian." Jenny took my hand. I rolled down the window. The smell hadn't stayed inside the building. "That bad, huh?"

"Just a lot." My heart started to race in the adrenaline surge of thinking about what could have been. "I was ready to blow them away just for the way they looked at you."

"I won't do that again. You don't have to worry. That will give me nightmares for years to come."

"You know I'll be right there with you. There's nothing to be afraid of that we can't handle. Me and Betsy Ross are here for you."

"You named your gun." Not a question.

"Rifle. I had a lot of time doing nothing out there. A lot of time. I could use some fresh water and maybe a hot meal."

"They were feeding the women once every two days, Ian. They had a closet barely big enough to turn around in where you got to read his manifesto or whatever the hell it was."

"Wasn't it dark in there?"

"Exactly. You couldn't read anything. All you could do is be in there, locked up. Quresh had created a living hell for his harem."

"The young girls?"

"I don't know. I didn't want to know, but they seemed less abused than the women. Probably replacements for when the older ones became undesirable."

"What are they going to do now?"

"We should help them," Jenny replied. "They are not in the right state of mind."

"You are exactly correct. I need to make a call as soon as we stop." I fumbled inside my jacket to get the GPS and handed it to Jenny. She activated it and tracked our progress down the road. "Let me know when we're a mile from town. We'll have to hoof it that last bit."

"I'm not sure she will be able to walk anywhere." Jenny brushed Becky's hair off her forehead and out of her eyes.

We rode in silence until Jenny said we were close. I slowed and eased to the side of the road, killing the engine to let the truck coast to a stop. I left the keys in it.

I used my untraceable phone to dial the number I'd been given by the Secret Service.

"Jimmy," came the tired voice.

"Ian here. It's done. And if you want bonus points, send counselors and people who can help out to the compound, the sooner, the better. Maybe a few nurses and food, too. We have Becky with us and will bring her to DC."

"You've done a great thing for America," Jimmy started.

"Stop it," I interrupted. "I did it for you because you asked. And after seeing that place, I would have done it regardless because it needed to be done. For the record, I didn't do a whole lot, but suffice to say that it was done in the right way."

"I'll get people on it right now. Call this number when you get here. I'll have you picked up at the airport."

I powered down my phone and set it on the tailgate with the rifle. I went through my pockets, pulling far more gear than I remembered carrying. It included two canteens, mostly collapsed since I hadn't refilled them before Jenny's call to arms, a GPS, my pistol, the rest of the fifty-round box of ammunition, and five extra rounds of fifty-caliber, along with a full magazine. I also had the pocket knife I'd purchased at the gun shop. I had my untraceable phone too, along with the two remaining protein bars. Jenny looked at them.

"Did you want one of these?"

"You have to ask?" I handed both to her. She pocketed

one for Becky. "He called me thick and said I'd benefit from missing a few meals."

"And you beat all three of them into submission because you are my well-toned babe. You know that I don't want to hear any insecurities about weight. You are beautiful and perfect as you are. I care that you are able to defend yourself, and you did."

"You're my forever champion." Jenny smiled before tearing the protein bar open and biting it in half.

"I am!" I removed the ghillie suit, leaving me in a t-shirt and shorts.

"What happened to you?" Jenny asked while chewing.

"Barbed wire." The punctures in my chest had bled but were mostly scabbed over, but they'd torn my shirt and left a mess.

With Jenny pushing and me pulling, we managed to get Becky out of the truck. She roused enough for us to give her water and the protein bar while we sat on the tailgate.

I cut the ghillie suit apart to make a cover for Betsy Ross. While Jenny kept Becky and Betsy company, I ran up the hillside about fifty yards to find a place to hide the remnants of the suit. I wiped down the truck after I returned.

Becky's eyes were hollow from what I could see under the truck's dome light. The sound of engines approached. My head snapped up.

"We need to hide." I slammed the door, and with Jenny's help, we got off the road and ducked into the shallow ditch. An ambulance and a sheriff's car with a civilian in the passenger seat raced by and continued down the road. "Time to go."

"Can you walk?" Jenny asked.

Becky nodded as bravely as she was capable of.

We strolled down the road toward town and our bed

and breakfast. Showers for everyone. We only had one bed, but we'd make do.

It was a little cool for shorts and a t-shirt. Becky wasn't walking as quickly as I wanted, but she kept going. Jenny limped.

"Why are you limping?"

"Hit my knee on a rock in my attempt to look sufficiently abused by my boyfriend and running away in a panic."

"Your boyfriend is a gentle soul," I replied.

"They didn't know that." Jenny winked.

"Who are you people?" Becky managed to say.

"My name is Ian, and you've already met Jenny. We do special projects for people."

"My dad?" she asked.

"I'm sure it'll surprise you when I tell you no, not the senator, but we are going to take you to him if that's okay with you. You are no longer a captive, and you make your own decisions.'

"My own decisions got me into that mess," she admitted. "It's time to face the music."

"We'll come with you, make sure there aren't any problems."

"Are you Secret Service?"

I laughed heartily. "Can you imagine me working for the government?" I joked with Jenny.

"Not at all, my love. Nor I."

I turned to Becky. "We're a private conglomerate."

She nodded. Jenny and I stayed on either side of Becky to keep her walking into town and down the road. We entered the bed and breakfast and looked for the proprietor to get our keys.

The old woman appeared. "Oh, my!" she exclaimed, gawking.

"We ran afoul of the wilderness and found this woman wandering. Would you have an extra room available?"

"Oh, my stars!" She held both her hands over her mouth. Jenny wrapped an arm around the old woman's shoulders.

"How about a second room?"

"We don't have any more rooms."

"Then we'll work with what we have." I rubbed the old woman's shoulder. She continued to stare.

We waited while no one moved. "Our key, please!" I said louder than I'd intended, but it snapped her back to reality. She shook her head and hurried to her office, returning with the key. Jenny smiled and gave her a hug. "Can I impose on you for a little ice? We took a nasty spill down one of your rocky slopes. Nasty."

"So nasty," I added.

"It is bad out there at night. What possessed you to do it?"

"When you're young, you think you're invincible, and you make bad decisions. Reality is a rocky slope and a fifty-foot slide and fall."

"What happened to your clothes?"

"Did we mention how nasty that fall was? I ended up in the middle of a fresh-killed wild boar. Do you have mountain lions around here?"

"We do!" Her eyes shot wide as her look changed from shock to understanding.

"Once we realized that, we knew there was no better place for us than the comfort of your place. You are a goddess. Ice, and maybe a sandwich?"

"Or four," Jenny offered.

"I'll see what I can whip up. You look famished," she said to Becky.

"I haven't eaten in two days," Becky admitted.

"Oh, my stars!" The old woman's hands shot back to her face for a moment before she recovered. "You kids run along. I'll be right up with everything we need to set things straight." She headed for the kitchen, calling over her shoulder, "Youth is wasted on the young."

In the room, we looked at our meager belongings. We didn't have much to spare. Becky needed the extra clothes that Jenny had, even though they wouldn't fit. She was little more than skin and bone.

"Why don't you catch a shower? Don't be too long since I suspect dinner will be here before you know it." Becky managed a half-smile before disappearing into the bathroom. In seconds, the water came on. It wasn't long before steam rolled out from under the door.

I grabbed Jenny and hugged her tightly. We kissed slowly and passionately. My hand drifted down to grab her butt and hold it. She reciprocated, holding me tightly. Things started to happen that would be embarrassingly obvious. I pulled away, and Jenny started to laugh.

There was a knock on the door.

"You get it!" I moved to the window and stood with my back to the door.

"You are the best," Jenny told the proprietor. "Come give me a hand, honey."

Through sheer force of will, I was able to strangle the titan and bring him under control. I strolled confidently to the door. Jenny tried not to snort, ending with a cough and swallowing hard. There were two trays piled high with breakfast sandwiches.

"Sausage, egg, and biscuit! My favorite. You truly are the best, Madame Housemistress." I didn't remember her name, which I should have.

"And a little something for the young woman. She

needs to build up her strength." She handed a thick shake to me.

"You made this just for her?"

"Ice cream and squeeze-chocolate blended with a little malt powder. It's something I usually have for myself."

"This is royalty-level pampering." I put the tray on the bed and gave her a big hug. She retreated smartly, and we locked ourselves inside.

Jenny put the ice on her knee, then we ate two sausage biscuits each, leaving everything else for Becky.

The shower ended, and Becky appeared wearing nothing but a towel. "I washed my clothes, but they'll need to dry," she announced.

"Get yourself something to eat. Miss Jenny, you're up next."

"I don't want the ice to melt. You'll take three minutes, so why don't you go ahead?"

I'd had to offer. I dug through my backpack to find that I had one t-shirt and fresh underwear and that was it. I had no other clothes with me. "We'll need to buy clothes before we get to the airport."

I looked at the two weapons on the bed. I couldn't take them to DC on the plane, and I couldn't send them to Chicago. I decided we'd sell them back to the gun store where we'd bought them. I didn't care about the money, but I hated to see two such fine examples of workmanship go to waste.

A siren sounded in the distance. The vehicle approached and continued past, then two more.

Once they were by, I hurried up and took a shower. I jumped out, dressed in the clothes I had, and turned it over to Jenny.

"I think we should probably get out of here tonight.

There's way too much company for my peace of mind," I whispered.

"I wondered. I won't be long." Jenny had a sundress in her bag and extra everything except shoes. I took the garbage bag out of the trash for our clothes and wiped the room down while Becky watched me.

"What are you doing?" She ate slowly but deliberately. She closed her eyes while she chewed, relishing a meal that hadn't been cooked in that hellhole.

"We're going to have to go tonight. It would be best if we weren't in this state come morning."

"And *you're* the good guys?"

"That's what I'm saying, but they keep asking pesky questions I prefer not to answer. One of the parameters of this contract was keeping things low-key. That means we need to leave. We'll throw in a big tip for the nice woman who brought us food in our time of need."

The shower ended and the blow dryer started. After ten minutes, I wondered what Jenny was doing and I had to knock on the door, hoping that she hadn't passed out.

She opened the door with her hair still wet. I was confused.

"Becky's clothes," she whispered. "Becky?"

I traded places with the young woman.

"I did the best I could, but I'm sure Ian is pacing because he's ready to go."

"It's like you know him or something."

"Just a lot."

"I'll be fine. It's amazing what a good meal can do. Have you tried that shake?"

Jenny shook her head.

"I haven't had anything sweet in forever."

"I'd say you're healthier because of it, but I'm not sure that's the case."

Jenny turned the bathroom over to Becky. When she reappeared, she made a face. "Worse than a wet swimsuit."

Jenny and Becky piled out of the room with our meager possessions. I carried the guns under the cover of the ghillie material while wearing my backpack. I did one last wipe, dropped my remaining cash on the bed, and followed the women out.

We waved at the proprietor. "We were able to change our flight, and now it's early tomorrow morning. Miles to go before we sleep. Spokane, here we come."

It wasn't in our best interests to have any more of a conversation with the old woman, so we hurried outside, loaded the car, and drove off toward Spokane. We rounded the block, returned past the B and B one road over, and continued on our way to Cheyenne. As usual, we drove the speed limit. We didn't stop.

Becky fell asleep quickly in the small back seat. Jenny was out cold, so I turned on Rush as a pick-me-up, opting for the entire *Moving Pictures* album. There was much to think about to help avoid falling asleep. I was as tired as those in my charge, but being the man I was, I assumed the duty to watch over and protect them. Once Jenny woke up, she could take the watch and drive.

CHAPTER TWENTY-THREE

*"Avoiding danger is no safer in the long run than outright exposure. The fearful are caught as often as the bold." –*Helen Keller

We drove south until we hit I-15 and then rolled with the truck traffic to Ogden because it was the shortest route to get out of Wyoming. The women slept soundly until we arrived, then I snagged a motel room with two queen beds. We still needed clothes, but this was a real town. We'd sleep, eat well, and go shopping.

In our room, Jenny used her phone to find flights out of Salt Lake City. We could be in DC by nine in the evening, leaving toward lunch. Jenny bought our tickets. I needed to sell the weapons and return the rental car in addition to everything else.

"Lots to do in the morning," I grumbled. Jenny stripped for bed, but not all the way. I frowned at her to make her smile.

"Soon enough," she guaranteed. "But why don't we fly

after another night? I don't think we can do everything before we'll need to be at the airport. There's no reason to stress ourselves out."

"Those are words of wisdom."

When Becky came out of the bathroom, she wore just her underclothes. I turned away. She crawled into the bed closest to the door and rolled over.

"Sleep well, Miss Becky," I said. Jenny was rejuvenated from her nap, but I was out cold the second my head hit the pillow.

I slept so soundly that when I woke up, I had no idea where I was. The room didn't have a clock, and I hadn't put a phone on the nightstand. I got up and dug through my backpack to find my burner. It was dead. I went through my clothes to find my watch in the pants pocket. It said five-fifteen.

Less than five hours' sleep. I was still tired, but there was stuff to do. I brought up my computer and used the data plan on the burner phone after I plugged it in and it returned to life. Modern technology made my life possible. It also forced me to carry around a variety of chargers.

I navigated through the layers and layers of security to find that in the short time I'd been out of the mix, a dozen new contracts had been dropped. And the government had paid the promised twenty mil. Nothing hit the national news, but in a smaller Idaho paper, they talked about how the female victims of Quresh had risen against him to free themselves. The investigation was ongoing while the victims of the cult were being treated for malnutrition and mental trauma.

I transferred ten million to my private account and dropped a note to Vinny that I was putting ten into the company.

He must have been online because my phone rang

within ten seconds after I dropped the note. I closed the computer and scurried into the bathroom.

"What?" I said by way of an answer.

"Grumpy. You should drink less caffeine."

"I've had no caffeine this morning, which reminds me, I should make a pot."

"Then by all means, drink more coffee. I wanted to tell you good work, Ian," Vinny finally said.

"Thanks, Vinny. Jenny did most of the heavy lifting on this one." I spoke into my hand, sitting on the edge of the tub and doing my best not to echo.

"Indeed. Why are you talking like that? Where are you?"

"I'm in the bathroom. Jenny and Becky are still sleeping."

"Becky?"

"The Minority Leader's daughter. We pulled her out of Hell's half-acre and are escorting her to DC."

"You're not coming back to Chicago?"

"Of course. That's where we live now. But gotta go to DC first, make sure our clients are happy. We'll be back in less than a week, I suppose."

"Good. We have one-way tickets a week from today. If you don't make it by then, Gladys will have the keys."

"Where you goin'?"

"Wouldn't you like to know?" Vinny jousted.

"Not really. Take that 'round-the-world cruise like we did. That was a lot of a good time, except that we were running for our lives. Outside of that, it was good. On a work-related note, I saw a lot of contracts got dropped."

"Busy, busy. There's no shortage of work. You'll have plenty to keep you occupied when you get back. I've scheduled your regular golf lessons. You'll be on the links and taking people's lunch money before you know it."

"It must be nice, being relieved of the burdens of the

world. You seem to be taking great pleasure in bringing me pain. The sadist in you is escaping."

"Nothing of the sort. It was always there. I've put the vehicles in your names."

"Um…" I didn't know how to broach the race cars. "All of them?"

"Both of them. You're not getting my race cars. They'll be secured in shipping containers this week and sent to our new home. You can't have those, no matter how much you beg."

"I'm pleased that you are pleased by my lack of being pleased."

"Did you get hit in the head or something?"

"Surprisingly, no, I did not. Came through mostly unscathed. Jenny got a little banged up, but nothing ice and sleep won't fix."

"Good to hear. Keep doing great things, Ian. Gotta run. Need to hit the gym before catching breakfast at the Club. It'll be a week of goodbyes. I've grown to like these old curmudgeons, even if they'll never accept me."

"It's okay, Vinny. You did what you could and stayed honest with yourself."

"I have two LeMans race cars. Who am I kidding?"

"But you don't have Daddy's money."

"True. Be good, Ian, and try to make it back here before I leave. There's something I need to tell you that I can't say over the phone."

"Sounds interesting. By the way, I have this righteous fifty-cal rifle and a new Sig forty-five. Is there an operator in Salt Lake City who could use them?"

"Ditch them. We don't want anything tying one operator to another. Don't fall in love with the tools, Ian."

"I tried to remind myself of that, but these are nice. I'll take care of it. Thanks, Vinny. Catch you on the flip side."

Vinny ended the call.

I took a drink of water. It was hard not to look at myself in the mirror. I was starting to look old. Maybe weathered was a better word. I flexed to feel the power in my muscles. We needed to get back into the gym, into a routine.

Play some golf. I laughed at myself. *You're becoming respectable,* I thought. The hit on Quresh and the Battleaxes had happened twelve hours earlier. I had lost track of time.

"You are what you were meant to be," I told the face in the mirror. "Few people will do what has to be done. You are one of those, but Jenny is not. Let her be respectable by stepping away from the pointy end of the spear. Dress her in silk and enjoy what life has to offer."

The door opened quietly and Jenny eased in. "I heard you talking."

"Damn Vinny, calling at all hours. He doesn't understand the concept of time zones." I pulled her close to me and held her tightly.

"You were talking to yourself. I heard the other stuff, too." She spoke with her head against my chest, not looking at me.

"I owe you a better life."

"You owe me jack!" she shot back, pushing me to arm's length and giving me her best glare.

"Who's he?"

Her hard façade crumbled and her face softened. "You are one of a kind, Ian Bragg. You're right that I don't want to go undercover like that ever again. It was horrific inside that building, as if all the joy in the world stopped at the door."

"Don't be angry that I don't want to put you through that again."

"If I remember correctly, I suggested it. You were

against it, I insisted, and you remained reluctant. It was my decision, and you respected that. I'll make a better one next time, but know that I'll do what I have to to support you and take care of the people who matter, like the President of the United States."

I held her, drawing energy from the warmth of her body and the emotional energy she always carried with her, much more than me. There was a gentle knock on the bathroom door.

Jenny opened it to find Becky standing there.

"I have to go," she explained softly.

"We're going to go together. We'll get on tomorrow's flight. It'll be okay."

She pointed at the toilet.

"Oh." We performed a minor kabuki dance to change places, and Jenny and I ended outside the bathroom. I turned on the lights so I could find the room's coffee pot. Nothing. "No coffee."

"It was in the bathroom," Jenny told me. "What were you doing in there that you never noticed the coffee pot? It's the two-cup version. We have three people." She smiled devilishly. She was still in her underwear.

I looked her up and down and shook my head. "You look righteously hot, but since we can't do anything about that right now, I'll get an extra cup of coffee from the lobby. I saw they had an urn when I checked in last night."

I put my shirt on, snagged a card key from the desk, and unlocked the door, checking outside to make sure no one was there to peek in when I headed out. I left Jenny with Becky to talk with her separately. Help her start to heal.

CHAPTER TWENTY-FOUR

"It is not the critic who counts; not the man who points out how the strong man stumbles, or where the doer of deeds could have done them better. The credit belongs to the man who is actually in the arena, whose face is marred by dust and sweat and blood; who strives valiantly; who errs, who comes up short again and again, because there is no effort without error and shortcoming; but who does actually strive to do the deeds; who knows great enthusiasms, the great devotions; who spends himself in a worthy cause; who at the best knows in the end the triumph of high achievement, and who at the worst, if he fails, at least fails while daring greatly, so that his place shall never be with those cold and timid souls who neither know victory nor defeat."
–Theodore Roosevelt

When I returned, we took our time getting as ready as we could to go clothes shopping, find a pawn shop to sell the rifle and pistol, and make sure Becky ate plenty. For a twenty-year-old, she was waif thin. Good food wouldn't hurt. If nothing else, a little ice cream would go down smoothly. It was hot out.

Our flight was for the next morning. So we went to bed early, arrived at the airport way early. Checked in, got screened, and settled in for our on-time flight.

The flight was smooth and unremarkable. Just as we wanted. The three of us rode in first class because that's how we liked to fly. Becky remained within a dark cloud. She needed time. Maybe her father had driven her to joining Quresh. I wondered if he would be able to help her into a happier place.

We were the first passengers off the plane, the benefits of being at the front of the plane. I dialed the phone number from memory while walking up the jet bridge to the terminal. It rang once. "We're here."

"Much earlier than I expected. I'll have you picked up in about five minutes. You'll recognize them."

By waiting a day, we were able to grab an early morning direct flight and arrived not long past noon. I had had enough of working through the night. I wanted more daytime playtime. I could feel the weakness trying to take over my body. I refused to surrender to the potato monster!

Our new clothes helped us blend in. Jenny still walked with a limp, but it wasn't as pronounced as it had been. I tempered my usual brisk pace to keep Becky between us.

Out the doors of Reagan International and there it was, the black-windowed Suburban. We casually strolled toward it with our minimal luggage, having sold the weapons and tech toys while getting rid of everything else we had taken with us out west. We went out heavy and returned light. It was our way.

The agent in the passenger's seat, I still didn't know

their names, jumped out to hold the door for us. Jenny went first, sliding across to the far side. Becky sat in the middle, and I glanced around the area before climbing in. The agent closed the door behind us, hopped in, and we were off.

"Don't watch. It's probably easier that way," I suggested to Becky. She chuckled and shook her head.

"I like the way guys drive. I like how you live life. You've given me the right things to think about. Windshield, not rearview. Know what I want, not what I think other people want me to want. You make sense." She looked at me. I pointed at Jenny.

"We're here for you. I'm afraid I rotate phone numbers fairly frequently, so I can't give you my number, but we'll stay in touch."

"I'd like that."

"You guys got any paper to write on?" I asked those in the front seat. They didn't bother answering. Jenny produced a pen and small note pad from her purse.

I wrote down the Chicago address and my phone number. "You are always welcome to visit us at that address. We have a guesthouse. And this is my number. It's not one that I give out to just anyone. Keep it to yourself, please. For me."

"Of course." Becky stared at her lap while we navigated the city traffic to get into the government district of the downtown area. We pulled around the back of the Senate building, where we were discharged to a small and covered entrance. Inside, we had to walk through a metal detector while getting our possessions x-rayed.

"If you'll follow me." A young man who looked like an aide rather than an agent led us through corridors and down into a less-used area of the building complex. We entered an area where uniformed capitol officers stood guard to keep casual visitors out.

Down a hallway and into a conference room where we were the only people. The aide left. "A glass of ice water?" I asked. A pitcher stood sweating on a side table. Real glasses were upside-down next to it.

I poured three glasses even though no one had answered. We didn't sit down. "Is it always like this?" I asked.

Becky shrugged. "What you see on television is different than what happens behind closed doors. You never know ninety percent of what it takes to govern."

"I hate bureaucrats," I blurted. "They suck the joy out of everything."

Becky laughed. "I knew there were other reasons why I liked you. My father cares more about other people than he does me. It's hard to accept."

"Let him be him. You be you. He cares a great deal for you. Most dads do, but sometimes they don't show it well." I had no idea how the Minority Leader felt about his daughter, but it seemed like the right thing to say. "Give him a hug if he shows up today and tell him you love him. You can never go wrong with that."

"Only if you do it first," she challenged.

"What?"

Jenny looked at me and pointed at my chest. "You said it. You own it."

The door opened, and an earpiece-wearing agent stepped in before moving aside. An older man dressed in a fancy suit entered. Behind him, Jimmy winked at us.

"Daddy." Becky stepped forward and hugged her father. He didn't hug her fully until after the door closed, then he embraced her as if he didn't want to let go. When she pulled free, her eyes glistened as she fought back tears.

"I am so happy that you're out of that place. I know I've failed as a father, but I'll start making that up today." He turned to me and held his hand out. "And I have you to thank for it."

I pushed past his hand to give him a hug. "I love you, man."

When I stepped back, the Minority Leader was staring at me. Becky dove back in. "I love you, Daddy. I put him up to it."

Jimmy's eyebrows were up, and he was shaking his head.

"It was our pleasure to take on this job, sir. Jenny," I nodded at my wife, "did the heavy lifting because she was able to get inside. You have her to thank for your daughter's freedom."

She held out her hand, having embraced my disdain for politicians and wanting nothing to do with a hug from the man. He shook her hand, covering it with his left hand in the traditional two-hand version politicians employed.

"Thank you. If you'll excuse us, I have time to make up." The agent opened the door for him, leaving Becky standing there. "James, please clear my calendar for the day. Becky and I are taking a drive outside the city. I think I'd like a dinner of blue crab."

"I'd like that, too." Becky relaxed as her father held out his hand for her. She took it, and with one last glance, they walked away. The agent left us alone with the Vice President.

"All's well that ends well," I suggested.

"We've made it a local matter, so DOJ isn't involved at all. If I were you, I wouldn't go back to Idaho anytime soon," Jimmy advised.

"Oh, man! We were looking at retiring there."

Jimmy shrugged. "Give it a few years. We will be funneling too much work your way."

"You seem bizarrely good with this now. What gives?"

"Reality gives, Ian. No matter how hard we try, not everyone deserves to live with the rest of us on the big green marble." Jimmy took a seat. I poured him a glass of water, and we sat next to him so the table would not be between us. "What was this guy like?"

I deferred to Jenny.

"He thought of himself as the savior of the downtrodden, looking to remake everyone in the image he wanted. He would not have been able to hold power over those women had it not been for the two women enabling him."

"His sisters," Jimmy said softly.

"Why didn't we know this before?"

"We just learned when they did the autopsies. They were related, so it was best that they met their end together in an uprising of their captives. From victims to heroes. The case will be closed soon without problems for anyone, although the authorities there are looking for a man in a Bigfoot costume, a thick girl—their word, not mine—and one of the captives named Becky."

Jenny's eyes narrowed at the revelation.

"Once they close the case, no one will search for you three. And without DOJ support, they'll never reach beyond Idaho. Well done, you two. What are your plans for the rest of the day?" He leaned back and crossed his arms, waiting for a response. To Jimmy, this wasn't small talk to put us at ease. He genuinely cared.

"I'm hoping for some quality time with the missus, but we'll probably visit Jenny's sister, who lives in Woodbridge."

Jenny nudged and shushed me.

"Me too, Ian. I have to schedule private time with all the events I'm supposed to go to. In a few days, I'll be heading overseas on a show-the-flag tour. I'll be gone for two weeks, so I better get that *quality* time in before I go." Jimmy offered a devilish look that made him appear younger than he was. "You changed our lives. For that, I will be eternally grateful."

Jimmy stood. We shook, then he hugged Jenny and left without a further word.

We straightened up the glasses before we followed Jimmy out. He was headed in the opposite direction from which we'd come. That left us alone in the hallway.

"What the hell?"

Jenny started walking. "Have you become so accustomed to getting the red carpet treatment that you get all grumpy when you aren't served champagne in a crystal flute? I'm not going to stand there and sulk because quality time can't come soon enough. Sometimes, Ian, you need to take matters into your own hands."

I grabbed her behind hard enough to make her jump. She turned and pushed me into the wall for a fierce kiss.

"We need to hurry," I said, taking her hand as we picked up the pace.

And almost ran into the President.

"You escaped?" he said with a tinge of his Southern accent.

"We didn't know we were supposed to wait. Jimmy and the Minority Leader have both departed." I didn't have anything else to say.

"I just found out you were here. I'll get a brief later from the Vice President on the details. Let me shake your hand for a job well done. A father is reunited with his daughter, and the nation is saved from another Waco."

"It is. A win all the way around. Just say no to gurus."

"I should have Justice make that into a coin." He shook my hand and then shook Jenny's. "Chris, make sure they get wherever they need to go. They should have the red carpet treatment, not running through the corridors of power, trying to escape the darkness that buries men's souls."

"Mr. President?"

He smiled close-lipped and headed out. The head of his security detail spoke into his cuff. "Remain here. Someone will be along shortly."

The small entourage disappeared down a side hallway and into an elevator.

"And here we are again. If we do it down here, will we get a special badge or something, like the Mile-High Club?"

"Don't you dare," Jenny cautioned, eyes twinkling under the government-issue fluorescent lights.

It was less than a minute before a uniformed officer hurried toward us to deliver the standard phrase. "If you would follow me..."

CHAPTER TWENTY-FIVE

"Never be in a hurry; do everything quietly and in a calm spirit. Do not lose your inner peace for anything whatsoever, even if your whole world seems upset." –St. Francis de Sales

We went from downtown straight to a hotel, and they allowed us to check in early.

After getting an appropriate workout and cleaning up afterward, we caught a cab to Jasmine's house. We had no luggage with us. When she came outside, she jammed her hands on her hips, much like her sister, and gave us her mom look. I had trained myself to be immune to it. I waved and walked off like I was making a call. Jenny grabbed me and herded me toward the front door with a heartfelt, "Oh no, you don't."

I smiled, but Jasmine looked mad. That put me on high alert.

"Why is my sister limping?" she demanded of me.

I pointed at Jenny. "I wasn't even there when it happened."

"He wasn't," Jenny admitted. "I fell on a road and hit a rock. Nasty kneecap bruise."

"Is that a bite mark?" She pointed at Jenny's neck.

"I was there for that one." I tried to look remorseful. I also wrestled with how much we could tell Jasmine.

"He was," Jenny agreed before holding up her hand. "We have a hard job, but it's one that requires us to be in shape and on occasion, to take some hits. My knee was my own stupid fault."

"Where did you go?" Jazz asked.

"Can't tell you that."

"What did you do?"

Jenny shook her head. "Can't tell you that, either."

"Is there anything you *can* tell me?"

"Pretty much, no." Jenny smiled radiantly. I nodded vigorously.

"But I get to see you twice in a week. That is how often sisters should get together." Jasmine hugged Jenny hard enough that she had trouble breathing. "Come on. I think I still have something leftover from lunch."

I looked at Jenny in alarm. She stammered, but nothing came out. We were doomed, so we resigned ourselves to our fate. In the kitchen, we were relieved to find cold leftover fried chicken from a local place. We were saved from having to eat Jasmine's cooking.

"I've been talking with Jack," Jazz started, "and we'd like to do something for you guys."

"We've had a lot of excitement lately and just want to go home and relax. We haven't even spent one night in our new home yet," Jenny replied.

"And work is building up," I added.

"If you just got done with a job, how is work building up?"

I wondered if it was a setup question since Jazz was a

wedding planner. "You know the deal. It's exactly like planning weddings. You've got the one happening right now while trying to keep next week's bridezilla happy while reserving a place for the week after and ordering flowers in between. There's probably a hundred moving parts with each wedding, so you don't have just a hundred things to do, but five hundred or six hundred. It's a constant list of checking stuff off and adding new items in. Same for me."

"You plan weddings where you get beat up?"

Jenny and I laughed at each other. "Can you imagine us planning weddings?" she joked.

"Almost, Jasmine. I expect the process is similar, that's all. The more time we spend at the pointy end of the spear, the less time we have to keep all those other plates spinning."

"'Pointy end of the spear?' Let me guess. You guys are mercenaries? Bounty hunters? That's it, isn't it? Oh, my God. Jenny!"

Jenny made her best bored face. "What we do is something you don't get to know. Ian is the best in the world at it, and that has a great deal of value to those who can pay. Don't press us on this; otherwise, we'll just have to leave and not come back. We can't tell you, so drop it." Jenny's voice changed from casual to firm as she put her foot down with her older sister.

"I care about you, that's all. So shoot me."

"I know you care. And if you press this, you put us at risk, so let's talk about cold fried chicken because Ian is in on your big secret."

"That I'm not a good cook? Everyone knows that, but Jack and Kate are worse than me. Back to my original request. We'd like to do something for you here at our house in a couple days if you can see your way to staying around. You're not going to stay at the house, are you?"

"I'm sorry, but no. It's less embarrassing to slam the headboard at the hotel."

I had to stop chewing so I didn't choke. I stared at the table. Sisters. Their entire goal in life was to give their spouses grief. By spouses, I meant me.

"Would you have any potato chips?" I asked. "Or Fritos?"

I tried to look innocent, but they were onto me. "Yes. We'll stay two days, but we need to get back to Chicago. A friend is retiring, and we have to be there before he goes."

Jazz rummaged through the kitchen looking for snacks but found nothing. "The kids have cleaned me out, sorry," she announced.

"That's not anything you hear at our house," I replied. "What did you have in mind for doing something?"

"What kind of surprise party would it be if I told you about it?"

"I don't like surprises."

"You'll like this one." Jasmine tried to stare me down.

"I won't."

"You will."

Jenny interrupted, "Now you're arguing like we used to. We'll be back when the time is right. In between, we'll explore what this part of the world has to offer. Ian?" Jenny stood and made to go.

"But you just got here!" Jazz waved her arms. I chowed through my piece of chicken as if I were eating corn off a cob. With a full mouth, I stood.

"When do you want us back here?"

"Two in the afternoon. We'll have dinner here. And you can lose the frowns. I'll have food brought in. You don't have to suffer with anyone's cooking. You guys eat out a lot, don't you?"

I continued to chew, shrugging instead of answering with a full mouth.

"We do, but I *can* cook. I spent a lot of time with Mom the last few years."

Words that would lead to another fight. "Time to go!" I declared with my hand over my mouth, and I ushered Jenny away before they could get into it. Outside, we realized we didn't have a vehicle. "Wave and we'll walk to the strip mall, then we'll call a cab," I whispered.

Jenny waved and we kept walking. It was our day to do with as we pleased.

"Are we going to play tourist?" Jenny wondered.

"Only as much as possible. Let's head to the Smithsonian. I've never been and think it will be a funky groove."

"A what?"

"A trippindicular total blowout."

"You're just making up words." Jenny one-arm-hugged me. Her limp was less pronounced.

"Or maybe we can take a load off that knee and ice it, then hit the gym for some upper body work before calling room service for the best the hotel has to offer."

"I like how you think, Mr. Bragg."

"What is Jazz planning?"

"I'm sure it's a wedding reception. It's what she does. We'll hang out under a canopy tent in the backyard and drink toasts while telling stupid stories. You'll regale them with tales of your misspent youth or time in the Corps, experiences they can't relate to. And then we'll leave, catching a flight home first thing in the morning."

"Home. What are we going to do about Vegas?"

"Go back. Clean it out, and let the landlord know that we've had to move. Life goes on."

"Sure. We'll pay the good man ahead for something like six months to give him time to put other people in there. Nobody likes a bad-news bomb. We were stellar tenants."

"We were and will continue to be," Jenny agreed.

The heat and humidity of northern Virginia were making us sweat. We stopped to call for a cab. "No more walking for you." While we waited, I shared my greatest revelation of the day. "Killing people is so much easier than dealing with relatives."

The appointed time came, and despite my trepidations, we jumped in the cab and made our way to Jasmine's house. Jenny seemed perfectly fine with it. I was dreading it. She stopped me from making airplane reservations for three hours after the "event" started.

"Why?" she asked, demanding an answer. She threw her hands down in frustration. "Take it like a man."

I started to laugh and continued to chuckle to myself while looking out the window away from Jenny's side of the cab.

She poked me in the ribs to get my attention. I was still smiling when I languorously turned my head to face her. "Yes?"

"You are impossible."

"Impossibly delicious. I'll do it since the rewards far outweigh the cost."

"What rewards?" Jenny tipped her head down to give me her teacher look.

"I was led to believe there would be rewards like

outside food. Maybe Fritos. Bugles? Do they have those anymore? I could eat a buttload of both."

We had been working out hard. It was nice to be back in the gym, even if it was only the hotel's workout room.

Jenny nodded slightly. "Fine."

It was the antonym of a safe word. It was my fire alarm and immediately put me on alert.

By way of an iPad on the dash, the taxi driver navigated the housing area's roads to deliver us to Jasmine's driveway. A few more cars than normal were on the street. Jack's ride was in the driveway. The gloom of mandatory fun returned and hung over my head. I paid the taxi driver, giving him a good tip because he didn't try to carry on a conversation with us.

We found Jasmine and a man I assumed was her husband Dylan waiting at the door. Jenny waved and hurried forward, not letting go of my hand as she pulled and I lurched forward. I trundled up next to her.

"Rewards," I whispered.

"Men," she countered.

"Just one. Incorrigible me." I kissed her, as I often did, but that brought the welcoming committee outside.

"I'm Dylan." The man looked like a librarian and stood the same height as his wife, with small round glasses. I shook his hand. It was soft.

"You're an interpreter. I applaud the mental agility that takes. I'm challenged in one language." He smiled at the compliment. "I'm glad to finally meet you."

Once inside, the planned event became obvious, with one glaring exception to my expectations. Jasmine had planned a wedding. The door stood open to the backyard, where a flowered arch stood behind a lectern where an obvious minister waited, keeping himself busy by reading a sheaf of papers.

"You need real clothes, mister," Jasmine said. "I guessed your size, but I'm probably right. I do this for a living. Upstairs. First door on the right."

"Sure. Thanks for putting this together for us. It means a great deal to me." I hugged Jasmine, then pulled Jenny to me for a separate hug and whispered into her ear, "Rewards."

She winked at me, and I went upstairs while Jasmine shuffled Jenny away. Inside the room, I found a tuxedo complete with shoes. It was too loose in the waist and too tight in the shoulders. I found this oddly annoying. I gave the impression of being less fit. Maybe she guessed based on my slovenly ways, which led me to think about snacks. It was on the bride to not be seen, so I removed the tux jacket and threw it over my shoulder to leave the room.

Giggling told me where my sister-in-law was, and I suspected my wife, too.

Downstairs, I found the first floor empty. The kitchen was filled with sealed dishes of food. I looked around to make sure I was alone before helping myself. Under foil rested a Honey-Baked spiral-sliced ham, warm and ready for the taking. I glanced over my shoulder while reaching in.

Jack and Kate strolled in from outside.

"Welcome to the family, my brother!" Jack tried to sound gregarious. I stuffed the ham into my mouth, wiped off my hand, and offered it. We shook like men. He wasn't as fit as he had once been and would inevitably lose any hand-gripping contest he tried with me. After a brief time, he surrendered. "I had to try."

"Of course."

The kids from both families were accounted for. The college-age kids were playing a ring-toss game with their younger cousins.

A team of caterers appeared in the kitchen and started moving the food outside. I tried to help but was shooed away. I put my jacket on, taking care to keep my shoulders back so I wouldn't explode the seam. I wondered how impressive that would be for the crowd while the preacher was reading the vows.

A gentle knock came on the front door, and Kate hurried away to get it. I checked the refrigerator for beer, but Jack suggested we shouldn't drink anything before the ceremony.

"I know you're right, but I want that beer."

"Then I would have brought more," came the reply in a familiar voice.

"Mr. Vice President. How did you know about this?"

Jimmy raised one eyebrow. "I have to go to all kinds of stuff to show the flag. It's nice to find a more intimate event like this where we can come and be among friends. And call me Jimmy like you used to."

"Of course. And Tricia. I'm glad you could make it, too."

The woman I had called the Wonderbeast stepped forward, looking like she had grown younger since the last time I'd seen her.

She pulled me into a hug. "Thank you," she whispered. "I don't blame you."

Tricia Tripplethorn knew I had killed her boyfriend, and she knew I had done it at her father's command.

"Do you get back to Seattle any?"

"We haven't been here that long. I'm still trying to get my feet under me."

A bell rang from the stairs. We dutifully turned our eyes to the procession of one: Jenny in a white dress, walking carefully to avoid falling. Her limp was gone, giving her the impression of flowing with the dress.

"Miss Jenny, I'm happy to marry you again."

"Jimmy," she said in surprise. "And Tricia. How did you..."

Jimmy tapped his nose with one finger.

"Take your positions!" Jasmine shouted.

Jack and Kate headed for the yard. "I guess it's showtime," I told Jimmy and Tricia before gazing once more at Jenny. She beamed at the look, although I was having a hard time coming to grips with the makeup. *Au naturale* was the look I was most comfortable with, and it suited her best, in my mind anyway. It was the look I enjoyed while she was still sleeping. It was the look she wore when we worked out.

It was the look of our life. Straightforward, no disguise except the biggest one of all: what we did for a living.

I walked through the yard to the tent, where I shook hands with the pastor.

"You got roped into this too, eh?"

"I'm sorry?" He closed the book he was reading—the bible.

"First time we got married was by Elvis. He sang an awful lot during the ceremony. You're not going to sing, are you?"

"I am not," the man assured me. "This ceremony is only scheduled to last two minutes from start to finish. There was some concern about lightning striking if we pushed it."

"You do have a sense of humor. Well done, Padre!" The pastors we'd had with us in the Corps came from the Navy, usually. We didn't have spiritual or physical care done by Marines. We were focused on one thing. Every Marine was a rifleman. I was obligated to mess with them.

I felt it was my duty. The few guests took their seats. Jasmine and her family. Jack and his family. Jimmy and Tricia, sitting among them all. Two caterers continued to set up while a Secret Service agent stood inside the house.

Another one was outside with us. All of that faded out of my picture as Jenny started walking toward me.

Sometimes, nothing else matters.

The ceremony was quick, as the pastor had promised. We said our heartfelt I dos, realized we didn't have rings, and made do without.

We cleared the short receiving line quickly before Jimmy held out a card for us. "We need to get going, but I'm glad we were able to make it." He stepped back and raised his voice slightly to talk to everyone. "It is our pleasure to know Ian and Jenny. They saved my life and made it possible for me to be in the position I'm in. The card is from the President. He begs your forgiveness that he wasn't able to make it, but he also owes you a debt of gratitude."

I blushed as much as Jenny and pointed at the family. "They don't know what I do because it's classified."

Jimmy smiled and didn't miss a beat. "Classified at the highest levels. See you next time you're in town, Ian." He and Tricia waved and walked into the house hand in hand. The agents disappeared with the Vice President.

I stuffed the card into my jacket.

"You're not going to open it?"

"We're going to open it, just not here. It probably has a pun because when he lets his hair down, metaphorically speaking, the President is one funny dude."

Jenny and I made eyes at each other. Jack and Jasmine looked like they were in shock.

"The ham is getting cold," I suggested.

After that, we didn't have any problems or hassles from Jenny's family. They put her on a pedestal, and she rode it like the Queen of Sheba.

CHAPTER TWENTY-SIX

"Don't dwell on what went wrong. Instead, focus on what to do next. Spend your energy moving forward together towards an answer." –Dennis Waitley

After landing at O'Hare, I dialed Vinny's number. It had only been five days since last we talked.

"Thanks for calling, Ian. We put my old car in long-term parking for you. It's where Chaz was parked."

"I don't have a key," I replied, feeling my chest tighten as I thought about Chaz dying there by himself at the hands of thugs who weren't good enough to carry out his trash.

"Use the code 59417. It'll let you in. Call me, and I'll activate it from here so you can drive yourselves back to the house. We're packed up and ready to go. When you arrive, come straight into the main house. It's yours now."

We walked briskly. Jenny was mostly up to full speed. Starting tomorrow, we'd go to a real gym and be models for staying fit.

"I don't know what to say, Vinny. It still seems weird. I hope to do you proud."

"You already have. Worry not and hurry up. The little lady and I are ready to start our vacation. It's been a while."

"I hope I'm not telling the next guy that. Mandatory mental-health vacations."

"It'll be a vacation every time you tee it up, Ian. See you soon."

We followed the signs, took the walkways, and covered over a mile before we reached the shuttle to take us to the long-term lot. A balmy Chicago evening sported a stiff breeze that made it seem much cooler than it was. I wore a t-shirt and jeans. Jenny had a jacket that Jasmine had given her. We'd be fine until we bought more appropriate clothing.

Jenny looked forward to mandatory shopping. I wanted to see how my golf game had degenerated. We'd both get our wish soon enough.

At the lot, we walked through the twilight under the dim bulbs of the pre-dark lamps.

"Careful," I said softly. Shadows appeared and disappeared between vehicles. We had to look for the BMW since we didn't have a key to click and make the lights flash.

"There," Jenny said. We tried the code on a car that looked like it. It didn't work. We peeked in the window to discover that it wasn't the right one.

"Lost?" a gruff voice said from behind us.

"Just trying to find one unlocked that I can wire to get us out of here. You?" I replied.

Three thugs. Different from those who had accompanied Detritus.

Different but the same.

They blocked our way. Jenny slid to the side and I eased

past, but not far enough where more than a single attacker could come at once. They knew what was up. The one farthest back licked his lips as he walked around the neighboring car to come in behind us. Jenny turned to face him.

"What would it take for no one to get hurt here tonight?" I asked.

"Give us your stuff, and you walk free."

"That's not going to work, you see, because a friend of mine was killed right out there by people like you. I'm still pretty mad about it. The right answer is, 'we were just funnin'. Sorry to bother you, sir, ma'am.' And be on your way."

He snorted and laughed, turning to face his friend to reinforce how funny he thought my answer was. When his head was sideways, I rabbit-punched him in the temple with everything I had.

Jenny charged, feinted, and kicked her opponent in the 'nads. She punched the top of his head as he fell and kicked him in the face once he was on the ground.

The talker was unconscious, falling as I pushed him into his friend, who frantically tried to get out of the way. He stumbled and fell, and the rough concrete of the garage deck caught his pants and kept him from sliding out of reach and getting up. I danced around beside him.

Jenny took a position on the other side.

"Why are you so stupid? How many of you punks do we have to beat into next week before you change your ways.?"

"I'll kill you!" He fumbled with his pocket. As soon as he took his eyes from mine, I kicked his hand, breaking at least two of his fingers. He howled like a lost dog.

I leaned close. "No, son. I'm going to kill you." I made a knife-hand and let it waver before his face. When he tried to slap it out of the way, I drove my fingers into his throat, but not hard enough to kill him. It made him gag and wrap two hands around his injured windpipe.

I stood up and spun to deliver a roundhouse into his face that flattened his nose and split his lip. He flipped backward and smacked his head on the ground. It sounded like a too-ripe watermelon.

"Time to go, my love?" I asked.

Jenny brushed off her hands and returned for her bag. She kicked the young man in her charge once more to make sure he would be in no shape to follow. I stepped to the first man and with the heel of my shoe, ground his fingers into the concrete. We dragged the third soul out of the way and tossed him onto his buddy sixty-nine-style.

We strolled down the lot until we found the car. The code opened the doors. I punched the button for the trunk, and we deposited our stuff inside.

"I'm not even breathing hard," Jenny said. "I guess it does get easier. I never doubted that we'd win that fight."

"That makes all the difference. Train harder than the real game. It wasn't even an easy day at the gym. Three punches and a couple kicks."

I called Vinny and the engine started.

"So very nice." I envisioned Vinny turning the phone off and putting it on the counter, cutting his final link to the Peace Archive.

The gas tank was full and the radio played, but it wasn't Rush. "We need to fix that," I said, nodding at the console.

Jenny ignored me. I'd have to get a Bluetooth burner and upload the Rush catalog so it would play automatically whenever we were in the car. The old player was just that: old. It was time for modern technology to join us without giving us away.

"A home, Miss Jenny. We aren't going to have to live life on the run. That will be odd. Us. Domesticated."

"You could use it," she replied. "You're still a little feral, but another five or ten years and we may get you decent enough to bring out in public."

"What would I do without my better half?"

"You know the way?" she asked.

"I feel like I should say yes, but that would get us lost, and I have no desire to spend any more time on Chicago roads than I have to."

Jenny humored me by bringing up the GPS on her phone and typing in the destination. She labeled it "home."

Not optimal for a burner phone. I couldn't relax my guard. Not yet. Maybe someday, but today wasn't that day.

I drove without needing the GPS. There weren't that many turns on the route, which we'd already taken a couple of times. I eased the Beemer up the driveway and punched the button for the garage.

We left our bags in the car and knocked on the door from the garage into the main house.

"What kind of idiot knocks before walking into his own home?"

"It doesn't feel like our home," I shouted back at the closed door before opening it.

"Keep that thought and hand it off to the next person. We've lived here for ten years, but I'll let you in on a little secret. I don't like Chicago weather or traffic. The airport is busy, and the people who work there are unhappy, unlike where we're going. Grand Cayman, here we come.

"And no extradition treaty, just in case something from the past sees the light of day."

"It won't."

Vinny hadn't been kidding. Their bags were packed and sitting by the front door.

"I feel like I don't know what I need to know."

"Ask Gladys. She knows everything."

"To include what we do?"

"Of course. You don't think Chaz and I ran this all by ourselves, do you?" Vinny laughed and made eyes at Vivian. "Here." He slid a key and piece of paper across the table. "That's to the safe in the master bedroom. It's under the small display table. You'll find additional support materials in there. Open it as soon as we're gone. It never hurts to have an inventory to work with. And good luck, Ian. I think the new government angle is going to work out best for the company, at least for the current administration. Change in admin, change in direction, so don't cut ties with anyone at the Club. Any final questions?"

"The Chicago police chief job and the New York City protection racket?"

"Those were handled while you were cruising the world. All taken care of. We're about twenty-one contracts in recouping our emergency shutdown cover. Forty-one million out, twenty-one million back in. It's all in the data once you get deep into where it's hidden."

"Just one more. Why did you keep doing this job?"

"You won't hear from us again, and you ask a question where you already know the answer. Interesting."

"No other question seemed to matter because at the end of the day, it'll always come back to why we do what we do. Moving forward without succumbing to the easy answer. It must always be that we only hit bad guys, criminals. Like the job we did for the President. We did it, and we did it right. Now the Minority Leader owes us, too."

"He's a contender for the big chair, so maybe you'll keep us at the forefront of those conversations for the next decade or more. The Archive will do the hard jobs that they can't be seen to do."

Vinny stood. I had hoped for enough time to listen and understand more of what drove him.

But it wasn't to be.

He used the untraceable phone to call for a taxi. Then he turned it off and left it on the counter next to a variety of keys and fobs. "Give it to someone who needs it."

With one last handshake and hug, they walked out.

"Wait. You said you were going to tell me something that you couldn't say over the phone."

Vinny hesitated before looking over his shoulder. "The safe. Everything you need to know is there." And he and Viv walked away, hand in hand.

We stood on the stoop and waved as Vinny and his better half climbed into the cab and left.

Once inside, we locked the door and wandered aimlessly until I discovered a whole-home sound system. I ran out to the car and picked up my music player, along with our bags. I dumped the bags at the bottom of the steps and spun up *Vital Signs*.

"Feels weird," Jenny said, looking out the windows at complete privacy. Woods surrounded the home to keep casual eyes from looking in.

We had some things in the guesthouse. We'd get those later.

I picked up the key and the combination. "We better do what Vinny suggested." Upstairs, the master bedroom was palatial. The table was empty and easy to move. We rolled up a Persian carpet to see the safe. I dialed the combination, four times around to the first number, three times back to the next, two to the third number, and then returned once until it caught. The key pulled the locks into the door, and I lifted it by its handle.

It was heavy, and I had to adjust to get a better angle on it. When it was open, small lights came on under the ledge.

Inside was a Sig Sauer of the same model I had just sold to a gun shop in Salt Lake City and five boxes of ammunition for it, with two extra magazines. "Self-defense for the discerning homeowners," I remarked. I pulled out a stack of files. Each was information tying a high-profile figure to a contract to make a hit. Blackmail for insurance purposes, a grim reminder of the precarious position our work put us in.

And a card that looked similar to the one the President had given us.

"Did you open the President's card?" Jenny asked.

"I did not. I forgot about it. You looked amazing, and I was helpless to resist."

Jenny stood and curtsied. "You're welcome. While I'm up, I'll get it."

She headed downstairs. I thumbed through the files. They went back twenty years.

The Archive had only been around for ten.

Jenny returned with the card and gave it to me. I slipped my finger under the seal and it popped open. It wasn't a wedding card, but Presidential stationery. On it was a string of letters and numbers. We looked at it askance.

"A password?" Jenny ventured.

"To what? That is the question. I guess we'll know when the time is right." I tried to memorize it but couldn't focus. I set it aside and returned the files to the safe. I opened the card from Vinny directed to *My Replacement*. It was stationery with the Club's logo.

In Vinny's handwriting was a simple message.

Make the scumbags pay. Kill them all.

THE END OF THE REPLACEMENT
IAN BRAGG WILL RETURN IN A FATAL BRAGG

While you're waiting for the next story, if you would be so kind as to leave a review for this book, that would be great. I appreciate the feedback and support. Reviews buoy my spirits and stoke the fires of creativity.

If you follow me on Amazon, they'll let you know when my next book is released.

Don't stop now! Keep turning the pages as I talk about my thoughts on this book and the overall project called the *Ian Bragg Thrillers*.
https://geni.us/IanBragg

FIRST UP IS PAUL ALAN PIATTS
WITH HIS TALE SURF SHOOTING

For fans of Ian Bragg, I offered to publish their fan fiction if I liked it. These stories do not represent canon in this universe, but I appreciate the commitment that our fans have to the incredible characters of Ian and Jenny. Thank you for being so invested in these stories that you want to see more of them:)

First up is Paul Alan Piatts with his tale *Surf Shooting*

The groundswell of a powerful storm thundered ashore in Southern California and drove high winter swells skyward. I'd learned to surf as a kid and decided to take it up again as an adult, but not today. After getting rag-dolled twice, I decided to call it quits for the day.

I tossed a farewell wave at a group of locals gathered down the beach, but they just stared. They'd tried the usual "this is our beach" crap when I first showed up. Insults on the water had led to fists on the sand and a broken nose for the one they called "Turd." Now they ignored me.

Who says violence solves nothing?

I noticed him as I walked up to my towel. He tried to look like a casual surf spectator, but his vibe was all wrong.

I shook out my towel and rubbed my face and hair as he approached.

"Pretty rough today, huh?"

I nodded. "Yeah, it's gnarly."

He was so average it hurt. Average height, average build. Plain clean-shaven face, regular haircut. Khaki pants, plain blue windbreaker. Mr. Everyman. I liked him immediately.

"What's it up to?"

He tried to look puzzled, but dollar signs flashed in his remarkably average eyes. "What's what up to?"

"C'mon. We're both professionals. What's it up to?"

He looked relieved.

"One-point-two."

"One-point-two? Nice." I gave an appreciative whistle. "So that means, what, three-fifty for you? Not bad."

I saw the doubt when his eyebrows bounced.

"That leaves eight and a half for the broker? Lotta money for no risk."

I let him mull that over while I peeled my wet suit down to my waist.

"Who's the broker? The Fat Man?"

There were only a few players big enough to handle a million-dollar contract, and the only one I'd upset lately was the Fat Man.

Everyman's eyebrows told me what I wanted to know.

"Who? Broker?"

"The broker. The guy who gave you the contract."

"Ah, I can't tell you that. What's it matter?"

"Just know that the Fat Man is a back-stabbing sonofabitch who will sell you out for a percentage. That's who you're dealing with."

He shrugged.

"Well, I have things to do. I'll see you around." I hefted my board and started walking toward my car, which was parked beyond the dunes.

"Wait! Wait a second!"

I stopped, and he moved between me and the dunes. He had his hands shoved into his jacket, and the bulge of a pistol was unmistakable.

"You can't leave."

"I have to. I have things to do. Can't surf all day, you know."

"But what about…what about this?"

I looked up and down the beach. People and dogs dotted the sand in both directions.

"What about it? You think you're gonna do it here?"

He looked up and down the beach.

"What's the proof, anyway? For a million two, there's proof, right?"

He nodded.

"More than pictures?"

Another nod.

"Fingers? Maybe a hand?"

"Head," he mumbled.

I laughed. "They want you to bring back my head?"

He hung his own head and kicked the sand. "That's what they said."

"And you agreed to that?"

A shrug and a nod. He was really starting to open up.

"Well, we both know you're not gonna shoot me and cut off my head on this beach. Too many witnesses."

He gestured toward the dunes with his hands still deep in his jacket. "Head up that way."

I strode through the sand, and he fell in a few steps

behind. The soft sand made for heavy going, and I heard him struggle to keep up.

"You okay back there?"

"Yeah, I'm good," he wheezed.

I led the way down the rocky path to the parking lot. There was a plain late-model tan sedan parked next to my plain late-model tan sedan, except mine had a board rack. I hit the fob button, the trunk lid popped up, and the headlights flashed a greeting.

I struggled to lift the surfboard onto the roof rack. "Gimme a hand, would ya?"

Mr. Everyman stepped back. "Screw that." His hand came out of his pocket with his pistol. "Drop it and get in the trunk."

"You want me to leave it here?"

He nodded.

"How long before somebody notices a surfboard sitting here on the ground?"

I sensed the wheels turning in his mind.

"How long before the cops check out my car, maybe open the trunk? People saw us leave the beach together."

He stood in silence.

"Exactly. Now, give me a hand with this."

I grunted as I lifted the board onto the rack. My hands slipped, and it started sliding down the roof. Everyman caught it before it fell to the ground.

"Here, let me—"

I was on him in a flash. I controlled his gun hand and hit him with a stiff-fingered throat strike. He gurgled and fell backward, and I slammed my knee deep between his legs. He moaned in agony as he curled up around his damaged balls.

I dug the pistol out of his pocket. It was a .22 target

pistol, a good choice for close-in work. I tucked the pistol into my wet suit.

His face was a sick greenish-gray, and flecks of vomit sprinkled his chin and jacket.

"C'mon, let's get you up. The best way to feel better is to stand up."

I hauled him up and leaned him against my bumper. He stared blankly, and I shoved him backward into my trunk. I drew the pistol and fired two shots into his forehead, then emptied the pistol under his chin.

I shoved the empty pistol back into my wet suit and slammed the trunk lid. After I secured the surfboard to the rack, I hopped in and made a calm, law-abiding exit from the parking lot.

I was due to hook up with Jenny in San Diego tomorrow, then we were going to pay a visit to the Fat Man.

NEXT UP IS TERRY WELLS-BROWN...

I knew someone would eventually try to use me to get to my husband. I mean, it had happened once already at the beginning of our relationship, and recently, another someone had a go at me. It made sense that it would happen again. Right?

What I didn't foresee was that someone being a tiny, slim, big-boobed blonde babe.

She'd introduced herself as Tina, and she was sugary-sweet. Her name alone made my skin crawl.

I wasn't sure what role she planned to take in Ian's life. My first and worst thought was she wanted my spot as his beloved wife, or maybe she wanted in on the business and thought I'd make it easy for her. Maybe she was trying to get close to my man so she could off him and had grandiose ideas of taking his place. Or maybe she was law enforcement, and she was here to take him and the organization down.

Honestly, it didn't really matter. She wasn't getting anywhere near my husband.

You see, truth be told, he's a contract killer. Not just any contract killer, but a good one, as in, he only kills bad people. He works hard to make sure all of his and his organization's kills are justified. How can you not love that? To top it off, he is the best thing that has ever happened to me.

I looked at the smiling woman who'd managed to sit next to me at the salon. This was the third time in a month we'd just happened to be in the same place at the same time. In all three instances, she had gone out of her way to strike up a friendly conversation, mostly about my home life and my husband.

Now, I know I might be a bit paranoid, but it was the thing Ian had taught me first and foremost: never take anyone at face value. And this chick was too good to be true. All of my internal alarms sounded with her from our very first contact.

I dropped the foot my pedicurist had been working on into the tub of hot water, lifted the other out, and rested it on the towel. I pretended intent interest in what was happening to my toes—anything to keep from having to look at Tina.

"Anyway, like I was saying, we should get together tonight if you're not busy?" She'd been talking nonstop since I sat down in the pedicure chair.

"Oh, I think my husband has plans for us tonight." I tried to sound distracted when in reality, all my senses were on high alert and tuned to her.

"Really? What?" she asked. She made the same move I'd just made—dropped her left foot into the bath and lifted her right out to present to the pedicurist.

"I'm not sure exactly. I just know he said we had something to do," I said quietly.

"What color are you getting?" she asked, holding up a bright red bottle of polish, changing the subject.

"I'm having French manicure applied."

"Oh, pooh! That's so ten years ago! You need to come into the here and now and put some color on your toes." She waggled the polish at me and instructed my pedicurist to use the red on my toes.

"That's okay. I'll stick with my out-of-fashion French manicure." This chick had some nerve. Who picked out another woman's toenail polish without asking?

"You sure? This would look so much better." She continued to wave the bottle at me and scrunched her nose. If we weren't going on a trip the next day, I'd have considered leaving without polish just to get away from this Tina person. But we were leaving, and I didn't think I'd have time to get my toes finished before we departed.

I was literally saved by the bell when my phone rang. When I looked down, I saw that it was Ian. I rolled my eyes and took the call.

"Hey, lover," I answered since I knew Tina would eavesdrop.

"Hey, lover, back." I could hear a smile in his voice. "I'm thinking of ordering takeout. I thought it might be nice to eat in since we have to be up so early. Whatcha feel like having, Miss Jenny?" I loved my husband. We really made a good team. I rolled my eyes to Tina, who was leaning as far toward me as possible in her chair.

"I want Egg Foo Young," I said.

"Two orders of General Tso's it is."

"Why do you even bother asking me?"

"Do you really want Egg Foo Young?" Ian asked.

"Maybe," I replied.

"Two orders of General Tso's it is."

I smiled to myself. "Sounds good, Mr. Man."

"When will you be done?"

"I'm not sure." I looked sideways at Tina, who was watching me intently. "I've got a new friend."

"Is this a real friend, or should I be worried?"

"I think the latter," I said and looked directly at her. "She seems very eager to meet you." Tina let out a deep sigh and slumped back in her chair.

"Do you need me?" I could hear Ian moving around. Probably getting ready to rescue me, which I did not need.

"Nope. I think I can handle this. I don't want you anywhere near this place...or her."

I hung up and shifted in my chair so I could read Tina's face while I had a come-to-Jesus discussion with her.

"I don't know who you are or why you think cozying up to me is going to get you close to my husband, but it's not going to work, missy."

Tina took a moment. I could tell she was thinking about her words before she spoke. "Look, I'm with the Peace Archive, and we want to use you and Ian as a successful team-building model for other couples."

I don't know what I had expected her to say, but that was not it.

ANDREW PERRY - THE MANTIS

For IT professionals who spend much of their careers waiting on computers, curiosity can be equal parts valuable and dangerous. Today as a young engineer is sitting in the dark working at a data center, this proves true. The roar of thousands of server fans is deafening, but for those who live in this world, the sound is often a comforting background hum.

Rick stretches as he pushes his chair away from the server-rack, which produces an audible groan. A network engineer by day, he is also an accomplished hacker whose expertise is navigating the darkweb. Computer engineers don't have a typical time when they are "at work", they're always working, and Rick makes productive use of what would otherwise be wasted downtime. He's constantly badgered to be billing for every minute, so why not help myself to a little more? He thinks. While waiting for a particularly large operating system patch to install and compile, Rick finds himself with too much time on his hands. In a place with a direct pipe to the interweb, the pull is too tempting. Plugging his laptop into a master router at the firewall level allows the proficient hacker to scour the internet with anonymity.

Sometimes Rick likes to just hang a device off of the web's edge and see what packets take the bait. He's had great success with gathering information regarding friends, coworkers, bosses, and others, that he has been able to use covertly. It is less like "fishing" and more like panning for fragments of gold debris hurtling by, until they collide with his router and are successfully scooped up. Once trapped inside this collector, the packets of information are analyzed and then prioritized for Rick's viewing pleasure.

All morning, Ricks router scoops up stray data packets of information. Each one grabbed provides clues to its origin. When he takes his morning break, Rick flips his laptop around and looks to see what he has scored.

"Hummm." Rick quickly reviews the contents. "Junk!"

Yet one of the packets is still calling for its mates (the packets immediately before and after). The data appears as some sort of redirected mail message with a non-standard encryption service on it.

Rick loves a mystery. A quick dip of his hand into his laptop bag produces top of the line hacker software code named "*the taken*" – Rick and his peers still call these illegal programs "Ice". They are hardcore nerds. Rick is a network engineer without a college degree, like all the best ones. He is in high demand despite his young age.

The very best stand out.

Unlike most of his friends, Rick is starting to grow out of the all-mighty siren song of online video games and is now actively spending time learning about different aspects of the actual world he lives in. This has been a powerful awakening for the young hacker and his quick mind is gobbling up everything of interest starting with mysteries on the darkweb.

Rick slots "the taken" and turns it loose. Thirty minutes later his ice has done its job.

Flowers. The message is something about flowers. Another dud. Rick almost deletes it. But the paranoid flows which race through his mind while he hacks, works automatically and he watches himself type the keystrokes necessary to view the site in question.

What he finds is no flower shop.

Rick glances left and right in the darkness. The blasts of hot and cold computer racked air serve to remind him that he is at work, but his job is no longer of any importance. The young hacker has sidestepped into something that has piqued his interest to the exclusion of everything else.

Here, in darkspace, he is viewing a menu. The contents of which might change his life forever. Most underside users have several tools to make their navigation of the broken web easier, while in Rick's case he has years' worth of accumulated malware.

In surprisingly little time he decrypts the message board and examines the available options. The list appears to be descriptions of people. There's also a location to bid on each of the people described. The programmer of this service is good, and Rick discovers that Blitzen is loaded. Blitzen is a nasty viral trap designed so that any wrong keystroke vanishes the contents of this board to Christmas town.

Rick is no luddite and carefully examines the information. There are pre-qualifiers to even review this message board.

Hacking is not for the faint-of-heart. Rick leans forward eagerly in the darkness of the data center. The blasts from the server fans continue to stir his hair. He pays this distraction no mind as he attempts to take in everything he is seeing. He reads service descriptions, including codewords, and basic details of required services. While he is watching, Rick observes that the auction-style board is seeing some sort of real-time action.

With a soft hiss and a "tisk, tisk, tisk" sound Rick executes the Picard maneuver on his keyboard, covering his tracks using the hidden and missing pieces of this most interesting of message boards.

The darkweb is home to all sorts of terrible service offerings. Spiders navigate successfully around webs by being smart and strong. On occasion other types of predators wander these dark webs. They don't fear the spiders. They know the spiders often lead to many types of prey and excitement. Six hours later Rick has gleaned enough information to understand how this bulletin board works, including an inkling of where the emails are originating from. *He thinks he knows what this site is for.*

Maniacal eyes glowing in the pitch black of the server room, Rick whispers and sends a message to the curator of these bidding opportunities. It is time to make his presence known.

I want in, he writes.

There is an almost immediate reply: *Who are you? What is your designation code?*

Call me Mantis. Rick smiles as he types.

AUTHOR NOTES - CRAIG MARTELLE

Written February 2021

I can't thank you enough for reading this story to the very end! I hope you liked it as much as I did.

When good people have to do bad things. I bring you Ian Bragg, my favorite hit man with a conscience and a better half.

Paul Alan Piatts submitted a piece of fan fiction that I liked, so I have included it above. Give Paul a hearty round of applause for his creativity. And Terry Wells-Brown added a few words about Ian and Jenny. Neither of these is canon for the Ian Bragg thrillers, but both stories are a testament to a growing fan base that is fully immersed in the universe.

I want to thank Patrick O'Donnell, a retired police

sergeant out of Milwaukee, who gave me insight into the hit within the neighborhood to make it as realistic as possible.

And to Andrew Perry for his schooling on the grossly misunderstood dark web. Okay. It's me. I have a minimal understanding of the dark web, but it's better now.

Also, a big thank you to Paul, Terry, and Andrew for their flash fiction – I think living in a different world is a great way to invest your time. Letting your imagination help keep the real world filled with color.

This book was a bit of a transition to the world of government contracts. That is where we've been going since the first chapter of book one. When authors tell you they have events planned far into the future, they're not kidding. I have book four in mind (not plotted yet) and a remote concept for book five.

My plan for Ian Bragg was that these first three books establish the foundation, and at some point in the future, I will offer the first three boxed at an extreme discount to draw readers into this series. That will be when there are a few more books available in the series.

We'll keep Ian's and Jenny's story rolling forward. I've added a short story: *The First Hit* to a thriller anthology that is only available from March 15th, 2021 to June 15th. Then I'll give the short story to all the fans of Ian Bragg, but it would be a lot cooler if you picked up the anthology and read it in there.

Thank you to everyone who has read this far. You are the reason I keep writing.

And in the winter in the interior of Alaska, there's not much else I can do. One of the triggers for my asthma is the cold and we tend to get extended times of extreme cold. Writing gives me something productive to do, especially as I get older with a bad heart and lungs, I need to keep my activity at a level that doesn't end me.

Lots of great auroras this year and my wife has diligently captured many from the peace and convenience of our own driveway.

This is a great place to live to see the wonders of nature. There is a certain amount of compromise that has to take place in order to stay here, but once those are settled, the beauty is nearly unrivaled.

Peace, fellow humans.

If you liked this story, you might like some of my other books. You can join my mailing list by dropping by my website craigmartelle.com or if you have any comments, shoot me a note at craig@craigmartelle.com. I am always happy to hear from people who've read my work. I try to answer every email I receive.

If you liked the story, please write a short review for me on Amazon. I greatly appreciate any kind words; even one or two sentences go a long way. The number of reviews an ebook receives greatly improves how well it does on Amazon.

Amazon—www.amazon.com/author/craigmartelle
Facebook—www.facebook.com/authorcraigmartelle
BookBub—https://www.bookbub.com/authors/craig-martelle
My web page—https://craigmartelle.com
Thank you for joining me on this incredible journey.

OTHER SERIES BY CRAIG MARTELLE
- AVAILABLE IN AUDIO, TOO

Terry Henry Walton Chronicles (#) (co-written with Michael Anderle)—a post-apocalyptic paranormal adventure

Gateway to the Universe (#) (co-written with Justin Sloan & Michael Anderle)—this book transitions the characters from the Terry Henry Walton Chronicles to The Bad Company

The Bad Company (#) (co-written with Michael Anderle) —a military science fiction space opera

Judge, Jury, & Executioner (#)—a space opera adventure legal thriller

Shadow Vanguard—a Tom Dublin space adventure series

Superdreadnought (#)—an AI military space opera

Metal Legion (#)—a military space opera

The Free Trader (#)—a young adult science fiction action-adventure

Cygnus Space Opera (#)—a young adult space opera (set in the Free Trader universe)

Darklanding (#) (co-written with Scott Moon)—a space western

Mystically Engineered (co-written with Valerie Emerson) —mystics, dragons, & spaceships

Metamorphosis Alpha—stories from the world's first science fiction RPG

The Expanding Universe—science fiction anthologies

Krimson Empire (co-written with Julia Huni)—a galactic race for justice

Xenophobia (#)—a space archaeological adventure

End Times Alaska (#)—a Permuted Press publication—a post-apocalyptic survivalist adventure

Nightwalker (a Frank Roderus series)—A post-apocalyptic western adventure

End Days (#) (co-written with E.E. Isherwood)—a post-apocalyptic adventure

Successful Indie Author (#)—a non-fiction series to help self-published authors

Monster Case Files (co-written with Kathryn Hearst)—A Warner twins mystery adventure

Rick Banik (#)—Spy & terrorism action adventure

Ian Bragg Thrillers—a man with a conscience who kills bad guys for money

Published exclusively by Craig Martelle, Inc
The Dragon's Call by Angelique Anderson & Craig A. Price, Jr.—an epic fantasy quest

A Couples Travels—a non-fiction travel series

Manufactured by Amazon.ca
Bolton, ON

40127388R00157